"Santosh Joshi is the *Dale Carnegie* of India and his book KEYS teaches you to keep your heart clear, live in the present and it inspires you to plan for the future."

Dr. Uday Nirgudkar - *Chief Editor, Zee 24 taas*

"Through his book, Santosh shows you a path out of your misery, through the effective HLP technique. KEYS is not just another book on self-motivation and life skills, but a guide book which helps in self-discovery."

Speaking Tree - *A Times Of India publication*

"KEYS is a very well knitted together book that succinctly encompasses everything you need to know to take your life forward. By using the techniques in the book, by imbibing its wisdom, each of us can unlock the prisons of our lives and coast our way to freedom."

Suma Varughese - *Editor-in-chief - Life Positive Magazine*

"The book KEYS definitely gives a direction to live a successful life."

Shri Nitin Gadkari - *Cabinet Minister, Govt. of India*

"I believe that all of us deserve to be happy. And we are not. Here are some tools and some insights that can change that pattern. And let us live in the now. As we must..."

Mallika Sarabhai - *Noted Indian Classical Dancer and Activist*

KEYS

Introducing

HLP

The Secret to a Happy and Regret-free Life

SANTOSH JOSHI

EMBASSY BOOKS
www.embassybooks.in

KEYS
© Santosh Joshi 2013

This revised edition published in 2015.

Published in India by :

EMBASSY BOOK DISTRIBUTORS,
120, Great Western Building,
Maharashtra Chamber of Commerce Lane,
Kala Ghoda, Fort,
Mumbai- 400 023.
Tel : (+91-22) 2281 9546 / 32967415
Email : info@embassybooks.in
www.embassybooks.in

Cover Design by the creative team of Think Why Not

Illustrations by Santosh Joshi

ISBN: 978-93-83359-71-4

Disclaimer: Examples given in the book are inspired by real life stories. We have changed the names and actual details to maintain and respect the privacy of the concerned persons.

Dedicated to my wife and soul-mate Aruna

I stand today only because you are by my side
As you held me during life's every tide
You give me the strength, the energy and force
The brilliant creative ideas, of which you are the source
No words can thank enough, for all you did for me
Your love, unending support, and trust deeper than sea
I can say now, what they say about success is true
'Cause behind my story, there is a woman like you

PREFACE

When I was young, we raised some pets at home. By that, I mean that we had a few birds locked up in a metal cage. Whenever I went near the cage, the birds would flutter their wings with the hope that I will open the door and set them free. But, perhaps due to my young age, I didn't understand the pain and the agony these birds were going through. I was very proud of my possession and even bragged about it incessantly.

Until one day, I found myself trapped in the enclosure of Do's and Don'ts. What a misery it is to be shackled by chains! That day I empathised with these ill-fated birds. I didn't waste any more time; I opened the door of the cage and said to the birds, "Go... fly high! Your place is up there!" pointing my finger towards the sky. As the birds soared high in the sky, so did my heart in joy and the peace that comes with doing the right thing.

After living in a set pattern, living the life that was designed for me and not by me, one fine day I decided to break free like the birds and pursue my dream destiny, i.e., to enrich others' lives. It was a difficult call as it meant completely downsizing my life. But the hope of achieving my purpose gave me the strength. I stepped in to an arena which was completely dark, holding the torch of faith. I set on my mission to help people heal themselves and discover their true potential. Since then, I have developed a few techniques on my own and gathered many experiences - some from my own life and some from the people who came to me for sessions - and I decided to put them all together in the form of a book.

During my workshops, I interacted with many people and found the cause of all unhappiness and misery centred in the regrets, worries, anxieties and insecurities of life. Rather than living the precious moments life offers, we either live in the past or the future, when the truth is the former has already gone and the latter is yet to come. I discovered that to live the present moment, we have to heal our past and plan for our future. This book will give you the means to do so, and enable you to live a successful, fulfilling, and a peaceful life.

My workshops reflected the HLP philosophy - Heal, Live, Plan - and participants, who had come to me with their issues such as relationships, health, career etc., found good solution to their problems. I found that the H, L, and P are the three most powerful KEYS to unlock the highest potential in each one of us, thus paving a way to a highly successful life. These keys are freely available to all of us. We just need to pick them up and open the door to our dreams. It was most rewarding to see positive and radical changes in the people who came to me who implemented the HLP philosophy. This gave me immense strength to move forward on my own journey.

Writing this book has been a journey for me from my past to my future. Each chapter has been a chapter of my life. Each and every word of this book has come from my heart and I believe that whatever comes from heart reaches the heart. I believe that we are all fellow travellers on this journey and should benefit from each other and help each other grow.

Though this book can be read in one go, I urge you to read one chapter at a time, relate to it, absorb it, digest it and then move ahead. I have created blank spaces at many places in the book with the symbol of 'thoughts'. This space can be used for putting down your thoughts while reading. At the end of each section, there is an exercise which will help you know yourself better followed by some powerful tools that can be used. All my genuine and sincere efforts will come to fruition, if this book touches you somewhere and pushes you to change your life for better.

During the process of creating this book, I have come to realise that each of us are unique and deserve the best we can aim for. Each one of us has the potential to reach the skies. If you read this book using your heart, instead of your mind, you will be a completely changed person – a person who walks through this planet joyfully and fulfils his destiny by taking complete charge of his life and leading a life full of happiness, contentment and peace.

Santosh Joshi
June 2013

ACKNOWLEDGEMENTS

This being my first book, I went through all the challenges, a first time author goes through. Moreover, I realised although I could talk on all the topics in this book for hours together, penning down those seemed like a humongous task at times. But there are some wonderful souls who came forward to make this mission a grand success. My deepest gratitude to all of them.

Aruna, my wife, for believing in me, more than I believed in myself. She stood behind me like a rock, supporting me in every possible way. She played a role of a worst critic and the best advisor.

I am blessed to have a family who was always by my side through thick and thin. I thank my parents for showering their unconditional love and blessings, and for their immense support and faith in my endeavour. I also thank Aruna's parents for their support and blessings.

The idea of this book came through, when Sanjeev Latkar and I were discussing on our favourite topic 'Life' in his office. He suggested, I write a book around this concept, and here it is. Thanks Sanjeev for your encouragement and support all through.

My heartfelt gratitude to two wonderful souls, Madhu Sahoo and Meirah Bhastekar, for trusting and showing confidence in me and my book. Since the topic was so close to my heart there was an abundant flow of thoughts and ideas. Putting these together in a constructive way was a task for me. Madhu and

Meirah helped me put these together in a very interesting way, using their literary skills.

Thanks Parveen Shaikh for a superbly designed website and the never ending support thereafter. I really appreciate your dedication towards work.

My heartfelt thanks to the creative team at Think Why Not for designing an exceptionally beautiful cover for my book.

There are a few people who were not directly involved with the book, but their contribution to my life's journey and hence the book is priceless. I wish to thank Vaishali & Rakesh Pedram, Priti & Amit Savoor, Ramki, Nitin Deshmukh, Puneet Gupta, Sonia Swaroop Choksi and Suma Varughese. All of you have a very special place in my heart and thanks a million for always being there for me.

This book will be incomplete without mentioning all those who have attended my workshops, talks, seminars and sessions. Thanks to each and every one of you for believing in me, and for becoming an integral part of my family. Without you, I don't exist.

My sincere thanks to Sohin Lakhani and Embassy Books for showing confidence and faith in my book and publishing it under their banner.

In addition to all the foregoing, I am filled with gratitude as I humbly prostrate at my Guru's feet, Nityanand Swami of Ganeshpuri. I was always divinely guided and protected throughout. At times, I was amazed at how the wisdom just flowed in when I sat to write. This book was only possible because of His infinite love and grace.

Table of Contents

The third KEY - PLAN YOUR FUTURE

THE NEXT STEP

Santosh Joshi

DIALOGUE WITH SELF

Knock-knock…

Knock-knock…

"Anybody home? Please open the door… I need to talk to you!"

The frantic knock at the door and a desperate and somewhat hysterical voice stirred me out of my deep sleep. I was slightly disoriented as I woke up, and found that my pulse was racing. I could literally hear my heart pounding in the stillness of night. I was sweating profusely. I came to my senses, as the clock struck two. Was it a nightmare? I wondered. Or was it simply my mind playing games?

"Who wants to visit me in the middle of night?" I said to myself and got out of my bed to fetch a glass of water, dismissing my thoughts.

Knock-knock…

Knock-knock…

"Please open the door, and let me in. I need you, please help me," said the pleading voice again.

That's when I realised that somebody was really at the door. The voice seemed familiar. Still, I was irritated at the stranger disturbing my peaceful sleep in the middle of the night. Reluctantly, I walked towards the main door to check on the stranger. Peeping through the eyehole, I was shocked at what I saw. In front of the door stood someone who looked just like me. Only he was younger and looked haggard. He was carrying a huge bag over his back that appeared to weigh him down. His clothes were in tatters and shoes worn-out. His child-like face was hidden behind what seemed like years of exhaustion. This sight made me nervous.

"Who are you?" I asked anxiously from the other side without opening

the door.

"I am your Past Self, please open the door and let me in," came the reply, with more desperation than before.

I was puzzled with this reply. Who is this stranger who looks like me, calls himself my past self and asks for my help; that too at an unearthly hour! Why does this past self have to come and rob me of my calm in the middle of the night? I could feel the resistance building up. I gathered my nerve and opened the door.

In a polite yet firm voice, I told Past Self, "Listen, I am sorry, but I cannot help you right now. Can you please come tomorrow afternoon? I need to get some sleep, as I have a couple of important meetings in the morning."

Without even waiting for a reply, I almost slammed the door. When I looked through the eyehole again, I saw Past Self turn away and leave, disappointed. I had lost my sleep by then and spent the rest of the night tossing and turning, thinking about this strange visitor who called himself my Past Self. As the sun rose, spreading its warm blanket all over, I got out of my bed feeling totally drained and gloomy. I made a hot cup of ginger tea for myself, and sat in my garden, sipping the tea, pondering over what happened last night.

I was blessed with a beautiful garden and a huge mansion and all that any human being would long for. I was always full of exuberance, focused on my goals and a go-getter. People were envious of me as I always appeared happy and cheerful. My mantra in life was 'Live in the moment'. I was truly grateful for all that I had in life.

But something changed that night, and I didn't feel the same. I felt haunted by Past Self. He had completely taken away my peace and calm. It was puzzling why the brief encounter with Past Self had frightened me so. It had stirred me deep within. Though I asked Past Self to come in the afternoon, I was not too keen to face him again.

I had to cancel the meetings planned for the morning as I was feeling low. I needed to change my state of mind. I decided to discuss this with my new found friend Future Self. Since Future Self and I were planning a few ventures together, I thought it would be appropriate to talk about this incident with him.

In the short acquaintance that we had, I found myself getting pulled towards Future Self due to his magnetic personality. Though he had a mysterious character, he always radiated hope. He exhibited enormous faith in his own potential and the universe. Future Self was always optimistic even in the darkest hour, and came up with positive and brilliant solutions for any problem under the sun. The only problem was that he was unpredictable most of the times. He did not behave the way I expected him to most often. Hence I was unsure if he would willingly help me.

I just picked up my mobile phone and dialled my friend Future Self's number.

"Hi Present Self, I was just thinking about you. How are you my friend?" said Future Self, in his ever enthusiastic voice. "What is it that is troubling you my dear?" he added without waiting for my reply. I knew that my friend had good intuitive sense, which made me trust him and the advice he offered.

"I am feeling very anxious and gripped by worry and fear," I said.

"But that is not your true nature my dear. My friend Present Self as I know him is always happy and full of life!"

"Yeah! You are right Future Self. But today the situation is different. Anyhow, I want to come out of this state. I want to be happy and energetic at every moment, again."

"So what's the matter?" asked Future Self.

I narrated what happened that night. Future Self lent me a patient ear.

Then on a very promising note, he advised, "The best way to deal with anything that is bothering you is to face it. Go and face Past Self and see what he wants to tell you. Don't assume things. If you get worried and anxious about anything, you will lose focus in life. You need to achieve certain goals. If you are scared and run away from Past Self, he will keep haunting you. So go and face him. The choice that you make at every moment will decide where you reach in the future. So have faith and march ahead fearlessly. Listen to your heart and just do it!" said my friend Future Self.

This profound wisdom from my friend gave me a lot of strength and courage to face Past Self with renewed vigour. I said to myself, "Yes! I can do it!"

As expected, Past Self promptly arrived in the afternoon. I opened the door, hugged him and gave him a warm welcome.

"Welcome my friend, please come inside," I said, after apologising for my rude behaviour the previous night. I asked him to sit on the sofa and I went to the kitchen to get some water. When I came back to the living area, I saw Past Self huddled up in the corner of the sofa, giving me a frightened look. He must have felt exceedingly startled by my changed behaviour.

"Tell me, how can I help you?" I asked lovingly, offering him the glass of water. I took a seat near Past Self, held his hand, and said "Don't be afraid. Trust me, I really mean to help you in every possible way I can."

At this point, Past Self just burst out crying. I allowed him to cry his heart out. After a while, he wiped his tears with both his shoulders and hands. Still sobbing, he said, "Present Self, I am in great trouble and I seek your help. In fact, you are the only person who can help me out of this situation. I am troubled by a lot of enemies. Few of them are Remorse, Guilt, Anger, Fear and Sorrow. They follow me everywhere and have made my life miserable. If they keep pestering me, I have no option but end my life. I just can't deal with them. They have even threatened to attack and ruin you very soon. I am petrified. I need your help in dealing with them. You are my only hope now." And Past Self started weeping again.

"Yes, it is a grave situation," I murmured to myself.

I got up from the couch and hugged Past Self tightly, and said, "Don't worry. I am with you, and we will handle this together. Everything is going to be fine. Have faith!"

I decided to put everything else on hold and give this situation my complete *attention and priority. We sat together and spent the whole evening making plans to deal with our now common enemies. I told Past Self, "The best way to deal with our enemies is to first acknowledge and accept them; and then make peace with them and let them go. The more we engage in battle, the more we will be hurt, as they are a mighty force. If we resist them they will persist. So the best deal would be to make peace with them and let them go."*

Past Self agreed to my plan and we started implementing it, targeting one enemy at a time. It was not an easy task. As we tried dealing with one enemy, the others would try to dissuade us from our goal. Though it took us quite some time and a lot of effort, we finally succeeded in our endeavour. My friend Past Self was completely at peace and now there was no possibility of threat from our enemies to him or me.

Eventually, all three of us, Past Self, Future Self and myself (Present Self) became thick friends. To celebrate the victory of our battle against our enemies, I hosted a dinner at my place. I was truly happy to see a contended smile on my friend Past Self's face. My friend Future Self was as bright as ever. His eyes were full of hope. It was a beautiful reunion of three long lost friends. We raised a toast to our friendship.

That evening, we vowed to be always present for each other, in any situation. After we finished dinner, Past Self quietly sat on the corner sofa, completely fearless and relaxed, enjoying the dessert. As I glanced at Past Self, he gave me a look filled with love and gratitude. With a satisfied smile on my face, future self and I got engrossed in planning our future. I experienced bliss like never before. This was the best day of my life, as I felt happy, peaceful and complete.

It is important for the three parts of our personality – past self, present self, and future self to be in harmony with each other. These are the three dimensions of life. Usually these three dimensions get disjointed with time because of the unresolved issues of the past, or the fears, anxieties and insecurities of the future. Living in just one dimension and ignoring the other two ultimately results in a fragmented life.

Many of us will ignore our past and think only about the present and the future; or ignore the future and spend lot of time brooding about the past issues. Some people will live only in the present, which is actually the best thing to do. However, their past issues are haunting them or they are too scared to think about the future. Key to a successful life is in integrating these three dimensions of life into one.

Here I introduce the HLP principle, meaning **H**ealing the past, **L**iving in the present and **P**lanning for the future. These are basically the three KEYS that open the gateway to a successful life – a life where all your dreams are waiting to be achieved. All the three keys are important, and we need to work upon them. This book will serve as a guide to do exactly this.

To be able to live a successful life, ask yourself these questions at every point in life.

- Do I ever get affected by bad memories from the past and the emotions attached to them?

- Am I happy, peaceful and content and using my best potential in the present moment?

- Am I often insecure and anxious about my future?

The answers to these questions will tell the extent of fragmentation of our *self*. They will tell us where we are living most of the times - in the past, present or future. If the answer is other than the present, then it is time for us to seriously start work on integrating our *self*.

In our lives, we are so complacent where we are, that only when we realise that there is no escaping the situation, we step out of the comfort zone. We must understand that when we enter the discomfort-zone from our comfort zone, it always leads to a bigger comfort zone, and the process thus continues.

What happens when we hear other people's success stories? Don't we feel motivated and inspired? Don't we feel that we can do it as well? Of course we do. Why then most of us unable to reach where we belong; to the top?

Here is the answer. Most people are not aware of the immense potential they have within. They are like sleeping giants, who have forgotten about their own powers; the power to take on the world, to achieve great success, to win. Even if they know about their massive strength, whenever they come across a difficulty or an opportunity in life, an inner dialogue with self begins. It is the dialogue between our own past, present and future self.

Our past self will bring to surface all the incidents in our life when we failed miserably. It will try to convince us about our lack of abilities in accomplishing the task. Our future self will make us anxious by projecting all the fears, in case we do undertake the task. Ultimately we end up not taking up the challenge. We are so ruled by our past and future that we miss the strength and beauty of our present; which is the only reality, the only truth.

We live life floating like a raft in an ocean getting swayed by the waves in all possible directions. But deep within, each one of us has the burning desire to take complete charge of his/her life. Only when we kindle this desire and take charge of our life, can we actually sail towards our goals. *The choice lies with us.* This book is the first step in committing yourself to becoming the change you want to see in yourself.

Heal your Past

Do we really forget what we've been through?
Or do we remember all, just pretend not to?

When we say "I moved on", do we really mean it?
Or just convince ourselves, not meaning one bit

Bygones are never really bygones, my dear friend
We just try to 'forget' the past, never putting an end

Past is important, as it teaches us lessons
And gives us insights, much valuable ones

But hurts of the past, we all need to heal
Offloading residual emotions, we so badly feel

It's good to heal our memories, and agonies of the past
As they slow our progress, as long as they last

We are like onions, with many layers of conditioning
Our real self is the centre, to which these layers cling

Conditioning pulls us back, from our highest goal
And makes us forget, the purpose of our soul

We can heal emotions, memories with painful feeling
By re-visiting the past, as re-living is relieving

Forgiveness is a great tool, to relieve us of baggage
Which we have been carrying, since a tender age

Each one of us inside, has a tiny little child
Who craves for attention, and is ready to go wild

It just needs our love, and a little pampering
Living that little child, makes us a happy being

So let's heal our past, and move ahead to achieve
And make 'travelling light', our motto to live.

"I think something is following me...
but what...?"

CHAPTER 1

BYGONES ARE BYGONES

The biggest myth

I thought it is forgotten, but my past was always there
Unknowingly following me, hiding from the glare
It is good for me to recognize this fact
It helps me in, putting together my act.

As I walked through the valley, I knew I was not alone. Even though it was quiet, I felt something follow me. I feared its presence and hurried through the valley gasping for breath. My journey was uncomfortable and miserable. The more I tried to run away from it, the more it chased me. But I was too afraid to turn back, so I continued hastily in fear.

When I reached half way through the valley, I got tired and was angry at myself for being afraid. So I took a moment, gathered courage and said to myself, "If I have to go any further, I am going to do it fearlessly; I will not take one more step until I have conquered this fear." Curious about what I would find, I gathered all my strength and turned back right that moment. I was astonished at what I saw.

It was my own shadow, nothing else! It had been following me quietly, creating fear and doubt and slowing my pace. I had nothing to fear as it was only a reflection of me; and when I realized that, I was no longer afraid. Then I walked ahead fearless and triumphant.

Identifying the cause of our fears of the past is what rids us of them and makes our journey better.

"Just relax. It's been a long time. No one will remember you, don't look so troubled, and cheer up," I reassured myself by repeating these words to suppress the guilt I felt deep within. I was equally excited and nervous about visiting my old school after 20 long years.

As I slowly walked through the main gate into the school, where I spent a wonderful decade of my life, I reflected on how amazing and carefree those days were. I looked around and saw that not much had changed. Children were racing around each other in the playground. Teachers walked through the grounds, serene and focused. My school was as vibrant as ever.

When I approached the principal's office, my heart was racing. I knew exactly what was bothering me, but tried to hide it with a broad smile, fearing someone might just figure it all out. The principal was friendly, and in a while, I enquired about the old principal and teachers of my yonder years. I learnt that most of them had retired, but our old physics teacher was still teaching a class at the school. The current principal insisted that I meet him. Reluctantly, not knowing a polite way to ignore his enthusiastic offer, I agreed.

As I walked to the staff room my pulse started racing again, the colour from my face drained. Pale and breathless, I entered the staff room with the principal. There he was, my old physics teacher, seated at the far end of a table, near a window, quietly reading a book. I walked up to him and introduced myself. He recognized me right away and smiled as he gave me a big hug. He said he was very proud of me as he knew I was doing well in life.

I thanked him for the compliment and said, "That is because of your guidance and blessings Sir. You know I wasn't good at physics."

My teacher replied with a smile, "It was my duty to teach you and your duty to learn, and I believe we both did our duties well!"

I thanked him and after spending a few minutes, I left the staff room. I sat on a bench near the playground and suddenly my eyes were filled with tears; tears of guilt and remorse, tears of anger at myself for what a bunch of friends and I had done to this teacher when we were in 10th grade.

As it was the final school year, my whole group was excited to leave school and get into college. It felt like we were finally going to taste real freedom. Freedom from wearing uniforms, freedom from being constantly reprimanded by teachers, freedom from being on time, doing homework and all the things that school-life demands. Our lives were about to change and a whole new world awaited us outside the walls of this school. Surely, a bit of mischief was not really going to hurt anyone?

And so we decided to play a prank. We had a group meeting to choose our target and what would be his ill fate. The next day was the last day of classes before exams began and the last class was physics. It was a hot summer day and as soon as our teacher walked in, he switched on the fan and sat down to wipe his sweat off.

Suddenly, something fell from above and landed on the teacher's head. We, the conspirators, screamed loudly, "Snake! Snake! Run, it's a snake!"

The poor teacher ran towards the corridor, and screamed, "Get it out! Get it out of my head!"

All of us ran after him to see how it would end. The teacher was looking down the ledge with dismay and despair. And when we looked at him, we were shocked out of our wits. Our poor physics teacher was bald. What we had thought to be a thick matt of black silky hair was actually a wig.

The wig that was the saving grace of a young man had fallen three storeys down, along with the rubber snake, which we had planted on top of the ceiling fan. The kids started laughing at the sight of this, which left him completely embarrassed. He came into the class, collected his books and left.

Alarm bells started ringing in our ears at the thought of what would happen if anyone found out we had done it. We could smell danger in the air as we looked at each other silently with guilty eyes. Later that day, we vowed not to say a word about it to anyone.

Contrary to what we suspected, nothing happened. The exams got over and on the last day of school was our farewell party. The principal addressed the entire class. He began by thanking the teachers and congratulating the batch for completing 10 years at the school; he said, "I'm very happy for all of you. As you leave, I wish you all, the best for your further studies and hope that you will make us and your parents proud."

Then he added, "I wish to take this opportunity to inform you all that a recent mischief has been reported to me. I even know the names of the mischief-makers, but I want to give them a second chance in the hope that they will change. Remember that when you leave a place, as you are doing today, leave with pride and good memories. Make sure that people remember you for the right reasons. It is very difficult to build a good reputation as it takes a long time; however, it just takes a couple of seconds to spoil it. So always choose your words and actions carefully. I hope, the students responsible for this mischief reflect on what they have done and how it has hurt the person who suffered embarrassment for no mistake of his."

The principal then continued his speech talking about other things, but by then I was deaf with guilt. This incident took place years ago, yet as I sat on the bench, I vividly recollected everything. How is it that I was still so guilty about something that had happened years ago? How can this feeling be powerful even today?

One thing was very clear though, I was still harbouring the guilt of that mischief, but most of the time pretended that it didn't exist. So then I questioned myself, am I still guilty of what I had once happily participated in? Is it possible that what we think of as old forgotten memories are actually skeletons in the closet, waiting to fall out at the very first chance? Are we then lying to ourselves? Are bygones *really* bygones, or are we living a myth?

The past is still there

All our lives are similar in a way. On one hand, we assure ourselves that everything is forgotten, that 'bygones are bygones'; and on the other hand, we walk through life worrying about the shadows of our past. These shadows follow us quietly and shock us when we notice them, which happens from time to time. Sometimes we are aware of their presence, but most of the time we fail to understand or recognize them. In fact, we can never really 'let go' of these shadows completely.

When we go camping in the forest, we usually light a bon fire. However, before leaving the camp site, we cover it up with mud to put off the fire. What we don't realize is although on surface the fire has been put off, it is still alive and burning underneath. And if not put out completely and quickly, there is a risk of the small bon fire burning out the entire forest. Just like how certain incidents from our past, which seem small and insignificant and we feel they can be ignored. Ignoring something will not make it go away; rather, it will surface in our thoughts again and again, causing repeated pain and anguish. And each time it resurfaces, the pain increases manifold.

The first thing to do is to accept the real possibility of an issue causing us unhappiness. Then, identify the cause of that issue(s) i.e. an event, a person or a place, when it happened, and the dominating emotion behind that feeling. This step is vital in the process of healing. As humans we operate only from two kinds of emotions.

Love-based emotions (happiness, compassion, courage and kindness) or
Fear-based emotions (anger, hatred, resentment and regret)

All our life activities are initiated by love or fear. When we are operating from a love-based emotion, we are happy. It is when we operate from a fear based emotion that we feel disturbed and bothered. And it is surprising, how easily we get disturbed by something that happened in the past.

Most of us will be able to precisely recall a particular incident from the past, the pain it caused and the time it happened. The fact that we can remember a particular incident so vividly clearly indicates how the whole incident is still embedded in our mind. That is the marvel of the human mind, it recollects everything.

Because every incident that occurs in our life is recorded and carefully stored away in our mind as a memory, which then becomes a part of our past. The mind is not biased when recording a memory; it does not discriminate between negative or positive, good or bad. Its job is to record and store. Therefore, we are able to recall most events quickly and accurately, the good and the bad ones alike.

The past is not to be disowned either, as there is much to be cherished from it. Whatever we are today is a result of our past — upbringing, conditioning, teachings, experiences, memories and relationships. In reality, nothing is good or bad (as we may label them), it's just a perception we hold. Every event is a result of the choices we make at any point in our lives and follow it up with a corresponding action. But some things are beyond our understanding, such as an accidental death, for example.

However, there are no coincidences in life, and nothing is accidental. Everything in our life happened or is happening for a reason. It may not seem so during that time, but in hindsight we will realize that reason. What we need to focus on, however, are the 'emotions' from the past that show up from time to time, causing pain and disturbance in our present. It is these emotions that need to be identified and addressed as they are the ones that cause havoc in our life.

I come across so many people who try to convince me that their past is of no significance to them. They claim to have forgotten the unhappy and hurtful events from the past, that they no longer bother them and that they have forgiven everyone who hurt them. They say they love living in the present, at all times. I wish they knew how far from the truth this confession is.

One of the biggest myths of our lives is 'bygones are bygones'. Bygones literally mean something gone by, in the past, no longer in the present. Every time we use the phrase 'bygones are bygones', we need to question ourselves and honestly answer if it holds true to the event or situation we use it for.

Have we really forgotten, completely let go of the pain and hurt caused by something that happened in the past? Or are we just not aware of its presence in our life? Or is it that we are aware but are trying to deny the existence of that painful past which is very much there? How can we be sure or validate that we are still holding on to the negative emotions from the past? A simple way to validate that 'bygones are not bygones' is to relate your emotions to a particular place, event or person and see how you feel. Think about suddenly bumping into a person who you have not met for a long time. What would your reaction be on suddenly coming face to face with him/her? What emotions would you relate to that chance encounter? Do you feel happy, sad or absolutely nothing?

The emotions that you feel at that exact moment on seeing that person will depend on the experiences you shared with him/her in the past. If you have had a bad experience, a flood of emotions such as anger, pain, and misery will come gushing out of you. This is enough to validate that bygones are not bygones.

A chance encounter

To illustrate my point, let me share another personal incident. Few years after I had left one of my first corporate jobs, I was trying to set-up my own business. I met a friend at a coffee shop to discuss a business proposal. On my way back home, I stopped at a music store to pick up a few CDs. As I was going through the rack of new arrivals, I suddenly came face to face with my arch-rival of that time.

I stood just inches away from a man who had caused me much agony in the past. He was the one who had very meticulously planned to blame me for something I had not done. I was being held responsible for something that was completely against my principles and work ethics. He knew I was innocent, but had some grudge against me. He was instrumental in my ouster from the job. In a matter of seconds, everything from that past flashed before my eyes. I was filled with so much anger and rage that I could have punched his face right there.

When he finally noticed me, he was speechless. We exchanged awkward smiles and he left hastily. After a while, I left the store, with the CDs tightly clutched in my hands. As I walked back home, I remembered everything this man had done to hurt and embarrass me. I was filled with immense pain and felt extremely angry at myself for not having said anything to him when all this actually happened, or when I saw him at the music store.

I went back home, and sat quietly on the couch for a long time. When my wife noticed me sitting in an unnaturally stiff way, she asked me what was wrong. I then narrated the whole incident to her and how angry I was on seeing him. My wife understood my pain, as she knew what I had been put through by that guy. She asked me to cheer up and said, "Listen it's been five years now. Isn't it time you moved on? Don't allow him to get to you like this... we live in the same city and you might bump into him again. Do you want to relive this pain again and again? Bygones are bygones, let it be."

For a long time, I thought about what my wife had said and asked myself a series of questions. It is one of the things I do when I come across a problem. I write down a series of questions and answer them to find solutions to the problem on hand. I asked myself what I would do if I came across him again, would I react in the same way.

Would I be as angry as I was today or would the anger lessen with time?

Do the painful memories of the past reduce in intensity with passing time?

Or do they just get suppressed until they are unleashed by a reminder of that incident and rise like a deadly serpent, ready to attack?

Easier said than applied, but bygones are *not* bygones and the sooner we realize this, the easier it becomes for us to find a solution. Ignoring the problem is like sweeping dirt under the carpet does. This only hides the dust where we cannot see it. *But the dirt is still there, and we are always aware of that truth.*

When the base of a wooden house is infested with termite, it has to be properly treated at the base; otherwise there is a risk that the entire house will eventually collapse. Similarly, there are no quick fixes to get rid of the heavy load of negative emotions that we carry in life. We have to take the necessary measures to rectify the situation. The longer we ignore a problem, the worse it will become.

Bygones are never really bygones, because everything that has happened in the past has an effect on who, what and where we are today. Everything we do today will have an impact on us tomorrow. What may seem good now may not be so, a few months later. Also, what may seem bad now may not be so either. It is important to revisit the past and learn the lessons from all that has happened. We must analyze how it plays a role in shaping our decisions, our thoughts, and our actions in the present.

The heavy burden of fear-based emotions which we carry from our past triggers many of the unhappy and unpleasant situations in our present. These suppressed emotions act as road blocks that slow our progress in life. There are many who live with a lot of guilt, not aware of the cause of their misery and pain. They should understand that it's easier to let go and move on; once we acknowledge that the past is still affecting our present and try to understand what needs to be addressed.

Unless we acknowledge the past, and until we learn the lessons, it will keep repeating itself, over and over again. The repetitive events in our life signal us towards an underlying problem, cautioning us to become aware. All we have to do is identify the pattern and work upon it.

The ultimate question you must ask yourselves is - *how do I want to live my life - in the bygone-lane or in the present-lane?* If the answer is the latter, do acknowledge and realize that you are consciously carrying the negative emotions of your traumatic past. That you are still holding on to them and these are truly the blocking stones on your path to being a happier, healthier and successful individual. This is the first step towards healing yourself of the past. Once you have this realization, the journey of transformation begins; turning you into your best, brilliant self.

Now that the realization has set in, that bygones are not bygones, what next?

At a glance

- *The past is still there, even if we tend to forget it*
- *Past emotions, hurts, anger, guilt, resentments pull us back*
- *It is important to acknowledge their presence*
- *We can learn from our past*

KEYS

"They say you are conditioned to run in circles....!"

CHAPTER 2

WE ARE LIKE ONIONS

Rediscover the real You

"Who am I?" When I asked myself, I heard a feeble voice
To understand its message, I had to silent outer noise
I realized it is coming, from deep within my heart
My 'self' lies under layers, that I need to tear apart.

When I thought of writing this book, I needed solitude. I needed to go to a place where I could be at peace with myself and write. A friend offered his cottage, somewhere in the outskirts of the city, in the forest.

What more could I ask for? This seemed like the perfect place. He informed me that it had not been used for a very long time and thus required minor repairs and cleaning. I told him how grateful I was of his gift and agreed to take care of the repairs. My wife was equally excited about me staying at the cottage.

The next day, I packed my bags and drove out. When I reached the quaint town, I was greeted by the caretaker of the cottage. With a big smile, he introduced himself as Khinchu. He said that it would take another 15 minutes to reach the cottage and his home was close by.

As we drove down, I noticed how scenic the place was and thought to myself, "Wow! This is the perfect place for me to write." The place was breathtakingly beautiful; surrounded by tall trees, wild flowers and a stream flowing so gently that you could barely hear it. Then the cottage came into view and my first reaction was, "Oh my heavens! This *can't* be it!" I looked at Khinchu and he smiled gaily.

When I went inside, I saw that the place was totally rundown and needed *major* repairs and cleaning. Although my mind asked me to turn around and go back, the surroundings had played their magic on my heart and I decided to stay. I immediately called my wife, who is an interior designer, and described to her what was before me. She jumped wholeheartedly into the chore, gave me some tips on how to go about restoring it and made a list of all the things I had to buy.

Now, I got really energized; it was just like I was back to school and doing a project. I went back to town and picked up all the things on the list. That night I was Khinchu's guest. The next day when we began work on the cottage, I realized this wasn't going to be the fun project I had imagined it to be. Khinchu had asked a friend to help us who agreed to, bless his heart. It took the three of us three days, to remove all the junk from the house. It cost us a cut on my leg, bruises on our hands and bodies as stiff as logs but we were successful. We were able to scrape off old paint from the walls and remove the old wooden flooring.

At the end of the third day, when I sat outside, sipping a cup of local *masala chai*, my thoughts went to how similar our lives are to the current situation. We are like the old cottage, conditioned to a certain way of life. As we grow older, we create belief systems of our own and sit cozily ensconced, locked up in the dense forest. Years of neglect and layers of dirt and moisture forms the fungus of conditioning. And eventually we start to rot.

It is only with great difficulty and through sheer determination that we can take up the task to restore and renew ourselves. It may be difficult, it may be painful, or we may get hurt and bruised in the process, but it **has** to be done. Living with conditioning, or belief systems is like putting fresh paint on rotting walls. The paint will chip off in no time.

The next few days were filled with excitement. We began work on the walls, the plumbing and the wooden floors. We put up new window panes and doors. We were humming, making jokes and bonding with each other, the way hard work bonds dedicated humans. It was an incredible experience.

When the cottage was restored completely, I thanked Khinchu and his friend for their help, support and enjoyable company. I could not believe that this was the same place I almost turned away from! It was the first time I had renovated anything, and I felt completely rejuvenated and proud of myself. Sitting in front of the cottage, I felt a sense of peace and calm that cannot be described but only felt. Similarly, when we remove the layers of conditioning, and get *in touch* with our *true self*, we too will feel completely rejuvenated and refreshed.

Who are You?

Whenever I ask people this simple question, 'Who are you?', they always start by mentioning their names, their physical attributes, what they do, their job profile and education. When I disagree, by moving my head side-ways, they go on to describe their emotional state, qualities, talents, abilities, likes and dislikes. The truth is we are none of these. Our true self is deeper and more profound than all these.

Have you ever peeled an onion? What do you observe as you go on peeling? You have to take off layer after layer before you reach the centre, or the core of the onion! Have you tasted just this core of the onion? If you have, you will know that it tastes very different from the outer layers. It is actually very sweet. We are all like that sweet core of the onion when we are born.

If you notice the face of a new born baby, you will see a glow, a sparkle and a magical kind of calm that surrounds the baby. This in turn fills us with joy, love and peace. Ever wondered what happened to the baby within you? Where did the glow disappear? What put out that sparkle? Where is the *real you*, that embodiment of love and peace?

The answer is simple; it is buried under numerous layers of conditioning. Over the years, these layers changed us from who we originally were to someone we no longer relate to. And it is time **now** to refurbish ourselves, by removing the deposits of negative beliefs that are no longer required in our life.

The layers of onion signify the layers of beliefs that we have been covered with, since the time of our birth. The first belief systems are passed onto us by our parents, in the form of dos and don'ts, right and wrong, good and bad. Have you observed a baby when it starts crawling and grabbing things? It experiences joy which radiates from its face. However, when the mother senses any trouble, she immediately stops the child, thereby stopping its natural instinct.

For instance, when the child is crawling towards the edge of the stairs, the mother (or any concerned adult) runs and grabs the child, stopping it from falling down the stairs or through her expressions and words tells the child not to go ahead. When we are young, our parents tell us many such things that are imbedded into our minds. To name a few, *don't run too fast, you will fall down*; or *don't laugh too loudly, it's bad manners*, and so on.

The second set of conditioning starts in school. When we go to school, our teachers give us a set of rules and regulations to follow. Don't speak loudly, don't play in the mud, don't pluck flowers, don't write on the walls, etc. Then as we grow, we hear more opinions about ourselves from others - *you are dark, you are fair, you are smart, you are dumb, you are good, you are naughty, you behave badly, you are well-behaved*. The list is endless.

Those are the early days of what we call 'Conditioning of the mind'. The belief system that we build slowly distances us from our true self. Layer after layer keeps adding up and we don't even realize it is happening. It becomes a part of our life; we identify ourselves with these belief systems and hold them to be true.

I remember, as a child, I was told, "You are not supposed to cry. You are a boy." Many, I know, are conditioned to believe that if they get up from the wrong side of bed or they look at their face first thing in the morning, their day will be ruined or something will surely go wrong. Really, how can getting up from the wrong side of the bed or looking at your beautiful face decide the fate of the events that occur during the day? It is a belief imbibed in us and something we have picked up while growing up. And because we believe in it, it manifests.

The amount of belief systems we keep forming throughout our lives is huge. These systems create a comfortable environment for us to thrive in hence, making it difficult to break out of at a later age. They also seem to rule our day to day behavior pattern.

The tiny chain

We all have seen an elephant in circus. You must have noticed the tiny chain by which it is tied to a pillar after the show is over. It looks so serene and comfortable in its confinement. Ever wondered why a huge elephant, which weighs over 1000 kg and has the strength to carry heavy loads, does not break the tiny chain and run away? It definitely can! Any day…. But the elephant is conditioned to think that it cannot.

How is this conditioning achieved? When the elephant is a baby, it is tied by the same tiny little chain, which it cannot break, even though it tries. After some time, it stops trying because it starts believing that it cannot break the chain. So, even after the elephant grows up and gains enormous strength, it doesn't try to break-free.

We are also conditioned to believe in certain things from the time we were born. We start believing what we are capable of and what not. . This is because we have been hearing people tell us what we can and cannot do. We believe everything to be true, and never try to experiment or take steps to change those views. Many of us spend our entire lives in such beliefs and never ever explore the store-house of potential each one of us is born with. Think of how you were as a child, and recall all the wonderful things that you did without any fear or inhibition. Are you still doing any of those things? If not, ask yourself, why?

Various studies have shown that until the age of seven, our brains are in a dream like state and the mind is absorbing everything from its surroundings, with no filters to differentiate anything. It's all just information which we record and store without processing. But as we grow, we start putting them in different categories, like good, bad, right, wrong, pretty, ugly, tall, short, and so on. Our sub-conscious mind accepts and stores, what we consciously believe. It does not discriminate between good or bad, positive or negative, it absorbs everything that we feed it with, consciously.

And so, if we have consciously convinced ourselves that we will fail, our subconscious mind will act upon that belief and yield according to our belief patterns. Our sub-conscious mind is a storehouse of memories, emotions and belief systems. It soaks everything like a sponge, without discrimination. Hence if a negative belief system is adopted, it will safely be stored away in the sub-conscious mind.

To be successful and find our true self, we have to get rid of limiting beliefs, and accept a new and empowering belief - "The future does not equal the past." If you have failed before, don't worry. Stand up and try again. Failing once doesn't mean that you are going to fail all the time. Understand that this belief system is a conditioning that has taken place over a period of time.

What we have to work upon is to shed it off, peel off the layers of beliefs that are limiting us from being our true self. It will be very difficult and may result in pain, just like when we peel off the layers of an onion. But if we want to reach the core, our true self, the layers have to be shed. No matter how painful, the conditioning has to be dropped.

The clay Buddha

In 1954, a new temple was built in Bangkok and a large Buddha statue made of clay was brought here from another town. While the statue was lifted by a crane, it slipped, fell on mud and developed a crack. The legend says, a temple monk had a dream the same night that statue was divinely inspired. So, the next day he visited the site.

While inspecting the crack, he noticed something glittering inside. He realized that there was something more to the statue than what was perceived and told the people around. They then carefully removed layers of plaster and clay to find a beautiful pure gold Buddha statue inside.

Apparently, this Golden Buddha statue was covered with clay and plaster when the Burmese had threatened to attack the city. The disguise was so convincing that no one ever suspected that there was something else inside. And for a long time, while it was still covered with plaster, it was thought to be worth very little. Today, the Golden Buddha statue is seen at Wat Traimit temple, which is one of Bangkok's must-see attractions.

Our true self is exactly like the golden Buddha which is hidden inside the layers of conditioning. Only when we are courageous enough to shed the layers will we find the 'golden self' hidden inside.

Lisa and her mother

Beliefs are created when we assign meaning to events. Many of the meanings we assign to the events of our lives are not based on truth. Lisa was always told by her mother to be silent and quiet. Over the years, Lisa started believing that she is unworthy of being listened to. However, the truth was that Lisa's mom had so much noise and residual pandemonium inside her that all additional noise annoyed her. Instead of realizing that, Lisa became a victim.

Many limiting beliefs are based on our (often child-minded) subjective, erroneous interpretation of others' actions and events. If someone we didn't know or care about, had done committed the wrong act, we would have assigned a very different meaning to it. Or ignored it completely. If a random woman asked Lisa to be quiet, she would have probably turned a deaf ear to it.

Nothing is inherently meaningful; and what others do is dictated by 'their' beliefs, 'their' stories. We are the ones who assign meaning to our experiences and from that meaning, we create everything we believe about ourselves. If this truth is accepted, we can begin to take control of our beliefs. We can then change our entire life for the better.

At a glance

- *Our true self is covered with layers of conditioning*
- *What we are today is the result of our past*
- *Our conditioning, belief systems form a major part of our personality*
- *Once we understand the layers, we can peel them off*
- *Only then we can utilise our true potential*

"There's no difference between us!"

CHAPTER 3

TRAVELLING LIGHT

Off-loading emotional residues

My own heavy baggage, dragging me from behind
As if I am walking, on a path steep and inclined
I slow down on my journey, to my chosen goal
My own past emotions, now taking its toll.

One afternoon, while working on the PC, I noticed that it was taking too long for a file to open. At first, I didn't understand what the problem was. As I closed the file, I realized that my desktop was filled with files that had been there for a very long time. I had not taken the time to clear them. It suddenly struck me that I had not serviced my laptop and to make matters worse, the anti-virus had expired!

After a nice cup of tea, I straight away got to work. I slowly and painstakingly had to open and check each and every file. Most of the files were unnecessary and many were even infected with viruses. I didn't waste any time in deleting them. There were a few important files which I saved elsewhere. In just 20 minutes, my desktop was clean and this time the file opened within seconds.

I'm glad I took time that afternoon to clear my desktop. Had I left it unattended, there was a possibility that with so many viruses on the desktop, my laptop would have crashed anytime. I would have also lost most of the important data, stuff that my workshops and seminars are dependent on. Immediately, I called my computer engineer and asked him to service the laptop and update the anti-virus software.

It is possible that many times we download 'viruses' into our lives and harbour them, completely unaware. Many of us carry unwanted emotions over the years that can prove to be detrimental. It is important to identify those emotions and get rid of them as quickly as possible. When we don't take time to clear out the unnecessary emotions and excess baggage from our life, it slows us down as well. If we don't keep a check and delete what is unwanted and dangerous, then we are surely headed towards a crash!

Heavy backpack

During a trek, I noticed my friend Karan carrying a huge backpack. So, I teasingly asked him, "Are you setting up a home in the mountains?"

Karan replied, "Oh trust me, I'm carrying all the essentials, and you will see how helpful they are when we reach the top."

After trekking for about 20 minutes uphill, Karan started panting and sweating profusely. At one point, he was unable to progress at all. So the rest of us had to take turns carrying the "essential things" in his backpack.

We reached the spot where we were to camp for the day around mid-day. When we looked around, we were speechless by the scenic beauty of the surroundings. The place was filled with wild flowers and fruits, and there was a beautiful waterfall that made the atmosphere serene. We quickly dropped our backpacks and went for a dip in the pond under the waterfall. After that, we sat in a circle and meditated.

Once the meditation was over, we went about plucking and munching on the delicious fruits, under the expert guidance of a friend. We were all having so much fun, that we totally forgot to unpack. Meanwhile, Karan was quite grumpy. He was removing things from his back pack in a fury, when I went over and asked, "Karan, what are you doing?"

Karan replied, "What a waste of my precious energy, I carried all these things, and we haven't used any of them. I wish I had packed light, I would have enjoyed the trek."

I said, "Well, it's never too late. Get rid of the unwanted stuff right now, the remaining trek will be easier."

Karan was not willing to do that. But soon enough, he realized it was really not worth carrying the heavy load further. So finally, he discarded all the unnecessary items. Once he gave away most of the things, his backpack was nearly empty and while climbing down, Karan had great fun and was always ahead of the group.

All of us carry such unnecessary baggage in the form of residual emotions. These may come from all our past experiences, which have affected us deeply and have left a visible impact on our psyche. And most of the times, these show up in the form of hurt, anger, resentment, guilt and fear. Whenever we go through an experience where we have felt one or more of these negative emotions, they are etched in our memory and travel with us at every moment.

In life's journey, when we carry excess baggage, materialistic or emotional, we are uncomfortable and unhappy. These emotions do not leave us easily; no matter how much we try. They have an immense impact on the way we behave or take decisions in the present moment. As a result, they also, adversely affect our physical, mental and emotional health. It's a great idea to shed the baggage, similar to what Karan did in the trek. However, this has to be a continuous process as we store new emotions in our mind, at every moment.

So how do we manage to carry these residual emotions for so many years? Here is the answer. When an incident occurs, the feelings pertaining to that incident get recorded deep in our sub-conscious mind along with the memory. Just imagine, if there was a video recorder that automatically recorded each and every moment of our lives, and at the press of a button we could watch any episode. It is similar with the memories that we hold deep in our sub-conscious mind. They resurface each time an emotional button is pressed.

The trigger can be in the form of (i) a similar experience, (ii) revisiting the same place, (iii) speaking on the phone with or meeting the person involved, or (iv) reading a book, seeing something in a movie or on TV, which relates even remotely to the original incident. In a nutshell, anything that reminds us of those feelings can act like a trigger. It is neither wise nor healthy to live with so much emotional baggage.

On social networking sites, you may often come across people with whom you never shared a good rapport with in the past. You may not feel like connecting with him or her. Well, that's absolutely fine, you are entirely free to choose who to "friend" with! Now pause for a moment, and recollect how this person's appearance on the mind-screen made you feel. At this point, ask an honest question, "Am I still carrying some residual emotions about this person?" In your answer lies the first step – identification. This will help you in understanding what you need to off-load or let go from your life.

Root cause of illnesses

It is astonishing to know how the unresolved issues and emotional residues can manifest in our physical body in the form of diseases.

Sometime back, my wife had developed a sore throat. As would be normal course of action, she went to the doctor and got a five-day course of antibiotics. However, after the five days, she was suffering and could barely speak. She even tried all the home remedies yet saw no improvement.

Incidentally, a few weeks before she got the sore throat, she had a misunderstanding with a close friend. She wanted to convey her wounded feelings to this friend, but didn't get a chance. This had been bothering her ever since. Still suffering from the sore throat, my wife decided to confront her friend. She called her, clarified the misunderstanding and resolved the issue. As soon as she finished doing this, she felt as if a heavy load had been lifted from her heart. The very next morning when she woke up, she was surprised to find that her throat was almost healed. She then realized that the underlying problem behind the sore throat was the emotion related to the misunderstanding with her friend. The moment she resolved the issue and let go of the excess emotional baggage, her throat started healing.

Many modern day diseases such as diabetes, high blood pressure, heart related ailments, skin disorders, sprout from the unresolved residual emotions that we carry. Unfortunately, we have been carrying them for so long that we don't even realize they exist and they become an integral part of our personality.

Residual emotions that we suppress always show up from time to time in our daily lives until we completely off load them from the sub-conscious level of our mind. For this, all we need to do is identify and get rid of them.

Only we can help ourselves

One evening, on the insistence of his wife, Kabir took her for a drive. Unfortunately, they met with a serious accident. Although his wife escaped with minor injuries, Kabir had to undergo a leg surgery. The doctors saved his leg but informed him that he would face difficulty walking throughout his life. Kabir was passionate about trekking and this accident totally shattered him. Today, petty things annoy Kabir and he ends up arguing with his wife at the drop of a hat. He couldn't understand why and how he could get angry so quickly at his wife, when in fact, he loves her dearly.

The truth is Kabir holds his wife responsible for his state today, and the arguments are a result of the residual emotions he was still harbouring deep in his subconscious mind. The emotions were being vented out as the angry arguments with his wife.

In a similar case, Mandira still harbours a lot of fear and doubt about the men she dates. She is extremely cautious, defensive and never trusts anyone completely. This is the result of a bad breakup she went through in an eight-year relationship. She did everything in her capacity to save the relationship. However, it eventually came to a point where she had to give up and they parted ways. The mistrust, fear and insecurity that she displays in her current relationships, come from the emotions related to that break-up. The emotions she is carrying, unaware, are ruining her chance to a happy life in the present.

Both Kabir and Mandira are destroying their present because of emotions from the past that may have no connection with them in the present. We are often so comfortable in that space of feeling victimised that we don't want to come out of it willingly.

Kabir's wife understands the real reason behind these arguments so she ignores them and makes every effort to keep him happy. Mandira's partner has moved on and has no clue of what she is going through. We need to understand that we, ourselves are ruining our chances of being happy by thinking about something that has long gone. We need to ask ourselves, is it worth it? Have we gained anything? Are we satisfied with the outcome? If not, then we must 'let go'. Remember that it is not only our present that stands the risk of being affected but we are very likely to mess up our future too.

Therefore, please pause and ask yourself - What is it that bothers me? When am I finally going to give up this baggage? How much more of my precious present and future life am I willing to sacrifice for the past?

It is most important to first acknowledge the enormous collection of residual emotions, which we are unknowingly carrying, and which are seriously harmful for our present and future. The next step is to clean or clear these emotions from our system. By doing so, we are giving ourselves a second chance to make a new beginning, to be happy, to be complete, to fulfil our dreams and desires and to be at peace.

At a glance

- *We all carry baggage of residual emotions from the past*
- *We must acknowledge and get rid of residual emotions*
- *These are root cause of most of our illnesses*
- *Only we can help ourselves*

KEYS

CHAPTER 4

RELIVING IS RELIEVING

Revisiting past memories

My past is very much, still part of what I am
My memories, emotions, even if I don't give-a-damn
I can revisit my past, whenever I wish to
To know myself better, and it helps me heal too.

As a child, I was terrified of the dark and could not stand being in the dark for even a moment. In the dark lived the monsters who would, I thought, crop up, grab me with their gigantic claws, and eat me up.

After I grew up, I had forgotten all about my fear of the dark until one day something made me realize that I still harbored that fear. I decided to overcome this fear by reliving it.

As I sat in the dark room, I finally faced my childhood fears head on. I recalled all the gruesome stories that frightened me and realized that it was only a creation of my mind.

When I had relived my fears I was relieved and even though I was still sitting in the dark, I was no longer scared.

On my birthday a few years ago, I received a parcel from an old school friend. I quickly opened it and found a photo album, the cover of which said 'All the wonderful memories captured here'. When I opened the album, the first picture was of my classmates and me from the first standard. Some friends from school had put together an album of old pictures from school functions, picnics, birthday parties and all the other times we had spent together as kids.

What a fantastic gift! Everyone at home suddenly got very excited to see the album. As we gathered around to look at the photographs, the old memories came alive. Each photograph had a unique story. I could precisely remember the details and also recall when it was taken. I had so much fun that day and just by going through the old photographs, I virtually went back to those moments.

It is amazing how powerful our mind is and what it is capable of. Just by going through an album, I could remember so accurately, the incidents and events from my school days. It almost felt like I was re-living, those days.

It is indeed a pleasant trip, walking through memory lane and reminiscing about the 'good old days'. The pertinent question, however, is what if we were presented an album of the bad memories? How many of us are willing to look at an album filled with all the traumatic, unhappy and bad photographs from our past? How many of us are willing to relive an *unpleasant* past?

Many people would avoid going to that lane and even reassure themselves and others alike that it is completely unnecessary and a waste of time. They see no point in remembering a past which has caused much hurt and pain. As mentioned before, our mind is not selective when storing the incidents of our life; it stores anything and everything that we experience. Therefore, just as we are able to remember all the good old days, filled with pleasant and happy experiences, we also remember the bad and unpleasant ones, from time to time. Yet, we try very hard to pretend to have forgotten them and console ourselves that they no longer bother us.

Our mind is a power house that stores all our experiences as 'memories', and is divided into two parts, the 'conscious' and the 'subconscious'. The subconscious mind comprises about 96% of the mind, while the conscious mind is only about 4%. This is most often compared to an iceberg floating in water, where only the tip is visible above. The vast portion which is under water is what our subconscious mind is like; while the conscious mind is like the tip of the iceberg which is above water.

The subconscious mind is similar to a huge safety deposit box in which are hidden all the knowledge, experiences, and all our hidden potential. Everything we have experienced from our past is safely stored in the sub-conscious mind in the form of memories and can be brought to our conscious mind by 'retrieving' them, i.e., by thinking about them.

Another interesting fact is that all our experiences are attached with emotions, which we go through at the time of the incident or experience. When a memory comes to our conscious awareness, the emotions automatically come alive. The idea behind reliving the past is to retrieve the negative or fear-based emotions that are stored in the sub-conscious mind and bring them to the conscious mind where they can be addressed and processed.

Why do we need to address these emotions? These negative emotions play havoc in our present life, affecting our decision-making abilities, our health, our relationships, our professional life, our day-to-day dealings with people and more importantly, our progress. They stop us from developing our full potential, depriving us from becoming who we truly are capable of becoming; a happy and successful individual.

Sometimes, it is easy to recall bad experiences of the past, depending on the intensity and the time of the experience. Other times, a situation or an event similar to the past experience acts as trigger to remind us of it. Whatever the cause may be, unless we identify and get rid of these negative emotions, we cannot lead a completely happy life. Therefore, it is crucial to revisit memories with negative emotions and re-live them, so that we can release those emotions and be relieved. And this forms the basis of *"Relive to Relieve"*.

By reliving a particular experience from the past, we actually release the blocked traumas or emotions associated with that particular memory or incident. If we can somehow go back to that incident and relive it in our mind, we can release the trauma and relieve ourselves from the effect of that trauma in the present moment. When we revisit these memories, they come to our conscious awareness or conscious mind where they can be processed and healed. Once the emotions are taken care of or released, the memory is automatically healed.

Having closure

Many times, people try to hide their true selves behind a mask, which does not suit them at all. But life has put them through such bad experiences that they find it easier to be in a disguise, as in the case of Maddie. She was 19 years old when she lost her parents in an accident. This incident changed her life completely, shattering all her dreams of a beautiful future. Over the next few years, she went through many difficulties and these turned her into someone she barely identified with. By nature Maddie was a very fun-loving and humorous girl, always full of smiles and laughter. But that was all in the past; now, she lived life as an angry, fearful and self-doubting adult.

When she came to me for a therapy, I asked her to narrate the whole accident. The more Maddie tried to think about the incident, the bitter she became. I realized that because the whole incident was unexpected, she could not have closure in the relationship with her parents and many things were unsaid. During the session, she got a chance to relive that memory and she could speak to her parents about all the things that she had wanted to, during the funeral. When she was ready, she bid them farewell and let them go.

Reliving this experience was painful to begin with, but once Maddie had made closure with what was left unsaid, she released that painful emotion attached to the memory. As a result, the memory was completely healed.

Healing wounds

When a wound is deep rooted, treating it on the surface is a superficial or temporary measure, as the problem lies deep within. If we have to heal the wound completely, the root cause needs to be treated; the wound will then heal and all that will be left is a faint scar. Yes, the scar will is a reminder of the wound, but it won't be painful. The memories of our past with negative emotions are exactly like that. Once we have retrieved, processed and released the negative emotions, they are healed. The memory of the experience will remain, but will not hurt or cause pain.

Linda was a natural host, who enjoyed planning and hosting parties, get-togethers and charity events. Her extroverted personality and go getter attitude drew the respect of all in her community. She was always the leader and centre of attention. Everything was going great for her family, until her husband lost his job. The global recession had set in and Linda's husband was one of the many victims of redundancy.

When he lost his job of 20 years, it was a hard blow for the entire family. He was a good person but losing the job was a very difficult thing for him to accept, especially at his age. Soon, he lost touch with his friends and became confined to his room. Linda realized that her husband was in depression and tried everything possible to be supportive and pull him out of this vacuum. But nothing worked, it became painful for her to see her husband sit quietly in a corner and do absolutely nothing.

One day, a family friend informed Linda that there was a good job opening for her husband and he should go for the interview immediately. Linda was very excited, but her husband was not. After much persuasion, Linda finally fought with him and forced him to go for the interview. A couple of hours later, the police called to inform her that her husband had met with a fatal accident on the highway. The police had traced Linda's whereabouts from the victim's belongings.

Six years after this unfortunate incident, Linda came to me for a therapy session. It was clear that she was living in guilt as she held herself responsible for her husband's death. During the session, Linda was able to relive the entire episode, release the pain, and forgive herself. She accepted that it was an accident and she had nothing to do with his death and slowly she was able to move on.

The tragic death of a loved one causes immense pain, anger and bitterness. In Linda's case, in addition to the pain of losing a loved one, she also felt guilty for being the reason behind it. I would like to point out here that healing is a process; and it takes time. We have to be prepared to let go of the painful emotions attached to an experience.

It is only when you are ready, that you can actually release that pain. What you have to understand and accept is that you have no control over something which has already happened. Nothing can change the past. But our willingness to let go definitely helps us to relieve the traumas. We can surely give this gift to ourselves.

Our mind is more powerful than we can imagine. It stores every single incident that has ever taken place in our life, like a master computer. What you may think as "forgotten" is never so. And at any point in time, we can retrieve the data, by metaphorically logging into it. However, sometimes it may seem impossible as we may not recall anything that happened to us at a young age. But just because we don't remember, does not mean it is not there!

Memories exist in our present day life through the behavior, action and attitude we display. Most of the times, we may behave in a particular way which is a contrast of who we really are. Many times, people around us and we ourselves may not understand, why we behave the way we do. This is because many of us are not aware that the behavior is streaming from deep within our sub-conscious mind.

Certain things never really leave us. When we re-visit the memories and live them again as if the events were taking place in the present, we actually release the emotions and traumas attached to those memories. The process is simple. We just need to bring the sub-conscious memories to the conscious mind and then experience each and every emotion we had experienced at the time of that incident. This process is also called catharsis or cleansing. By doing so, we are getting a second chance to have closure.

It is very important that we have closure, for our sakes as well as our loved ones'. Nothing is gone until we completely *allow* it to. And when we let go of a traumatic event from the past, we heal inward and allow ourselves to be a healthier and happier person.

Have you ever noticed, how, while reading a book, sometimes we want to go back to the pages that we have already read? As if we have missed something important, as if something within us had urged us to re-read a particular part of the book. When we go back to that chapter and read it again, we feel a sense of completeness, and then we are able to continue reading the rest of the book peaceful and happy.

It's the same with life. Our life is a great story with so many mysteries ahead, but until we completely let go of the traumatic past memories, rooted deep in our sub-conscious mind, we will not be able to continue the rest of the story happily. When we have an option to live a better life, why choose a bitter one?

The reason I emphasize on reliving is because the root cause and the solution to most of our problems lies within us. But since we are unaware, we are unable to do anything about it. Sometimes, the answers are right there at the back of our mind, safely and secretly stored away, without us even knowing that they exist.

Given a chance, each one of us would like to let go completely of the traumas and negative emotions of the past. Given a chance, we would like to be completely happy and carefree. Given a chance, we would like to edit the script of our life to make a happy ending. The question is, is it possible? Yes, of course it is! And the key to unlock the demons and monsters and destroy them lies in our hands. Let us give ourselves a second chance to live a life that truly represents us.

At a glance

- *By reliving a past incident mentally, we can release attached emotions*
- *It is important to have closure with the past*
- *We must be willingly ready to let go*

CHAPTER 5

INNER CHILD

The fountain of joy

I want to dance in rain, blow bubbles of soap
I am the inner child, full of life and hope
I like to run and play, and shout and sing
And scream with joy, as if no one's listening.

One evening I came home from work extremely stressed and angry. At that time, I was still working in the corporate setup. I'm not the sort of person who gets angry easily, but that was an exceptional evening. The continuous travelling, endless meetings, reports, deadlines and constant bickering from bosses, had finally taken a toll on me. I entered my home in a rage and got into an argument with everyone at home.

That night, I had no appetite, shunned dinner and asked everyone to leave me alone. As I retired to bed late, I calmed down and started to question my behavior. I felt extremely guilty. The next morning, I began the damage control by apologizing to everyone. As I drove to work, something inside me kept screaming to take a break. So that weekend, I decided to go alone for a nature walk to a forest near my home. I watched the sun rise, slowly turning the dark blue skies into sweet orange color. I noticed how breathtakingly scenic the forest was, as I walked leisurely taking time to soak in the beauty of the place.

The aroma of the grass was sweet and the morning dew looked

like tiny little pearls scattered all over the grass, the tall trees looked like giant guardians of the forest and the ground was filled with wild flowers of all kinds and colors that looked like a carpet woven on earth, from a distance. The gentle sound of the stream flowing nearby felt like melody to accompany the singing of the birds that were chirping in chorus. It felt like the forest was welcoming me along with the dawn. I took a few deep breathes of the fresh air and stood still for a while, in awe with the beauty that surrounded me.

As I looked around, I spotted a bunch of beautiful butterflies sitting on a berry shrub. My first thought on seeing the butterflies was to run and catch them. But when I went near the shrub, they flew off. I looked around to see if anyone was watching me and when I realized that I was alone, without wasting a second, I started running after them. The various colors of butterfly wings fluttering in the air were like hundreds of tiny rainbows forming momentarily in front of my eyes. It was simply an astonishing exhibition of life within nature. I ran behind them with all enthusiasm, going up and down the hillocks. After sometime, I stopped running and just watched them.

As I sat down, completely breathless, I laughed out loudly, dumbfounded by the beautiful display of life in front of my eyes. The experience was awesome and filled my heart with joy. Although I had been running after the butterflies, I was not tired; I felt fully energized and completely rejuvenated. I relaxed, in the lap of nature, and it struck me that I had gone back in time to when I was 10-years-old.

As a kid, I used to enjoy chasing butterflies in the hope of catching one. I had not done that since I was a kid. This experience completely rejuvenated me and brought back so many wonderful childhood memories. I had reconnected to the inner child in me. The inner child was always inside me, but ignored for too long. This new found enthusiasm was because I had allowed the inner child to come out and take over the adult in me.

Can you recollect similar incidents which gave you tremendous joy as a child? Things you thoroughly enjoyed doing and had enormous amounts of fun with, like catching ladybugs, climbing trees, plucking berries, eating raw mango, getting drenched and dancing in the rains, playing hide and seek, playing football in mud, playing doll house, hiding under the bed, coloring, blowing candles on your birthday and making a wish, bursting balloons, licking the ice cream off your fingers, wrists and elbows as it melts, making sand castles, collecting sea shells or stamps, blowing soap bubbles, building a castle with cards.

The list is endless. Just making a list of the fun things will bring back such wonderful and joyous memories. Imagine how much more fun you would have, if you could actually do them again?

Do you remember how excited you were just blowing candles on your birthday? Being the centre of attention, everyone singing the happy birthday song for you while you smiled from ear to ear, waiting to cut the cake. The cake cutting was such a *wow* moment then. It was the moment you waited for the entire evening, followed by the birthday gifts which you received with a big "thank you," and tore open the wrapping paper, to unveil the delights that will be yours. Those were such fun, simple and exciting days.

But times have changed; you grew up and became a responsible adult. For some, it would be embarrassing if people found out they were excited about a simple thing as a birthday. Some even find it a total waste of time.

I vividly remember that, as a little boy, I enjoyed lying on the floor and watching an army of ants march in a single neat file carrying sugar and disappear into a crevice. I watched them with awe and curiosity and wondered where they where they lived. I really enjoyed doing that. I wonder how my wife would react if I were to do that now.

As children, we were so innocent, we had so much fun doing simple things, like running around aimlessly or screaming on top of our voices. As years went by, we stopped doing these things and grew up into so called "responsible adults". It is as if a rule book of 'dos' and 'don'ts' was handed over to us and all the fun things we liked was listed under 'the don'ts'. It would be considered absolutely crazy if we were caught doing anything 'childlike' or as we so often hear people say 'childish'.

Funnily enough, as "sensible adults", we see the same army of ants as pests that are harmful. It's not like the ants that have changed, but our outlook towards them definitely has. The point is we no longer connect to the ants in the same way or for that matter to any of the simple things that we used to as children. And that is because we are no longer connected to the inner child within our hearts.

The child within

The inner child is the little child we were, who still resides within us, who desires to be nurtured, cared for and loved. It is the fun loving, happy, joyful, humorous *us* when we were young. It is also the emotional, sensitive, creative and imaginative *us* whom we have controlled and silenced. It is a part of *us* which is hurt, neglected, abused, ignored and hidden from view. This child is just below the surface, causing us to be anxious, worried and fearful of mistreatment.

The inner child is that part of us which was left behind somewhere, which never grew up although, we physically did. It is simply defined by the qualities it represents and the behavior it exhibits, such as joy, freedom of expression, fearlessness, honesty, trusting, carefree, spontaneity, mischief, etc. All these and many more positive characteristics combined are a true portrayal of the inner child.

However, these attributes start disappearing slowly from our lives as we grow up, and other new ones cover them, completely redefining our personality. This is similar to a sunken boat getting covered with layers of algae.

It is possible to know whether our inner child is active or not. If we (i) lose ourselves in children's fun activities or enjoy playing with children's toys; or (ii) cry during an emotional movie; or (iii) over-indulge with our own children; or (iv) love visiting theme parks designed for children; or (vi) get emotional looking at old photo albums, home movies or scrapbooks from our childhood, or even

(vii) seek to please the senior members of our families, then our inner child is still active and we should try to keep in touch with that deeper part of us.

The inner child exists in our subconscious mind. It is a concept used in psychology to indicate the innocent, child-like part of human mind. The term is often used to talk about one's experiences during childhood and its residual effects. We can clearly picture what the little child looks like and how the child is feeling and acting.

Over the years, memories stored in our sub-conscious mind, the layers of conditioning, the belief systems and the excess baggage of negative emotions such as bitterness, pain, anger, guilt, resentment and fear, act as a knife which gradually cuts us from our inner child. It is important to note here that this transition varies from person to person. That is because every individual is different, their experience is different and their ability to deal with a particular situation is also different, depending on their circumstances.

Societal norms, family values, belief systems, social and financial stratum and many other factors play a great role in shaping an individual. The inner child comes into being by our denial of our true feelings, especially when we try hard to live up to others' expectations. In doing so, we hold back our child-like responses, thinking that we always have to be 'serious' about life. We do not feel the freedom to play and act childish. We feel that we are being loved for 'what we do' rather than 'who we are'.

Kavya's loss

Kavya was a young girl of 20 when she got married and a true example of a person who's in touch with the inner child. Her days were filled with laughter, jokes, and stories. There was never a dull moment in her life. She paid no heed to people who made fun of her child-like behavior. Those who resonated with her, found her full of positive energy and life. She was the star of every picnic and party, and children loved to play with her.

After 3 years of marriage, Kavya had a baby. Her pregnancy was not a smooth one. During that time elderly ladies, with many years of experience and full of strict rules surrounded her. She was soon restricted from doing many things she enjoyed, but she had no choice but to follow.

Her husband noticed the first changes in her behavior and attitude towards people and situations. Her opinions were different now; she no longer laughed out loud, joked around, or enjoyed the simple things she liked. He took this as a phase that would get over once the baby arrived. The arrival of the baby was a joyous moment for all in the family.

The new mother was happy, but not cheerful or excited. I once asked her why she was not her old bubbly self, to which, she replied, "I'm no longer a kid, I'm a mother now, and can't behave like a child anymore!"

Gradually, she distanced herself from her inner child and donned a new role of a mother. It's a beautiful thing to be a mother; in fact, it is one of most delightful miracles in the world. But that does not mean you disconnect from your inner child!

What do you think happened to that child in you? The child that was the real you, the child that was full of dreams, the child that was afraid of nothing, the child that was willing to take on risks and adventures, the child that laughed, and screamed and ran. Most of us look back at those good old childhood days with fond memories, but say, "Well I'm all grown up, I'm an adult now, I have responsibilities. I have so much to do, bills to pay, errands to run, reports to complete. I have a duty towards my company, my family, the society. I cannot sit around and blow bubbles all day, that's crazy and ridiculous!"

If this is what our answer is, then it confirms only one thing. We no longer feel connected to our inner child. This is because we have ignored that child, and are not connected with it, we don't believe it exists. But that child is very much alive. In fact, that child is screaming to get out and be acknowledged. That inner child that we have ignored for so long is the solution to many of our setbacks in life today.

What has changed? As we grow up, various changes take place in our lives. The additional responsibilities, change of role, change of place, the various incidents, our societal conditioning. Like when we are told,

"Stop behaving like a child, you are a grown up now,"

"You have to study hard and get 98%,"

"You must get into the best college,"

"You must at least have a six figure salary. You must join a multi-national company,"

"You must get married now,"

"You must have a child now."

The endless list of do's and don'ts which are handed down while growing up, gradually and unconsciously distance us from the inner child. Sometimes, resentment towards the people who have stopped us from doing what we really enjoyed as children also acts as a barrier between us and the inner child. More so, if those people are still around in our life. And when we can no longer connected to that inner child, we no longer feel its presence in our lives and when we no longer identify with it, we draw an iron curtain between the adult and the inner child. Then comes a time when we refuse to acknowledge the existence of that inner child altogether.

The inner child is a part of us that is not complete. It is a part of our being, which we have left somewhere in the past, in the process of growing up. The inner child is ignored and deprived of doing what it enjoys most and that's why we often feel incomplete as adults. This incomplete part of us, unless healed or attended to, creates an unfulfilled life. It often pulls us back from the path of our success. We can connect to the inner child anywhere, any place, any time we want to. We just need to be willing to do so.

Tips to heal the child within

The first step towards healing the inner child is to acknowledge that we are disconnected from it. We have to recognize the problem in order to find a solution for it. Here are few questions we can ask ourselves:

Do I often feel irritated, sad, angry, sacred or shy?

Am I unhappy in my relationships?

Do I fail to express myself openly?

Do I have low self-esteem?

Do I often feel hurt?

Do I often feel angry or jealous?

If most answers are 'yes', this validates that our inner child is hurt and has been ignored for a long time. Our current state of life and the behavior we exhibit determines the extent of damage to the inner child.

Acknowledging the problem is only the tip of the iceberg. The real and important step to healing the inner child is to identify the cause. If the inner child is hurt or damaged, then the adult, who carries this inner child, will be living in resentment, anger, pain and fear. We need to go back to our early childhood days and slowly walk through; step by step carefully identifying the issues, events and people that were instrumental in hurting or causing damage to our inner child. For example, if as a child, we were loud, always laughing and shouting, but were constantly reprimanded for that behavior, we slowly get conditioned to believe that speaking or laughing loudly is considered bad behavior. And as a result we grow into adults that abide by that erroneous assumption and more so advocate it to others.

Once we have identified the reasons for ignoring our inner child, the next step is to accept. Accept that our inner child is hurt or has been disconnected. Accept that the past cannot be changed; however, it can definitely be healed. The healing can only take place when we whole-heartedly and honestly accept ourselves with all our flaws.

Acceptance forms an essential part of the healing process of the inner child. It is okay to feel angry, hurt, that we have been ignored. Remember that healing will not happen overnight, just as the damage was not caused overnight. We have to be patient with ourselves and give ourselves the time.

After we have accepted the traumas our inner child has gone through, it's time to release those traumas and reconnect to the inner child. Talk to the inner child! Find out what is that one thing that would really make us happy. There is a simple yet beautiful process through which we can analyze why and under what circumstance we have drawn the curtain between the inner child and ourselves. Once we are able to identify that block, that fear, which is holding back the inner child in us, we will find new energy and enthusiasm, like I felt that day in the forest.

By being connected to our inner child, we can overcome the fears we are harboring, explore our true potential with new horizons and achieve anything that we always wanted to.

At a glance

- *There is a child in all of us*
- *We disconnect ourselves from that child as we grow up*
- *One of the main reasons of our miseries is this disconnect*
- *We must try to reconnect to that inner child*

"I firmly believe that forgiveness is the best revenge.....!"

THE GIFT OF FORGIVENESS

Set yourself free

I want to be free, from guilt of the past
My anger and regrets, and shadows they cast
I want to forgive, and let go once and for all
It's for my own self, and I must take the call.

A few months back, I met an old friend. He had come to town for some work and we decided to have lunch. As we were eating, he suddenly said, "It doesn't pay to be honest, the world is full of crooks, and one needs to be manipulative."

Five years back, Sam had been falsely accused of taking a favour and asked to resign from a company that he served for 15 years with honesty and dedication. Sam was a hard-working and honest guy. I could see that he still suffered from that incident. He was hurt and depressed and this was affecting his present life, both at work and home.

With great difficulty, I talked him into coming for one of my workshops. After the first day of the workshop, I made him talk to me about what was bothering him. Once he poured his heart out, I asked him to write down everything he felt, especially the names of all the people who had hurt him. An hour later, he had filled pages.

After taking a look at his "released rage", I said, "Sam, you are filled with so much of hurt, anger and bitterness. Do you realize that by constantly talking about them you are still connected to all those people involved with the incident? If you wish to live a happy life, you need to 'forgive'. It may not be easy, but it is possible. Until you have forgiven, you will not be able to move on. The choice is yours; do you want to carry the entire burden around? Or leave it behind right now?"

Sam seemed quite eager to leave it all behind. I asked him to tear up the papers on which he had written down all his troubles and burn it up. I told him to forgive each and every person from the bottom of his heart while doing this exercise. After a month, when I met him, I saw in him my old college friend, the one who was cheerful and happy one.

Cutting the strings

Forgiveness is like the sword which cuts the ropes of bondage of our past negative emotions, which we unconsciously carry, day-in and day-out. Forgiveness is a conscious decision to let go of resentment and thoughts of revenge. The experience that hurt or upset us might always remain a part of our life, but by forgiving we will lessen the grip it has on us. This allows us to focus on other positive aspects of life.

It is a tool that sets us free, to soar high towards our ambitions, without the baggage of our negative emotions. Forgiveness helps us disconnect from our past bad experiences and the emotions set therein. This helps us move towards our ultimate goal or purpose of life. It is through forgiveness that we open the cage, in which we are trapped, to set ourselves free. When we forgive, we have closure for the unresolved issues of the past. Forgiveness can even lead to feelings of understanding, empathy and compassion for the one who hurt us.

Forgiveness doesn't mean that we deny the other person's responsibility for hurting us, and it doesn't minimize or justify the wrong. By forgiving, we are not condoning or approving the act itself.

We are releasing ourselves from that hurt. The person we find most difficult to forgive, is the one we have to let go of the most. Forgiveness brings a kind of peace that helps us go on with life.

Many of us can relate to the irritation caused by a dust particle in the eye, especially when we are in the midst of something important. We stop whatever we are doing and try all kinds of remedies to get rid of that tiny particle that's bothering us. Until that happens, we can't see clearly. And only when we see clearly, can we focus.

The anger, the irritation and the discomfort we feel at that moment due to that tiny dust particle is minuscule compared to the burden and hurt we have been carrying for years because we have not forgiven. It is like thousands of tiny dust particles getting into our eyes and putting us through unbearable pain and discomfort. Are we willing to undergo that cleansing, get rid of that burden, so that our vision is clear and we can focus on the present and future ahead? If we are ready, then, it is time to forgive.

Forgiving and letting go is all about us. It is about making peace with our inner self. Even science attests to this phenomenon. As per some studies, when we forgive from the heart, certain hormones are released from our endocrine system, which are extremely beneficial for our health and well being. When we forgive completely and from our heart, the reminiscence of negative emotions is wiped from our being.

The crystal vase

We often live in pain and guilt because we hold our loved ones responsible for trivial issues, and carry that burden for years.

One day while playing in the house, Mary and her brothers broke an expensive crystal vase. The eldest of the three siblings, Mary, stood still with fear along with her younger brothers Jim and James. Her mother, Jane came running into the living room, looked at the broken vase and started crying. "I'm sorry, Mum," said Mary. Her mother went over to Mary and slapped her. This was a very special vase; it was a gift from Mary's father, who had died a year back. The loss of her husband, little money and three kids to care for had turned Jane into a bitter widow.

Jane collected the broken pieces, while crying, and kept them in a box. Then she looked into the little girl's eyes with anger and said, "You have broken something very precious and it can never be replaced. I used to think of him all the time looking at the vase, and now it is gone. I will never forgive you for this, Mary".

Years passed, but the relationship between Mary and her mother was never the same again. Jane always found a reason to be nasty to Mary, and Mary knew why, but never said anything. Jane had been living alone since the kids had moved out. One day she got a call informing her that Mary had met with an accident.

When Jane arrived at the hospital, both her sons and Mary's husband were waiting for her. Her son James informed her that Mary was in very bad condition and that she might not survive. Jane went to the room Mary was in and sat near her bed. For the first time in so many years, Jane started crying.

As she held on to her only daughter's hand, Mary slowly opened her eyes and smiled. "Don't cry, Mum," she said in a feeble voice. "I'm not in pain, I'm glad you came. Please forgive me for the vase; I know you have been upset with me, all these years."

Jane, still crying, kissed her daughter's hand and said, "I love you honey, and I know I haven't been fair to you, I forgive you. I forgive you completely and I know it was an accident."

Mary passed away peacefully in her sleep, the next day. After the funeral was over, James informed his mother that it was he who had broken the vase that day. Jane had forgiven her daughter, but she still had to forgive herself. Sometimes, we carry burdens, which we realize after many years, were just not worth it.

Forgiveness is the act of releasing ourselves from a painful burden. A burden that we carry for years together which weighs us down. This leaves us standing miles away from where we could have reached in life, had we forgiven. When we release this burden, we have made peace with the pain and are ready to let go.

Karishma's plight

Until we are at peace with ourselves, the burden follows us everywhere in life as a ghost, as in the case of Karishma. Her mother in law and her never agreed on anything. This caused many fights and gradually created an iron wall between them that was never broken down. Recently during dinner at her best friend's place, Karishma talked about how her mother in law would have found fault in each and everything, from the dinner menu to the décor, to the people that were invited.

Her friend listened to her with patience and said "Karishma, she's been dead for three years now. I feel you need to just forgive her and put an end to this constant bickering. It's almost like you carry her around wherever you go. It's not healthy at all. You become so bitter and angry each time you speak of her. Talking about all the wrong things she said or did won't change anything now. She's gone, make peace with her at least now. Let her go. "

That night, Karishma went home and cried her heart out while recalling all the things her mother in law had said or done to hurt her. After crying for a long time, she went outside and looked at the sky and said aloud "I forgive you unconditionally for all the hurt and pain you have caused me. I release you from my life right now. I've made peace with the hurt and pain that you caused me, rest in peace, I forgive you!"

Sometimes intervention is highly important in the process of forgiveness. Most often, we are not even conscious that we are carrying so much hurt and pain from the past, like in the case of Karishma. Only when her friend pointed it out, did she realized the burden she had been carrying all along.

Understanding why we need to forgive is 80% of the job done. This involves a continuous introspection. The balance 20% is the actual act of forgiveness. When we understand, forgiving becomes very simple. Only when we forgive 100% do we grow into happy and complete individuals.

Ever observed, how many times we say "Sorry" in a day? Now think, how many times do we really mean it? Asking for forgiveness is equally important and plays a huge role in living a fulfilled life.

Give yourself the gift of forgiveness

Guilt is an emotion that we experience when we hurt someone. It is a heavy burden to carry around day in, day out. It starts showing very quickly in our behaviour towards everything in life. We tend to give justifications for everything or become extremely defensive. This behaviour arises, most often, out of guilt. Most of the time, we are not able to relate to this pattern of behaviour or connect to the guilt inside us and hence go on living in ignorance.

Living with guilt is like allowing a poisonous creeper to grow around a healthy plant. No matter how much you trim it, it will grow back again and eventually engulf and kill the tree itself. This is how guilt works in our life, like a poisonous creeper, preventing us from blossoming into beautiful and happy individuals and from achieving our true potential. What is important is to uproot the poisonous creeper from our lives completely and throw it as far away as possible.

At times, we don't find anything wrong, and assure ourselves that everything is fine. We convince ourselves that there is nothing to feel guilty about, or that we may have been too hard on ourselves. We conveniently ignore the guilt, which is like a deep-rooted wound that on surface seems fine. But in truth, it is actually growing inside us and will eventually prove to be fatal, if not treated quickly. Firstly, we need to acknowledge its existence. Confront it with courage, operate on it with faith and treat it from the root. Once we have done that, we will feel liberated; as if a soothing lotion has been applied on the wound.

Like in the case of Jelita, whose father-in-law suffered a lot in the last five years of his life, because he did not ask for forgiveness. Jelita did everything possible to be the perfect daughter-in-law. However, her father-in-law always had something to accuse her of. As things got worse, Jelita and her husband moved out.

Jelita visited her in-laws regularly and never once complained or fought back. Deep in his heart the old man knew that Jelita was a nice girl, but his own awful nature compelled him to fight with her. He was always in and out of the hospitals, but the doctors couldn't diagnose any major problem. When the doctors finally saw the end coming, they informed his family members. The old man asked for a priest to come and pray for him.

As the priest prayed, the old man said, "Father, I want to be forgiven for all the wrong things I have done in this life."

The priest said, "If you truly want to be forgiven, apologize to the ones you have hurt."

After a lot of contemplation and hesitation, the old man asked to speak to Jelita. He said to her, "I know I have been mean to you all my life. I have intentionally said and done so many things to hurt you. I have also made you cry. And I know that today I suffer because of my own deeds. I'm so sorry Jelita, I beg you to forgive me. I can't take this burden anymore."

Jelita accepted the old man's apology and said that she had completely forgiven him. In his last few days, the old man was full of life. He joked and laughed with all who came to visit him. It was astonishing how much he had changed from the old mean and grumpy man he was. He died in peace.

The act of apologizing, saying 'I'm sorry' is an overwhelming feeling. It releases us from an iron cage in which we have been trapped for years. Only those who have had the courage to ask for forgiveness can relate to it. However, remember not to attach any expectations to it. Because there is no guarantee that the other person will forgive, there is no point questioning why we are not forgiven. What is important is that we are willing to ask for forgiveness. And just by doing that we are released from the guilt that we harbour inside.

What is more important is that we are healed, and are ready to move on to achieve our full potential. That is the miracle of forgiving and asking to be forgiven. Both are life changing virtues and lead to greater spiritual and psychological well-being, and healthier relationships. This results in a life of less anxiety, stress and hostility which is the root cause of hypertension and depression.

We always have a choice and we can either choose to live a life filled with hurt, anger and guilt or we can choose to forgive and see our true self blossom.

At a glance

- *Forgiveness is the tool by which we can cut strings of the past*
- *Forgiveness releases us from a painful burden*
- *Forgiveness is about making peace with our own self*
- *Forgiveness is only about us, to let go and move on*
- *We always have a choice - to forgive and forget*

CHAPTER 7

HAVE YOU HEALED YOUR PAST ENOUGH?

All of us have a past. As we move ahead in time, the preceding moment becomes the past. The unresolved emotions from the past pull us back, depriving us of the joy of present and the zest for the future. It is extremely important to assess ourselves from time to time, to know if we have completely healed our past. This chapter contains a small exercise to help you analyse this.

Take some time out for yourself and find a quiet place. You can put on some nice relaxing music. Just shut yourself from all sorts of disturbances and outside noise. Switch off your mobile phone, put off your doorbell and make sure that nobody disturbs you.

All you need for this exercise is a pen/pencil. You can also use blank sheets of paper. Once you start the exercise you need to be honest with your answers. Take your time to think. Answer the following questions in a *Yes* or *No*.

The answer cannot be a *'May be'*. You can also note down certain incidents from the past that triggered your answers or certain things which you feel you need to resolve. Make a note of it on the blank sheets.

After you finish the exercise, go back to these notes and try to resolve or heal them one by one, using the 'Powerful tools to heal your past' given in the next chapter.

This is an invaluable gift you are giving yourself. So, get set...
Go!

	Yes	No
1. Do you try to avoid talking about your past?	☐	☐
2. Do you think any conditioning or belief system is stopping you from doing what you like?	☐	☐
3. If someone makes you angry/upset do you go down memory lane and recall all the times this person made you feel like this?	☐	☐
4. When you are alone and think about unhappy past incidents, do you get upset?	☐	☐
5. Do you feel guilty about something which has happened in the past?	☐	☐
6. Do failures in the past stop you from taking steps towards new venture?	☐	☐
7. Are you afraid of taking risks?	☐	☐
8. Do the traumatic incidents of your past still haunt you?	☐	☐
9. Do you blame others for your current situation in your life?	☐	☐
10. Is it difficult for you to let go and move on?	☐	☐
11. Are you afraid to recall and resolve traumatic memories?	☐	☐
12. Do you resist doing something that you enjoyed doing as a child?	☐	☐
13. Is there anything you have done in the past for which you have not completely forgiven yourself?	☐	☐
14. Is there anyone you have still not forgiven for hurting you in the past?	☐	☐

15. Do you see yourself as the same person today as
     you were in the past? □ □

If the answer to 10 or more of the above questions is *No*, then congratulations! You are on a forward journey in life. You just need to consciously continue the healing process to keep yourself healed of your past. However, if 10 or more of your answers are *Yes*, then you have a second chance right now to heal your past.

After you finish assessing revisit the questions where the answer is *Yes*, refer to the notes you have made and work upon them with the tools given ahead.

CHAPTER 8

POWERFUL TOOLS TO HEAL YOUR PAST

Given below are some tried and tested powerful tools that will help you in healing your past

- **Relieving through forgiveness** – Visualise any painful or traumatic incident of the past which you need to heal, as if it is happening in the present. Imagine that incident in smallest possible detail, for example, what time of the day it was, who were the people present, the location, what were the feelings the incident generated, etc. Get into all the details of that incident. Feel all the negative emotions you felt at that time. Acknowledge them. If you feel like crying, that's fine. Let all the emotions flow out. If you are feeling guilt, ask for forgiveness from those whom you have wronged. See that they have forgiven you. Remember, it is important to ask for forgiveness. Just asking for forgiveness relieves you of the burden you are carrying. It is also important to forgive yourself completely. Similarly, if you are emotionally hurt in a past incident forgive all the people who have hurt you. You need to move on. This exercise will help in offloading lot of emotions that pull you back, such as anger, guilt, remorse, hatred, sorrow, etc. It is possible to heal yourself from any of your past traumatic incident, even if it involves people who have since departed. The basic pre-requisite for this exercise is that one should be willing to let go, through forgiving or asking for forgiveness. Visualising a painful memory in its complete detail as if it is happening in the present, helps to bring the memory to our conscious mind. This helps in relieving the painful emotions through re-living the past memory.

- **List making** - Make a list of all the people, places, things and incidents that bother you. Against each of the above, write what is it that bothers you. Once you've written it down, tear the paper into small pieces and say, 'I let go' while tearing. Once you finish this, flush it or burn it. Repeat this for 7 days and see the result yourself.

- **Cord Cutting** – This is a very powerful tool. Visualise that there is an invisible cord that connects you and the person whom you would like to let go off from your life. Feel the connection with that person through this cord. Ask the universe to give you an imaginary pair of scissors and imagine a pair of scissors coming in your hands. Now with these pair of scissors, cut this imaginary cord and see the person moving away from you to his/her own journey. Thank him or her for their role in your life, and for teaching you valuable life lessons. The person you imagine could be living or even departed. This can also be done for a situation. Sometimes you are too attached to a negative situation from the past that haunts you. For example, you could be a witness to some tragic incident, such as an accident, riots, etc. In this case treat the situation as an entity and repeat the above exercise.

- **HOPE Technique** – Sit in a comfortable position and close your eyes and breathe as deep as you can. Concentrate on the breath and count 15 to 20 breaths. Now lightly tap on your left shoulder with right hand. As you tap, think of one or more of your painful or negative memories. Visualise them filling the left side of your body. Feel the pain or traumatic emotions due to those memories as you do so. Then with your left hand, lightly tap the right shoulder. As you tap, think of one or more of your most positive or happy memories. Visualise them filling the right side of your body. Feel the happiness or positive emotions due to these memories as they come out. Now again tap the left shoulder with the right hand, and see all the negative emotions and memories flowing like a liquid out of your left hand and fingers and absorbed by the earth. Feel the vacuum created in the left side of your body due to this. Now tap the right shoulder and see the positive emotions in the right part of your body filling the entire space in your body. Feel the positive emotions, happiness, joy, courage, love, confidence, peace, etc filling in your whole body. Then visualise any symbol in front of your eyes, it could be any shape and colour of your choice, or a positive symbol you associate yourself with. Now repeat the affirmation three times, "This symbol fills me with all positive emotions" and open your eyes. Whenever you feel troubled with any negative emotions related to the past, you can remember this symbol, and can feel yourself getting filled with positive emotions. This symbol could even be a sound or a certain word, or just a deep breath. This technique is called HOPE (Holding On to Positive Empowerment), because one can use this any time to come out of negative emotions and instantly feel positive and happy.

- **Banish clutter.** Cleaning your house of clutter is a very easy and quick way to heal yourself. The old, broken things in the house may carry emotions associated with some traumatic memory in the past. Many times when you just look at something, you are flooded with unpleasant incidents or memories attached to it. It is like a chain reaction, many times leading to completely unrelated but negative memories as well. It helps to get rid of all those old, soiled and broken articles in your house, connected to such memories. You can immediately start feeling lighter by doing this.

- **Change of scenery.** A change of house, or town can also help some times to move away from a bad past and help in healing faster. It also metaphorically means you are moving on and leaving the past baggage in the past.

- **Make amends** - If you have not been in touch with someone over the years due to some misunderstanding in the past, take an initiative to call up and clear the misunderstanding. If you have to say sorry, then do so. If someone apologises, accept it gracefully. The idea is to shed the baggage and move on. It really does not help us in the long run to keep these misunderstandings or grudges in mind. What matters is being free to move forward. We must put a logical end to any such past emotional baggage to travel ahead lighter.

- **Explore like a child.** - Make a point to try something new every day. It could be a small thing, but has to be something you have never done before. Try out anything new, a new way to the office, a new person you speak to, a new thing or word or phrase you learn. You can even do something that you have been doing over the years, in a new way. This exercise frees you from the bondage of 'shoulds' and 'should nots'. These shoulds and should-nots become a part of our conditioning and play a major role in forming belief systems. The point is to break out of conditioning layers or patterns. Be good in experimenting.

- **Do what you enjoyed in the past** – Many times we grow old very fast and label certain things as childish, that we used to enjoy doing once upon a time. If doing a certain thing gave you happiness when you were a child, it will surely make you happy even now. The secret is to keep your inner child happy. Go ahead and blow soap bubbles, make castles in the sand, make paper boats or aeroplanes, climb trees, dance in the rain, or do anything that you loved doing as a child.

- **Spend time with children** – Children connect us to our own childhood. The more time we spend with them, the happier we feel overall. It helps us in shedding our inhibitions about doing certain things, which has probably built over the years knowingly or unknowingly. This exercise also brings out the inner child in us.

- **Pamper yourself** – When something goes wrong we hold ourselves responsible and bury ourselves under heap of guilt, anger, fear, hatred, jealousy, resentment. We also punish ourselves at times and engage in self-sabotage which ultimately adversely affects our self esteem. This process needs to be reversed. Tell yourself "it is ok" and move on. Pampering yourself in whatever way you can helps in moving on. Go and have an ice cream or pat yourself on the back. You can even buy yourself a gift or give yourself a spa treatment. You can find creative ways to pamper yourself. The underlying rule is, whatever makes you feel the best.

- **Positive Affirmations** – Positive affirmations are like having an energy drink. It will fill you with instant energy. Each time a negative thought comes to your mind just drink a thought of positive affirmation and recharge yourself. Here are a few affirmations to help you in the process of healing the past.

  ✓ *I love and accept myself the way I am*

  ✓ *I let go of all my hurt, pain, fear, anger and guilt*

  ✓ *I completely forgive myself and others who have hurt me*

  ✓ *I am always surrounded by loving and positive people*

  ✓ *I am always divinely protected*

Live your Present

We must live our present, 'cause present is a gift
Living every moment, does make a deeper shift

Each one of us, has a life purpose, a task
This is revealed to us, whenever we ask

Our purpose is hidden in things, we love doing most
We must try to find that destination of life, at any cost

Once we know the direction, we must start the walk
And leave it to the universe, to open our life's lock

"Just do it" is the mantra that can take us ahead
Get-up and get-going, and quickly leave the bed

With no fear of taking risks, we'll certainly succeed
Our passion giving us energy, and the courage that we need

It doesn't really matter, what is our aptitude
The only thing which takes us far, is our attitude

Ships look great, while standing on the shore
But that's not what ships, are really made for

Once we start walking, let's not stop for anything
Let failures be our strength, to never give up and keep going

This is the moment where, we find our true happiness
Choice lies with us, to live life large, or live less

It's important to be thankful, for all we have in life
Gratitude gives us the power, to overcome our strife

With our head held high, with towering self esteem
Let's make our life a success, and achieve our dream

This is the only moment, when we can move ahead
It's time to take action now, on whatever has been said.

"Why do you say I am not going to be in the present moment....?"

CHAPTER 1

LIFE'S GREATEST GIFT

The Present moment

Present is where life is, neither future nor past
This is the moment where, my destiny's die is cast
Living in the now, leads me to my peace
Where all my mind's chatter come to a cease.

When I bought my first car, I enrolled myself in a driving class. After 3 weeks of training and securing the driving licence, it was time for me to hit the road on my own. I still remember the first day of my driving independently, as that taught me life's greatest lesson. I was able to drive smoothly on the highway. But as I went on to a by-lane, the road went uphill. With the very sight of the road, my pulse started racing. The traffic congestion was relatively high that day. The space between my car and the cars immediately front and behind was hardly a couple of meters.

Just then, my worst nightmare came true. As soon as I started going uphill, my car engine stopped and all my fears mushroomed inside me. Using my full presence of mind, I immediately applied breaks. I had to restart the car in order to move ahead. After putting the ignition on, I had to lift my feet off the brake and without losing even a fraction of a second, put it on accelerator and push it for the car to move ahead.

Now that was 'the moment'. If my attention drifts slightly from the present moment, my car would just go sliding down hill and bang the car behind. So I had to be fully present in the moment. I realised that I was very anxious about the consequences before even taking the first step. I had to first calm my pulse down by taking few deep breaths in the midst of honking from behind. Then I gathered my consciousness to that moment and finally succeeded in moving the car ahead. I realized then what 'living in the moment' was.

Most times, we either live in the past or in the future. It is as if we are driven by some mysterious compulsion to live through memories from the past or anticipation of the future. These compulsions occur mainly because the past gives us an identity and the future holds promises. We either feel guilt or regret about the past, or worry or stress about the future; and thus completely miss the moment we are living – The Present Moment.

At every given moment, we are climbing the uphill of life. There are many things from the past that pull us down, and believe me, it's very easy to be pulled back as we are on a slope. We can't even afford to stop, as a matter of fact, there is no way we can stop. If we don't push the accelerator every moment, there are all the chances of us going down-hill. The real art lies in how successfully we are present at that moment and move ahead without being pulled back.

As a common saying goes, the moments that are gone make the 'past', the moments that are yet to come is called 'future', but this particular moment, which is "Life", is called the 'present', the "gift". It is only in this moment that we are living, we are alive... Both past and the future are illusions, really. The *Now* is all there is. Life is happening in this very moment. Life IS the 'present moment'. Every moment is an opportunity for us to create our future and at the same time define our past; as the present moment becomes the past the very next moment.

During an emergency or in the middle of life threatening events, we are automatically living in the present. It is a natural process. Our personality which contains our past and future gives way to the present consciousness. Our response to the emergency situation then comes out of this state of present consciousness, which is extremely still and watchful at such times.

Suffering is optional

Kavita is a 35-year-old single woman, who lives alone in the maximum city. When I met her after a long time, she looked completely worn down and visibly stressed out. "Is there something that is bothering you, Kavita?" I asked gently. She was stumped by my question, as she didn't expect it - she is the kind of person who usually puts on a brave face in public.

"How did you guess?" she exclaimed. With tear-filled eyes, she started to pour her heart out, "I feel very depressed and anxious nowadays. Do you have a solution for my problem?"

"Yes, I do" I said, "Just be".

Kavita seemed quite irritated by my suggestion. "You must be kidding!" she retorted. "My life has been very traumatic. I am haunted by the memories of my past. I am just not at peace with myself. I am now jobless and I don't know what's going to happen to me in future. And you are telling me to 'just be'? That just sounds ridiculous to me".

It was clear to me that Kavita was purely exhausted by carrying so much baggage of her past memories. Since her mind was going through so much of turbulence, she was also under a tight grip of fears and insecurities. I said to her, "Kavita, you are depressed because you are not letting go of your past baggage. And your anxiety is the result of your fears and insecurities about future. So you are either living in the past or in the future."

"So what do I do?" She asked.

"Just be, be present in the moment." I said. After a pause, I continued, "You see, only when you are just being in the moment, you can get rid of stress, anxiety and depression. You need to understand that the fears and insecurities about the future is only your projection. It is just an assumption. Whatever you fear about your future may or may not happen. It may just be your fears playing on your mind. It is not a reality."

"Reality is only this moment," I added, "and in this moment you are just talking to me.... that's it. These fears can be conquered by developing faith in ourselves and trusting the process of life. Remember, your thoughts in this moment are going to create your future. If you have fears and insecurities about the future, it will eventually turn out to be that way. You are creating your future every moment."

I was glad to notice that Kavita was listening to me attentively. I continued, "Similarly your past is past.... already gone. It no longer exists. It's a bygone. It exists only in your memory now. If those memories are haunting you, you need to handle them. Don't resist them. Accept those memories to be a part of your life.... life which you have lived. If they have caused you pain, you need to heal them. It is very important to protect and heal the wound with lot of self love and forgiveness; otherwise, the wound becomes very vulnerable. Forgiveness is a very important healing tool. You need to forgive yourself for allowing people to hurt you."

Kavita was now completely immersed in self-introspection. She absorbed each and every word that I was saying. "That's the reason I say, 'Just Be'. By just being, you can handle all your issues in a better way. Because by being in the moment you are disconnecting yourself from the negative thoughts about the past or future. It is okay to feel hurt. But don't get attached to that hurt. Just experience it and move on. That is the beauty of being in the moment."

"Moreover, our thoughts have enormous power. They do manifest. So scan every moment for the thought it is carrying. Every present moment is the vehicle for the thoughts. It has the power to swing you in any direction. So choose every thought very carefully. Appreciate every moment and be grateful for each moment. Being alive at every moment in itself is a miracle."

"Thank you so much. I think I got it now, I am really grateful to you for making me understand this" said Kavita, with tears rolling down her cheeks, but with a peaceful and contended smile on her face.

Like Kavita, many of us get so bogged down by the miseries of the past and the fears of the future that we refuse to live in the present moment. And when such a series of present moments pass away in front of our eyes, we say that our life is full of miseries. When the truth is, it was only 'us' who created that life. As they say, "Pain is inevitable, but suffering is optional". The choice is all ours.

Many times it is our perspective towards life that makes us decide whether life has been fair or unfair. Look for beauty, and there it is... look for despair, and there it is! Even if there is a problem, the solution often lies in itself. We just need to introspect and discover it. There is no good or bad in life. It is a subjective term and is viewed in the perspective of time. Something which is 'good' for someone can be 'bad' for someone else. Or something 'bad' in the present may turn out to be good in the future.

Whenever we are not in the present moment, we are either in the past or in the future; and both are 'illusory'. As a result, we totally miss the opportunities the present moment presents before us. We are actually unfair to ourselves by not being in the moment. We are depriving ourselves of the pure happiness that present offers. The present moment is the only gateway through which we can go beyond the limited confines of the mind. This is where our complete life unfolds, and the only factor that remains constant. There was never a time, or will never be a time, when our life is not 'Now'.

Being with the breath

Breath is something that happens every moment. But unfortunately most often we are unaware of its presence. We just take it for granted. When we are living in the past or for the future, thereby feeling depressed, angry, guilty, stressed or anxious, fearful, then our breath changes its rhythm or pattern. It becomes shallow and fast. If we become conscious of this change and then restore the rhythm by deep and slow breath, we can instantly bring ourselves to the present moment.

Being conscious about breath is the key. Try focusing on the breath, while taking slow deeper breaths. Following the breath, as it travels in and out of body feeling the abdomen expand and contract with each breath, is a great way to begin any meditation. The focus will then gently shift to the inner feelings. When we breathe in deep and slow, it takes our awareness to the breath, and brings our attention to the present moment.

Illusive time

There is a fine difference between our perception of the physical time and the illusive or mental time. Whenever we take note of our past events, or apply the lessons learnt from past mistakes in the present situation with positive feelings, or heal our past in the present, we live in the physical time of NOW. However, when we dwell in the past mentally, letting the anger, guilt, remorse or self condemnation take over, we live in the 'illusive' time, which links us to the false identity.

Similarly, whenever we set targets or goals and work towards them, we again live in the physical 'present' time. But if we are anxious about the future events or gripped with fear, then we live in the 'illusive' time. There is nothing wrong in learning from the past mistakes or healing the past, and taking appropriate steps for the future by predicting from patterns or established laws, as long as we are doing this in the present, or in the physical time of now.

Be careful of the slip from the physical time into the illusive time. When one lives in the illusive time, he does not take advantage of his full potential (which only comes out during the physical time of now). Try to let go of this tendency of unknowingly slipping in to the illusive time.

Experiencing the Moment

Many times rather than experiencing the present moment we are either fast forwarding or going reverse. For example, if we are late for a meeting, we will be completely disturbed mentally. We are so anxious that our mind will either immediately rush to the future, thinking about the firing we may receive from the boss; or thinking how we got late because of morning issues at home. Either way, we are not living in the moment and experiencing it as it is in the present. We can learn to be in the moment and experience the present. For that, one should first learn to free the mind of its habitual caught-in-responsibility, self-absorbed, stress-filled state.

Sometimes the true value of the moment is never really appreciated or even known until it becomes a memory. Every one of us is running. We are either running towards our pleasure; or we are running towards acquiring more and more knowledge. It is important to be still sometimes and not run in either of the directions.

As an experiment, take a lunchtime walk to a park to feed pigeons. Be so fascinated with the pigeons, their eating habits, the other people feeding them, and the foliage that you forget what just happened that morning and don't pre-think the afternoon. Your mind will relax, your heart will pick up, you'll smile at people, and they will smile back. Or on your next coffee break — really take a break and just have coffee. That's all. Don't talk on phone. Don't check emails. Don't visit anyone. Just taste the coffee. Look around. See your surroundings as if for the first time. With wonder in your eyes.

Sometimes it is very important to 'be' and not 'do'. When someone says, "I am feeling very angry, what do I do?" I say, "Don't do anything, just be. Doing something in such a situation will only make the matters worse. Just experience the anger and that's it." "Just Being" is also a very powerful form of meditation and also the easiest to understand. Just Be….. wherever you are, whatever you are, whatever the situation is, whatever time it is, just observe the moment, be in the moment, live the moment. If we practice this every moment our life itself becomes a meditation, similar to a necklace made of beautiful pearls of present moments.

When we become conscious of 'being', we then really live the present. Our Being becomes conscious of itself. And 'Being', 'Consciousness' and 'Life' are synonymous. Did you ever realise why we are called "Human Beings" and not "Human Doings"...? That's because our primary objective or purpose is to be, to experience, to live, to be conscious and not to do or perform anything. Doing comes later. Since doing involves mind, it creates an illusion of separateness, a continuous conflict within and without. This creates a terrible habit, almost enslavement to constant never ending cycles of thinking.

When we identify ourselves with our mind, we actually create a false facade of judgements, definitions, labels and concepts that actually blocks all our true feelings. It creates a separation between all our true relationships whether it is between me and myself, me and my close ones, me and nature, me and the universe. It is our mind which creates this illusion of separation between us and the other, completely disregarding the fact that at deeper levels of existence we are all one with the other.

Catch the watcher

Whenever we just try to observe the thoughts for some time, we will find that there is someone else watching or talking to us. This is a spontaneous process which continuously keeps on happening in our mind, a continuous form of conversation or discourse. Most importantly, we never realise that we can stop this process and go into that stillness or peace deep within us. This someone or the voice judges or interprets the situations we are at most often either by imagining negative outcomes (anticipating future giving rise to anxiety) or in terms of past events (falling into negative judgement trap). What this does in fact is that it drains us completely and most often becomes the cause of our physical diseases.

However, we have the ability to come out of this process and save ourselves. As soon as we start observing our own thoughts as a third person, we are in present moment. We must pay attention to those repetitive thought patterns which are causing us untold miseries, without being judgemental or condemning. Just watch. This makes us a witness of the events, feelings, thoughts and emotions and frees us from the bondage of attachment with the same.

The best way to do this is to "Catch the Watcher". Try to catch the one inside us who is watching our thoughts. Then catch this catcher, and so on. Ultimately we find ourselves very deep in the sub-conscious, and actually come out of the negative thought patterns. We can actually feel our deeper self in doing so. We will realise that the power of those impulsive thoughts on us has actually reduced and we will no more identify ourselves with them. This will also open up something beautiful within us – the state of "no thought", a gap between thoughts.

Initially this gap may be small, but slowly you will find that they become extended. This happens once you start experiencing this more often. This is the time when one naturally starts living in the present moment. This also becomes a naturally meditative state where we experience deep peace and stillness. However, this should not be confused with lack of alertness. In fact, we are more alert or more fully present during these times as we feel full of life and energy. This way, we can actually practice to separate ourselves from the mind. It's also fun doing this... try it and see!

Silence and gratitude

"Silence is golden" goes an old proverb, the origin of which is obscured by the mist of time. When we focus on the silence outside us, we can find the silence or stillness within. If we pay more attention to the 'silence' around us than the sounds, we will realise that all the sounds come out of silence and go back into silence. Silence is the beginning and the end. Silence allows the sound to be.

Silence is an opportunity to rest deeply and to truly investigate the vast simplicity at the core of our being. Silence is the peaceful place where we can find the wholeness of our true nature. Excusing ourselves from everyday activities and going into silence from time to time, is a great exercise in the present moment awareness. That is when we can allow each experience to flow through us. It is a way to notice our abundance or goodness in others. We can apply this perspective in everyday life to experience life in the Now.

Gratitude

Gratitude is an important virtue that helps us live in each moment happily and to be present in every moment. Famous saying goes, "I was sad that I did not have the shoes until I saw a man who did not have feet." If we are grateful for each and every small thing, life itself becomes a beautiful journey. Saying "thank you" every morning, for the things that we have in life gives us immense energy to cruise through the challenges of the day. Feeling grateful brings our focus on the present moment.

At a glance

- *Past and future are illusions.*
- *Present moment is what life is all about*
- *Our first job is being in the moment or experiencing the moment*
- *Observing our breath is the best way to be in the present moment*

KEYS

"Lost.... and found...!"

CHAPTER 2

DISCOVER YOUR PURPOSE

Be passionate about it

I want to know, what is my role
Am I just a part or I am the whole
I want to know, the larger plan of the universe
Discover where I fit in, and find my life purpose.

When I changed my career to a full time life coach and healer at the age of 40, many eyebrows were raised. After all, anyone who is in an enviable position like I was in the career is not expected to give it all up at this age. Being a mechanical engineer with seventeen years of experience in reputed national and international conglomerates, I had risen to this position through shear dedication and hard work. Hence, no one initially approved of my decision to plunge into a new career so late into my life. They thought I had gone crazy!

A lot of unsolicited advice came my way. Some out of concern, some out of fear, yet others out of sheer ignorance. I realised that every person operated out of his own space, his deep rooted conditioning and his own experiences. To the majority, it was a foolish decision to make a career change at this age, and that too in something that I was not qualified for. Many dissuaded me from walking the path by high-lighting the pitfalls, while a few just decided to wait and watch the situation, deliberately avoiding talking about it. This is exactly how the human mind works. If we fail while taking risks in our life, we form an opinion that "one should not take risks in life." It's like if we don't understand stocks, then we advice others never to invest in stocks, and so on.

I get scared when I hear people giving advice to children about their career and life. Our neighbour once told us, "My nephew is a champion in chess at national level, but now, I have advised him to stop playing chess and just focus on his studies, because all that matters in life is how much you score in your exams."

I was flabbergasted! What a prejudiced view about qualifications! Why didn't that gentleman think in this way - May be that child is here on earth to excel in chess. But just because of advice from someone, whom the family respects, the child quit playing chess. I came to know later that the child was unable to focus on studies as well.

The uncalled-for advices I received, did not really bother me much. Deep down from my inner consciousness I knew that I had found my inner calling – my purpose in life, which is "to heal people out of their traumas and to help them discover their true self." Although it took me 10 long years to accept and acknowledge it, I had firmly decided to follow it now with deep conviction and passion, irrespective of any obstacles or hurdles, whatsoever. I knew that overcoming these roadblocks was the only way to shorten the distance between my life's purpose and me.

Purpose of life - what is it?

Many times we are so caught up in the dos and don'ts of life that we just turn a deaf ear to our inner voice, and disregard our inner feelings. However, deep within, each one of us knows our true purpose in life. It is a 'knowing' that comes from within. We just need to be aware and pay attention to it. As we grow up, we comfortably slide into the fixed patterns laid by our parents and the society.

We are conditioned to believe that certain things are right and certain things are not. We form our own constitution of life based on the way other people want us to live and their experiences and beliefs. We completely forget what we truly want from our own life. In the bargain, we forget our true potential and lose the passion to excel.

Being a Past Life Regression Therapist has given me an opportunity to understand our process of coming to this birth and its deeper aspects. I have come to understand the fact that we decide our purpose of this lifetime even before we are conceived inside a womb. We decide what we need to achieve and need to learn. Accordingly, we choose our parents, our place of birth and our situations in life, which are all conducive for us to achieve or learn what we had decided before.

Even the so-called challenges (which are actually positive roadblocks for our own development) are leading us towards that purpose of life. Events that look unfortunate or challenging at human level of understanding are actually the events which take us to a higher level in the overall evolution of our soul through many lifetimes.

When do we know?

The process is so designed that we remember our purpose only till we are about two or three, or till we start forming complete sentences when we start talking. Child prodigies such as Wolfgang Mozart, Pablo Picasso and Shirley Temple are few of the many known personalities who exhibited their extraordinary talent and passion at a very young age. These people could connect to their purpose at an early age and then follow it. However, as we grow up, slowly our memories start fading. We get trapped in the layers of conditioning. That 'knowing' gets buried deep inside us, till we realise that we are not happy the way we are living our lives. We continue feeling a vacuum in life which needs to be filled, but never try to give enough thought and time to that feeling. We feel disconnected from our inner self, our inner core, our inner being. Because of the disconnection from the inner self, most often we start seeking real happiness in external gratification. We want to buy a car, house, get married, and earn wealth, etc., thinking that these things will give us real happiness in life.

There is absolutely nothing wrong in seeking or acquiring material possessions. Each one of us has the right to live life in all the comfort and luxuries. The actual problem arises when we identify happiness with these and become a slave to our desires. The list of our desires then becomes endless. One desire leads to another and each gets bigger and bigger. In the process, we also fall prey to the competition and comparison of these things with our peers, friends and neighbours.

We thus fall in to the vicious cycle, which only causes pain and tremendous amount of stress. It is only when our body starts giving us signals, that we realize that all these years, our desires were getting fulfilled at the cost of our health. We still carry on with fulfilling our long wish-list, thinking that one day we will be truly happy and satisfied. Only when our body stops supporting, do we wake up as if from deep sleep.

Questions and answers

Our body is in total despair by then, attacked by all the modern so-called lifestyle diseases. We find ourselves confronted with questions such as, "Am I really happy?", "Is this what I wanted from life?", and funnily enough the answer to all these questions is a big NO.

Soon we realise that despite having a great job, all luxuries, a loving and caring family, we still feel discontented and unhappy. We start questioning life itself. Why are we living? Why do we have to go through all the challenges in life? Why can't life be the same for everybody? Why is there so much of disparity in the world? Why am I not happy? However, at our deepest level, our real questions are, Why am I here? What is my purpose?

This is exactly where the quest to find our 'True Purpose' starts. And when we find our true purpose, all the "whys" are replaced by "hows". That is the time when we really start living, 'adding life to our years and not simply years to our life', as it is commonly said. It is never too late to realise this fact. Any time in our life is a good time to start. Once we realise our purpose, it becomes our prime responsibility to take corrective steps in the right direction.

The purpose of life could be different for each person. It could be,

• Developing certain virtues such as kindness, patience, courage, honesty, truthfulness, love, surrender, trust, service to others

- Learning to handle negative emotions such as fear, hatred, anger, pessimism, need for control, revenge, blaming others for failures

- To develop an attitude of forgiveness or gratitude

- To learn a certain form of art

- Serving people or even learning to get served

- Developing relationships

- Overcoming a challenge in the form of a physical disability, extreme scarcity or financial burden, addiction (drugs, alcohol, etc), bad relationships, social status or class, upbringing, unusual circumstances (parental divorce, molestation or rape etc.)

- Earning name, fame or money

- Learn to give unconditional love

- To spread happiness, knowledge or awareness.

The purpose of life is different and unique for each one of us. It is beautifully woven in the script of our life. We do know our purpose deep within us. We just need to calm ourselves to listen to our inner voice. When we are silent and calm from within, our life's purpose is slowly revealed to us.

Changing courses

Many times there are repetitive patterns in our life or certain road blocks which are an indication that we just need to change our course. There could be a deep learning or wisdom coming from a particular repetitive event. Sometimes we may even need to take a U-turn. If even after repeated indications, we don't learn or change our path, the universe puts us in a place where we are left with no choice. These are the moments when our true purpose may be revealing itself. We seem to be so trapped in the invisible cage of conditioning and dogmas that we forget life is all about freedom.

It is an irony that although we know that death is the eternal truth, "we live as if we are never going to die; and die as if we have never lived." Many times it is our encounter with death that ignites our will to live life to its fullest potential. I have seen this happening with people who have had near death experiences (NDE).

Kim's story

Kim was a happy-go-lucky person who owned a successful garment export business and enjoyed an enviable status in society. She would always show off her new assets such as her Bentley Convertible, the penthouse apartment she bought in a posh locality, or her diamond studded necklace gifted by her husband on her 40th birthday. She was completely immersed in the material world and left no opportunity to proudly display her material possessions. Until one day when she was admitted in a hospital for a surgery.

While on operation table under the influence of anaesthesia, she suddenly found herself floating at the ceiling. She realised she can see her own body lying on the table while doctors are desperately trying to revive her. It dawned upon her that she is probably dead, and then she started frantically trying to get back inside her body. At one point, she blacked out and woke up after a day, alive and on the mend.

After a few days, Kim was discharged from the hospital. She didn't know whether what she saw during her operation was a hallucination or not, as no one told her about it. A few weeks later, she came to know that this incident actually happened, through one of her close friends who knew the doctor present during the operation. She realised that she indeed was clinically dead for a few moments on that operating table!

The near death experience made such an impact on Kim that she is a completely different person now. She came to understand that the material pleasures never last and started to search for the deeper purpose of her existence on earth. She started a charity organisation where she helps poor and under privileged. She also started teaching destitute children and visits old age homes to help the old people.

Death as a reminder

I vividly remember attending a funeral of one of my close relatives about ten years back. It was a sudden death and everyone was deeply grieved. During the cremation, I started an internal dialogue started within myself. It was as if I was actually face to face with death. It was like a volcano of thoughts and feelings erupting out of my mind. I was restless. "Oh! Even I am going to die one day! Then, why am I here? Am I going to just live in vain and die, or there is a purpose of my being here? Who am I? What happens to me after death? What would people say about me when I am no more?" These questions would not leave me alone.

Sometimes the extreme moments of sadness opens a doorway to our purpose of life. Especially in the face of death, all external desires, expectations, ego, fears just fall away like worn out clothes, leaving only what is truly important – our true self. We realise that there is absolutely no reason not to follow our heart. I could feel my deeper self trying to break free from a cage. "I don't want to live an ordinary life," I said to myself. This incident led me in search of the deeper meaning of life and its purpose.

Purpose and Passion

Often, we find a call for our passion, by choice or accident. There comes a time in each of our lives, at least once if not more, when we feel, "I wish I could do only this throughout my life." For instance, people who go hiking and explore the mountains, wonder if they can continue doing that for the rest of their life, or when we indulge in something creative, such as painting and completely lose track of time, or while singing we experience that inner bliss. These are the real sign-boards that show the way towards our purpose.

When I started on the path of self-discovery, every time I entered a bookshop I was drawn towards the self-help section and would end up buying only those books. About 90% of the books in our library are self help books. I realized that while I was with a group of friends, our conversation would slowly drift in the direction of healing of life issues. I was obsessed with this subject and thought about it constantly. I realized that this was something very close to my heart, I had found my passion. I had found my inner calling and just wanted to follow my heart without any compromise.

If you find something you are really very passionate about, it often leads to your purpose. Once that happens, you won't have any excuse. You will simply do it, whatever it takes. When you start on the path to your life's purpose, you will be completely at peace with your inner self. You will simply 'know' that you have found our purpose.

When we are on the path to our purpose, we are helped by the universe in every possible way to reach our goal. Once we are on the purpose we will find a lot of synchronicities taking place in our life. We suddenly come across the right books and attract certain people and situations in our life.

The problem with duality

We live in the world of duality. We look at everything around us as one or the other. For example, things in our life are either good or bad. We believe in darkness or light, cold or heat, black or white, negative or positive, wrong or right. We judge every event, person, situation or experience in our life in the same way, either good or bad. However, when we are working towards our purpose, this concept of either/or does not seem to work. At a higher level of consciousness, from where we operate when we are working towards our purpose, everything that happens – or does not happen in our life – has a reason behind it.

We understand that darkness is nothing but just the absence of light, cold is nothing but the absence of heat, black is the absence of any colour while white is the presence of all colours, whatever looks negative is actually lack of positive, and nothing is wrong as everything is right. Only because we live in the world full of dualities, we go through a life of suffering. Our suffering comes out of ignorance of this basic fact that we are in the universe which is always supportive, guiding us toward the purpose.

The big picture

We automatically get pulled towards something that takes us to our purpose. We often get a déjà vu experience. Since I was a child, I had visions of talking in front of a huge crowd at a stadium, guiding people into meditation. Somehow I knew from within that this is what I am supposed to do. When the time came, my life took a beautiful turn and I met a few wonderful souls on the way, including a few who I hardly knew, who went out of their way to help me follow my purpose in life. This was one sign for me that my life was going on the right track.

The universe works on a larger purpose. You can isolate a drop of water, but when the drop is from an ocean it is a part of the whole. This drop cannot be seen as separate from the ocean. Similarly, we are also a part of the humanity altogether. We are a part of the whole. The universe does not see us as different from itself; it sees us as its own part. Our individual purpose is in fact magnificently integrated into the purpose of the universe.

The life of every single human being has a larger meaning, which is why it becomes even more important for us to know it and work towards it. We just need to trust the process, and not judge it from our limited perspective. Our higher self always knows and will always guide us towards our purpose. What we think is wrong at a given point in time, may be good for us in the larger plan.

At a glance

- *We all come with a purpose to be fulfilled in this lifetime*
- *The purpose of life is different and unique for each one of us.*
- *We are helped by the universe in all possible ways to reach our purpose*
- *Our higher self always knows and will always guide us towards our purpose.*

CHAPTER 3

CHOICE IS YOUR BIRTH-RIGHT

Exercise it

Every moment is a cross road, and I have the choice
To move towards my purpose, & listen to the inner voice
I can choose my path, to greatness and life goal
Making the right choice, gives satisfaction to my soul.

I once heard an interesting fable about a man who paid a heavy price for the choice he made. On a winter day, he had gone on a hike to a mountain. Due to bad weather, he was not able to get back to the base camp at the foot of the mountain.

As night approached, the weather became worse. The harsh cold winds and the darkness of the night made it difficult for the man to climb down. As he was descending, he stumbled and rolled down the mountain. Afraid that he would surely die, he started screaming for help in the dark, as he fell.

Suddenly, as he crossed the cliff, his hands touched something that felt like a branch and he grabbed it. He felt relieved when he realised he had come to a halt. He started shouting for help with the hope that someone will hear him and come to his rescue. There was no response and to make matters worse it was a pitch dark winter night, so he could not see a thing around him.

When he was tired of hanging in the air for a long time and felt that he would die soon. He started praying, "Please help me God, please save me, I don't want to die, I want to live." To his great astonishment, he heard a soothing voice that said, "My dear child, I will save you, just let go of what you are holding and you will be saved."

The man thought his mind was playing tricks with him and he was hearing voices. Again, the voice said, "Son, do not delay, just have faith and let go, you will be saved." This time too the man told himself; "Don't let go… hold on tight… your mind is playing tricks with you. If you let go you will die. Don't listen to the voice."

The next morning, when the villagers came out of their homes, they saw a man hanging from a tree just a few feet above the ground. He was frozen and dead. The villagers were talking amongst themselves, "Poor man, why didn't he jump to the ground. He could have easily found a house and taken shelter. He could have been alive!"

The journey of life is like climbing a mountain. The destination is the peak. Each one of us is born to reach the top and has all the potential to do so. But as we climb, there are many forces which pull us back; these are in the form of distractions, emotions, ego, desires, fears, doubts, etc. At each step we have a choice, whether to let ourselves be pulled back by these forces or march ahead. The higher we go, the stronger these forces become; and hence the greater the agony when we fall down.

Choice is our birthright, and we must exercise it. The choice we make at every moment during the journey determines our speed and the time we take to reach the peak - our ultimate goal, our purpose in life. We are all born on this planet with a purpose, to be lived during this lifetime. We may have set certain goals for ourselves to reach or achieve during the life span. Once we have decided on what we want to achieve or where we want to reach, we set on the path towards it.

Free will

As human beings we have been bestowed upon with a wonderful gift – 'free-will', i.e. intellect along with the power to choose. Having discovered our purpose, choice plays an extremely crucial role in finding the right path. It is our choice that either takes us towards our purpose or away from it. Our life graph is marked with tiny dots of the choices we make at every given moment; and each moment is a crossroad. At every moment, we have a choice to move towards our goal or away from it. Series of such choices marks our path, which when analysed shows the direction in which our life is moving. There is always a choice and free-will to change our direction at each moment, if we find we are going away from our purpose or goals.

There is another dimension which plays a vital role in the choice making process. This is the inner-feeling or guidance that comes from the 'knowing' or from our heart. It is commonly said, "When you are stuck while making a choice, listen to your heart. The heart is always right." Our heart knows exactly what is right for us.

Choices

The choices we make are often labelled as right or wrong, depending on the consequences. For example, a heavy smoker has been advised not to smoke due to his ill health. The next time somebody offers him a cigarette, he has a choice. If he accepts the smoke, he falls prey to his desires and hence further deteriorates his health. If he refuses, he is develops courage and strength, and gives himself a chance to live a healthy life.

However, there is no 'right or wrong' in absolute terms. We can define this in a different way though. Any choice which is in sync with our goal or purpose and takes us further towards it is 'right' for us. Similarly, any choice which is not in sync or not favourable to our goal or purpose and takes us away from it is 'wrong' for us. The whole system of free-will is so designed that even if we make a choice which is not in sync with our purpose in the present moment, the very next moment is our next chance to correct ourselves. But the most important point of choice is the 'now'. The gateway to our highest potential and the highest possibilities is only in the 'now'.

The domino effect

The domino effect is a simple chain reaction that occurs when a small change causes a similar change nearby, which then will cause another similar change, and so on in linear sequence, by analogy to a falling row of dominoes standing on end. The domino effect also relates to a chain of events. (Ref. Webster's Dictionary)

Let us say you have an important presentation to make early in the morning for a big client in the office. You miss the alarm and frantically wake up to realize that you are terribly late. In haste, while shaving, you cut yourself. Looking at your cut, your wife lovingly offers to apply antiseptic lotion, but you simply yell at her as you are agitated. Your wife gets upset and with a foul mood goes to wake up the kids and scolds them for sleeping till late, the kids not knowing the situation wake up in a grumpy mood, crying. You somehow manage to get ready and leave home and get into your car.

While reversing the car, you hit your neighbour's car. Hearing the noise, the neighbour comes out and enters into an argument with you. By now you have not only lost valuable time but are on the verge of losing your mind too. You drive fast, but since you are already late and anxious, you jump the red signal only to be stopped by the traffic police. You try to argue but have to finally pay the fine and move ahead.

After reaching office, your anxiety increases when you see your colleagues and the client already seated in the conference room waiting for you. You feel embarrassed and guilty. Eventually, the presentation does not go well and you lose an important contract. You call your subordinate and fire him, putting the blame on him for improper inputs in the presentation. At the end of the day you are filled with remorse, guilt and anger. Finally you label the day as a 'bad day'.

Good days and bad days

But the truth is that there are no bad days. It's the choice that we make which results in a good or bad day for us. In the example above, at every juncture you had a free will to choose your reaction to the situation. Although you got up late in the morning, you had a choice between getting anxious and maintaining calm. When your wife offered to apply lotion you had a choice to operate out of love instead of anger. When your neighbour started arguing with you, you had a choice of politely accepting the mistake and saying 'sorry'. This would have helped in keeping your anger in control. While driving to the office, you had a choice to drive at a slower speed so that you don't jump a red signal. When you arrived late at office you had a choice to feel guilty and angry or to accept it and apologize for being late. One choice always leads to another and every time you had a choice to correct the previous one, by choosing differently. Thus the domino effect could have been completely avoided.

Now imagine the gravity of this domino effect on your life. If you call a day full of wrong choices a 'bad day', what will you call a life full of wrong choices - a 'bad life'? Life beautifully presents us with an opportunity at every moment to correct the past wrong choices. Exercising the right choice means taking responsibility of the wrong ones and correcting them in the very next moment.

Suppose you are driving from one city to another and you arrive at a Y junction, the road ahead bifurcates into two and there are no signboards to guide you. You take one of the two roads and after driving about 100 km you realize that you are on the wrong road. What will you do now? You can either take a U-turn, come back to the point where you made a choice and take the other road; or you can find the nearest road that connects to the road that leads to your destination. In our life, however, we cannot take a U-turn and come back to the point of choice. We have to make corrections from wherever we are and find the path taking us back on the road to our goal or purpose.

To live by choice or by chance

While driving, we are very cautious and make sure we take the correct road that leads to our destination. So why can't we be even more cautious when making choices that lead us towards our purpose, the ultimate goal?

We always have a choice. Our reaction to the situations in our life is our free-will. Many times, we just step back and allow life to happen to us rather than taking life in our hands. We blame our destiny instead of creating our destiny. We live by chance and not by choice. All the great achievers or the people who have lived their purpose have always lived by choice and not by chance. By making the right choices they opened the gateways that helped them reach their goals. They always focused on their goals and made choices that took them further. Thus they also created their own destiny.

To make changes or find excuses

Finding excuses is always an easy way out but not the right choice to make. Well, many of us face this on a day to day basis. For example, we choose to lose the excess body weight, as we realize it's a threat to our health and of course our public image. We decide to make a change – the right choice. We understand the gravity of the situation and after all, none of us wants to fall sick. So we enrol ourselves in a gym for a year after a lot of deliberation, and decide to follow a strict diet plan.

Everything goes well for a first few weeks (or even just a few days). Slowly lethargy sets in and we come up with amazing and creative excuses for not going to the gym such as, "Work is worship for me, I can definitely skip the gym", or "I am very tired today, I must take sufficient rest," and so on. Eventually we also start indulging in junk food giving the excuse, "I will just have it today, after all you should enjoy each and every moment." And so we start off on a spree of making excuses - the wrong choice. We are conditioned to take the path of least resistance, which ultimately proves to be our bane.

To be manipulated or be motivated

When I chose to follow my purpose, some of my friends thought that it was their moral duty to point out all the pitfalls in the career I had chosen. One of them very bluntly said, "This is not your cup of tea. I don't think you will succeed in this. You are better off in your job." When this came from the person I adored and respected, I was disheartened. I began to lose focus on my goal and allowed the self-doubt to sink in.

However, I knew deep within that I was on the right path. After spending a few days in dejection, I realized that I had a choice of either to be dejected or to be motivated. I chose to be motivated. I just told myself, "I take complete responsibility for my life choices and the consequences thereafter. If someone tries to deviate from this path, I will spring forward with double the zest. I choose to be motivated to excel and not to be disheartened by anyone's perspective about my life choices." And here I am writing this book, a result of the choice I made at that point in life.

To excel or to compete

We live in the world of competitions. Most of us will experience competitions at each stage of life. When a toddler goes to kindergarten there is competition for admission, as the child grows there is competition in school, after studies to get a job one goes through intense competition and then in the job there is competition to survive. One just cannot seem to get over these struggles till the fag end of life.

Even to be termed as successful in the eyes of society, one has to compete; as success in people's eyes is all about how much material wealth one gathers. In the process, we end up in an endless, self-defeating, or pointless pursuit of either peers' adulation or approval of others around us. This pursuit could even be to attract attention of people around us, our friends, colleagues, relatives, sometimes even parents; as gaining attention seems to make us feel important in their eyes.

Eventually, we become slave to the competition. As is commonly said, 'the trouble with the rat race is that even if you win, you're still a rat.' We always work hard to be one step higher than others which gives rise to bloated egos. Unknowingly, we try to prove ourselves superior to others. However, the problem with this whole system of competition is that although one is trying to be or do better than the other, there is no effort to excel. We fail to excel because we are working only towards the standards set by somebody else. This competition induces a lot of stress and also drains our energy levels.

We all have enormous potential within us from the time of our birth.... each one of us, without exception. This potential, which can be used to reach excellence in whatever field we are in, is wasted when we compete against each other. While competing, the whole focus is on being better than the other and not on excelling. In order to excel, we need to set our own standards and milestones and work towards achieving them. We always have a choice to excel or to compete. If we choose to excel we come out of the fray (or rat-race) and free ourselves from the bondage of competition.

Anger or love

When we operate out of anger, we build walls; when we operate out of love, we build bridges. We always have a choice, to operate out of anger or love in any given situation.

Kapil is a doctor who works in a famous hospital in Mumbai. Whenever we met I always found him frustrated and full of anger. He said it was the work pressure that is getting too much for him. One day he came back home early from the hospital as he had severe headache due to migraine. He was resting in his room, when suddenly his 10 year old kid came inside, ecstatic and shouting at the top of his voice. "Yes! I have made it," he said, "Dad, I got selected in my school cricket team" and started dancing.

Kapil was already in a foul mood because of the bad headache. He got enraged and snapped at his child, "What's there to get so much excited about? Don't scream like this and go to your room." Feeling dejected, the kid entered his room and slammed the door behind him. This incident affected the kid so much that he stopped playing cricket. I heard later that when Kapil came to know about this, he felt extremely guilty and just could not forgive himself. Operating out of anger always leads to guilt and regret, and sometimes the damage is irreversible. We must stay away from anger, as the only person who gets hurt the most is us. The choice is ours.

Fear or courage

Courage is an extremely important ingredient of a successful life.

"Everything you want is on the other side of fear" or "Your greatest treasures lie beyond your greatest fears" are common sayings, which are so very true. Courage is not just physical bravery. Courage could range from physical strength and endurance to mental stamina and innovation.

Fear is a negative emotion which acts as an iron wall to one's progress, and to overcome this wall one needs courage. Fear is something that has the capacity to completely destroy a person, whereas courage has the power to pull one out of the worst situation. We must choose to have the courage to be honest and truthful, to ourselves and others, to do the right thing in life, to take responsibility for our actions.

We must have the courage to say 'no', when we have to. We must be courageous to ask for what is rightfully ours. Choosing courage to accept certain truths about us, without being fearful about the consequences, is a great way to live successfully.

To have faith or doubt

Faith is something that fills us with peace, serenity and understanding while doubt inflicts us with frustration, anger, remorse. Faith opens many door-ways to reach our purpose, while doubt always pulls us back. The choice is ours, whether to operate out of faith or doubt.

Self esteem or self pity

Suppose your boss, in a fit of anger says, "You are good for nothing; you mess up everything you do." Here you have a choice, either to take offense and indulge in self-pity thinking you are really a mess or to tell yourself I know I am the best at what I do, boss must be in a foul mood today. This applies to every situation. We often fall prey to self pity and low self esteem. This eventually, pulls us down and takes us away from the path of our highest potential. The choice lies with us whether to take these situations or comments seriously or just let it go, and believe in our true worth.

To forgive or to blame

Blaming anyone does not take us anywhere. If someone hurls an abuse at you, you have the choice to take it or leave it. Nobody can hurt you unless you allow them to do so. Forgiveness is a practice that takes us up the ladder and above the person who has hurt us. When somebody hurts us, we always have a choice, either to forgive that person or blame him. Everything has to do with you, not the other person or situation.

During my corporate years, one of my subordinates created serious misunderstandings between me and my immediate boss. This strained our relationship which was otherwise very friendly. Once I found out the real culprit of the rumors was the subordinate, I angrily confronted him and he accepted his mistake and apologized for it.

But it was not possible for me to forgive him. I was feeling the hurt and betrayal continuously in the next days, and as I got more affected, my productivity went down. This eventually started affecting my health adversely, while he led a happy life. Finally after couple of weeks, I let go of the hurt and completely forgive him. That's when I experienced peace.

Acceptance or resistance

Sometimes it is good to accept the things we cannot change and move on in life. The more we resist something, the severe the issue grows to be. Resistance also causes friction and a considerable loss of energy and prevents us from moving towards our goals.

A gentleman brought his son to me for healing. The son ever since his childhood wished to become an artist, but his father had forced his son to study engineering. I later came to know that becoming an engineer was his own unaccomplished desire. The son had gone into severe depression and had developed several physical ailments for giving up his dream of being an artist and doing something he never liked.

Finally the son gave up everything including his studies. Had the father accepted what his son wanted to do, things would have been completely different. Because he chose to resist his son's wishes and forced his expectation on him, it resulted in son choosing to go against the wishes of his father, and stop doing anything at all. Finally, the whole family was in despair.

Remember, by exercising our choice we are creating our future. And by making the right choices we are moving towards our purpose or goals one step at a time, every moment. **We are always where we choose to be.**

At a glance

- *Once we know our goal, we must choose our path*
- *Choice is our birthright, and we must exercise it.*
- *Trust your heart - it knows exactly what is right for us.*
- *Be courageous to ask for what is rightfully yours.*

CHAPTER 4

JUST DO IT

The time is now

I know my goal, my life's destination
My purpose, my chosen path, my vocation
I have to take the first step on my stride
Only when I dare, luck'll be on my side

The little baby eagle watched with awe as its mother flew fearlessly high up in the sky. It knew that it is also meant to fly. After the initial struggle, the day finally arrived when it was ready to soar high in the sky. Without any fear or hesitance the young eagle took off with pride, never looking back.

In a little village, surrounded by beautiful mountains and lakes, lived a boy. Every day on his way to school he would pass by a lake and watch other little boys dive into the lake from the top of a hillock. For the little boy, this was a daring and heroic act that he was eager to try out but could not. His mother had strictly warned him against trying this stunt, as she thought it was too dangerous and could prove fatal. This warning was enough to scare the boy and he never tried the stunt. But every day he passed by the lake, he secretly wished to try it out. However, he never attempted it.

After many years had passed, an old man was narrating his childhood stories to his grandson, sitting near the same lake. Suddenly, his grandson said, "Grandpa let's take a dip in the lake. We'll go to the top of that hillock and jump from there."

The old man immediately reacted by telling the little boy how risky it was to try this stunt, but the boy replied with all enthusiasm, "Oh come on, Grandpa, it will be fun! Don't be afraid, I'm with you." Saying so, his grandson pulled the unwilling grandfather by the hand and took him uphill. Looking down at the lake from the hill top, the old man remembered how his mother had scared him about this little stunt.

He then told the story to his grandson. The grandson said, "Well grandpa, it's not that high, it will be okay. Just see how I do it and follow me. You have nothing to be afraid of." The boy then jumped into the lake and called out to the old man, "Come on grandpa, just do it! Don't think too much and don't waste time... You have been waiting all your life to do this, this is your chance... don't lose it!"

As he stood there, the old man thought of all the years of his life that had passed by. He had wasted so much time and thanks to his grandson, now was the moment he can finally try. He took a deep breath, looked down at his cheering grandson and said to himself, "Just do it."

And the old man jumped into the lake. When he surfaced from the water, he was laughing like a little boy and his grandson was clapping for him. "You did it grandpa, you did it!" he said jubilantly

The old man, even as a little boy, knew that it was safe to plunge from the hilltop, as he had seen other boys do it. But his mother had *instilled* the fear of consequences in him so he never gathered the courage, even later in his life, to try it out. Only when his grandson *assured* him that he would be alright, he went ahead without any fear.

The same is true for our life as well. We tend to avoid doing things simply because we give too much importance to other people's perspective. We are guided by others' opinions never actually daring to try things out ourselves. We stop ourselves, thinking we will fail or get hurt because that's what people tell us. By doing this, we live someone else's version of life, restricting ourselves and following standards set by others and not us.

Take the first step

After identifying life's purpose and making the choice to walk on that path, do not waste even a single moment waiting around or mulling over the decision. 'Just do it'! A car is stationary when parked and only starts when you turn on the ignition key. We too are initially in a state of inertia when we find our goals. Kick start the ignition by taking the first initiative, release the hand break by lifting the veil of fears and put your life in gear by self-motivation and determination. Then push the accelerator to start off your journey!

If you stay too long in the state of inertia, there is a high possibility that you may never take off on your path towards your goals. When we have just found our highest goal in life, we are like young saplings that require nurturing. There are many dangers lurking around such as fear, doubt, unsolicited advice to wither us. The only way to survive is to overcome these by holding on to our inner strength and having faith in our abilities.

Fast forward twenty years into your life. Then look back and ask yourself, how do you feel? If you are feeling happy about the decisions you took, that's great! But, if you feel regret for not having pursued your chosen goals, then you have all the reasons to 'just do it' now. By not doing so, you are running the risk of not living your life completely.

Imran's tale

A few years back, my friend Imran, got his driving license and was very excited to drive around by himself. It gave him the feeling of being in control. However, his father would always caution him with words such as, 'be careful', 'take it a little slow', 'avoid the highways right now', 'since, you are new to driving, don't drive every day'. Frustrated with all the unsolicited advice, Imran eventually decided to give up driving and now prefers travelling by public transport.

The point is, even when you are well-equipped and ready to take on the journey of life, you will face adversities and roadblocks. Remember, you have chosen your path after adequate deliberation. Believe your inner voice, which will guide you throughout your life. Keep telling yourself, "This is my path, my purpose, my goal, my life. I should not wait any longer. I have made a choice. I must take the first step towards my goal ASAP!"

All great things begin small. Even though the road ahead may not be clear now, you must believe that you are on the right path. Vasco da Gama, the great Portuguese explorer, led a fleet of four ships and a crew of 170 men when he set sail to find India. En route he faced many difficulties, but he finally achieved what he had set out for, when he discovered the sea route from Europe to India in 1498.

Had Vasco da Gama sat around thinking and weighing the pros and cons even before setting sail, he would have probably never sailed. But he knew what he wanted to achieve and did not let anything distract him. Our goal should be the central focus of our life and nothing should be able to pull us away from it.

Overcoming negative feelings

Many times a strong feeling keeps nudging us to begin our path, but we are either too scared or too lazy to respond. To suppress that feeling, we often engross ourselves in our daily routine. We sideline those feelings and thoughts, and continue living our life as if they do not matter. However, in the process, we risk never finding out what would have happened if only we listened to our inner voice.

It is very important to ask ourselves how we feel from within at the thought of pursuing our calling. Our inner strength will always guide and help us to take that first step. We must not stop exploring new ideas and opportunities. Our natural human fears of failure, embarrassment, being judged or change may try to stop us from trying new things. But it is our prime responsibility to rise above these fears.

A successful and deeply joyous life, ultimately, is a collection of small and unique experiences. The more unique experiences you have, the more interesting your life will become. Hence, it is imperative to seek opportunities to have as many new experiences as possible. You must also make sure that you share these with the people you care about.

When I first thought of writing this book, I did not ponder much on whether it would sell or not, whether people would appreciate it or not. I just wanted to share my life's experiences with everyone, connect to people, reach out to them and help them discover their purpose in life. From that first thought to the time I actually started writing the book, there were many challenges and hurdles that I faced. But soon I realised that this was not just any passing thought, it was an inner calling, because each time I ignored the voice that urged me to write, I felt restless and disturbed. So I listened to my inner voice and started writing.

I realised that the challenges and hurdles I faced earlier were my own fears and self-doubts trying to stop me from pursuing my passion. And when I tackled them with courage, they just disappeared. I had very little professional writing skills, but I believed in myself. I also kept complete faith on the universe to guide me at every step of the way. I knew that writing this book would take me closer to my life's goals. Each time I sat to write, I felt extremely happy and blissful. Once I made up my mind, I did not allow anything to discourage or distract me.

Humans are gifted with a wonderful faculty, the intellect which helps us choose or make decisions. But there's a big difference between knowing what to do something and actually doing it. Knowledge is completely useless without action. The problem arises when we are too scared or sceptical to take the first step. Understand that no one in the whole world can guarantee what's going to happen in the next moment. This moment is all you have. You can decide only in this moment to take that step towards what you long to do. We discover the real joy when we start walking the chosen path. Nothing comes easy in life, but when we make up our mind to just do it then we have to take the first step. There may be tough times, even discouragements, but nothing should deter us from taking that first important step.

Mistakes are golden

The advantage of living in our comfort zone is that we never have to take any risks. The disadvantage is that we will never know how life would have turned out had we come out of our comfort zone and taken a risk. It is okay to make mistakes. As a matter of fact it is great, as mistakes happen only when there is action – when we are doing something or taking some steps. It is a sure indication that we are not still or stagnant, that we are actually trying to succeed. Remember, what stagnates, eventually rots and stinks!

Mistakes are also great teachers, as they teach us important lessons. We cannot expect to be perfect unless we make mistakes, correct ourselves and learn from the experience. In life, it is all about taking chances, and never about getting chances. Opportunities need to be created. Yes, the outcome cannot be guaranteed, but until you try, how you find out? It is better to try and fail and try again, than never to try at all.

Don't miss the opportunity

I happened to read a story while surfing on the internet once. The source of the story is unknown but it is worth being shared here. It goes as follows. A young man wished to marry a farmer's beautiful daughter. He approached the farmer to ask for his daughter's hand. The farmer looked at him and said, "I'm going to release three bulls, one at a time. If you can catch the tail of any one of them, you can marry my daughter." The young man agreed to do so and waited for the first bull in the field. The barn door opened and out came the biggest, meanest looking bull he had ever seen. The young man quickly decided that this is definitely not his bull.

So he ran over to the side and let the bull pass through the field, out of the gate. The barn door opened again. The young man was stunned to see an even bigger and much more ferocious bull than the first one. The young man said to himself, "I have to wait for the next one if I don't want to die young." He immediately ran to the side and let the vicious animal pass through the field, out the back gate.

The barn door opened for the third time. The young man was extremely happy to see a small little creature. This was the skinniest bull he had seen in his life. "This is my bull!" he said to himself with a beaming face. As the tiny bull came towards him, the young man lunged at its back. To his astonishment, this bull had no tail!

There will be opportunities at every corner of our life. But always keep in mind that they will not wait indefinitely for us. We need to recognize them and then grab them with both hands. Once you let them pass, they are gone forever. Worse, someone else will grab them before you do and you will lose out to him.

We should also strive to cultivate the winning habit of creating unique opportunities for ourselves. Some opportunities are easy to take advantage of, some are difficult. It really doesn't matter. If we get bogged down by circumstances, we will always find excuses. The idea is to live life beyond excuses and live an extra-ordinary life. Enterprising persons will see opportunities in everything they come across. They will keep eyes and mind open to grab even the smallest opportunity. If something goes wrong, they will not be disturbed but will find ways to overcome the challenges. They have the courage to see things differently, to go above the crowd.

Sometimes we really want to pursue our goals, but we don't have the resources to pursue it. There is a saying, 'When universe guides, it also provides.' As odd as it may sound, have complete faith in the universe. When you are on the path of your goals or purpose, it will help with everything that you require, at the right time.

The escape velocity

When we throw an object in the air, the gravity pulls it down. The faster you throw it, the higher it goes and longer it takes to come back to the ground. If you keep increasing the speed, at some point the speed is fast enough for the object to escape the gravitational pull of the earth. When the object is thrown at that speed, it does not come back to the earth. This speed is called 'escape velocity' in physics.

How does this relate to our life? Well, we all experience the gravitational pull while starting something new. Say for example, I decide to get up early in the morning and go for a run every day from tomorrow onwards. I set the alarm for 6 am before I go to sleep. In the morning, I experience the enormous pull of earth's gravity when I am trying to get up at 6 am. The bed is like a strong magnet, and I am being dragged towards it as if my body is made of pure iron. I somehow manage to go past the first challenge, get ready and successfully complete my commitment to myself.

I successfully follow the running schedule – I run for the first three days until I start experiencing the fatigue and initial muscle pain because of no exercise for a long time. This really complicates the issue for me, as it feels like now my bed, along with the magnetic pull, also has strong glue applied to it. To top it up, I find the excuse-making part of my mind has started working overtime. I can observe excellent, unmatchable excuses coming to me at great speeds. I finally draw the conclusion that I cannot get up, with my present resolve and determination. I stop going for the run on the fifth day.

In the above example, my resolve is the speed at which I launch myself to fulfill my commitment to myself; in this case, the morning run. The stronger my resolve is, the more days I was able to continue my run. To be consistent in doing this continuously over a long period of time, I really need to have the resolve which will break all barriers. I compare this with the 'escape velocity'. Only when I am able to get myself free from the mental and physical obstacles, will I be consistent in moving towards my goals, with matchless speed.

Constant unswerving efforts and perseverance takes us to that uppermost slot of success in life. If we pursue something with dedication, give it our heart and soul, it becomes a habit. To make a new habit, I encourage you to continue doing the same for at least 15 days, which is how long it takes me. This may change from person to person; but the resolve to continue doing something over a long period has to be cultivated using our will power and how much we want that habit.

According to Newton's first law of motion, an object in the state of rest continues to remain at rest or an object in the state of motion continues to remain in motion unless and until an external force is applied to it. The rest state is called inertia. In common parlance, we also call it lethargy. Many times it is sheer laziness that stops us from pursuing our inner calling. Lethargy has no cure. Self motivation or will-power is the only cure to break free from this confinement and leap out.

Fear of change

Change is sometimes extremely difficult and poses a huge hurdle in front of us. We are like a bird that has been living inside a cage for a long time; even if the cage is opened, the bird will not fly away. It has been conditioned to live inside the cage, which is its safety net or its comfort zone. We too become so ensconced in our present environment that it is nearly impossible to pluck us out of that cushy comfort zone.

The only thing that is constant is change. We must welcome change and be open to new challenges and opportunities. We must take a moment and look around us and ask ourselves, "Are we really where we are meant to be?" If the answer is, "No," then it's time to fly away and embrace change.

Fear of being judged

Many times we are too embarrassed to follow our passion, because we are afraid of what others will think of us. For example, imagine that you are a young executive working for a big business house. You decide to quit your cushy job and pursue singing as a full time career. How do you think people around you will react? The answer is simple. Many including your family and friends may ridicule you for such a decision. They may even label this as a serious mistake and you as crazy. But just remember one thing, if your heart says this is your true passion and it really makes you happy, then what others say becomes irrelevant. Gather the courage to face the world and just do it!

Fear of failure

Be an optimist. It really helps. We must see or visualize ourselves succeeding at whatever we undertake. If we visualize failure, then only failure is what we get. Fear of failure comes as a result of either our past experiences or experiences of others around us. Sometimes we get discouraged by seeing others fail having taken a similar path. We assume that we will fail too. We must always remember that this is our journey and it will have its unique new enriching experiences. Each one of us is here with a unique purpose which we must follow, against all odds. Do not be afraid to walk on your own path, even if it means diverting from the set rules or paradigm or dogmas.

When we want to pursue something new, self-doubt ay creep in. Remember, if you feel the inclination, it means you also possess the ability to make it happen. I again recap here that the universe has already made big plans for us and has gifted us the necessary abilities to pursue our goals. The apple seed does not know its potential to produce apples, but the farmer does!

Once there was a man who prayed to God to let him win the lottery. Every day, he prayed sincerely, but nothing happened. But he still continued praying. After listening to his prayers for many days, God was frustrated and appeared before the man. God said, "My dear child, I have been listening to your prayers for so long. I want to help you win a lottery. But can you please go and buy a lottery ticket first!"

The problem with many of us is, while in a state of inertia, we expect an external force to magically make us begin or start our path. But that's not how it works. We have to personally take the initial step towards our goal. Once we have identified our life goals and chosen to pursue them, why let anything stop us now? The more we sit on it, ponder or doubt, the more time we waste and delay the process of completion. Do not allow anything or anyone to discourage or distract your focus. Life is short, yet amazing. Enjoy the ride.

At a glance

- *Once we have chosen our path, we must take the first step*

- *Never delay anything - just do it!*

- *Mistakes are great teachers, so even if you falter, you will learn.*

- *Believe your inner voice, which will guide you throughout your life.*

- *A successful and deeply joyous life, ultimately, is a collection of small and unique experiences.*

"Mr. Truly Unstoppable..."

CHAPTER 5

BE UNSTOPPABLE

Realise your highest potential

I will keep moving, come what may
No challenge or difficulty can block my way
Not ready to give up, on any day
Even if I failed before, I'll win today

Like a river I flow, meandering around all the hurdles that try to stop me, making my own way I move forward fiercely. It is my destiny to reach my goal, to merge with the ocean and I will not be stopped. One day, I will merge, overcoming and triumphing over everything that stands in my way because, I'm unstoppable. I know that the only way to reach my destination on time, overcoming all hurdles on my journey is to ride on wheels that are unstoppable.

It was 20th of October 1968, the final day of Olympic Games that were being held in Mexico City. On that hot Sunday afternoon, the men's marathon started with 74 participants. Only 57 could finish the race in the end. At 7 pm, almost an hour after the last runner had crossed the finishing line, medals had already been awarded, even the games closing ceremony had already been completed, the announcer asked the remaining guests to stay back.

Suddenly, a lone runner entered the stadium moving slowly. The audiences were amazed at what they saw next. John Stephen Akhwari of Tanzania was covered with blood when he hobbled in the stadium.

He had fallen down while running and got himself badly hurt. His knee was dislocated and he was bleeding as he had hit his head in the fall. He was asked many times by the authorities to quit the race but he did not. He fell many times, still dragged himself to finish the marathon, limping. The response of the crowd was overwhelming with a huge applause and cheers. His body was exhausted and injured, but his determination was not.

When he was asked the next day, why even after sustaining serious injuries and knowing that he would not win a medal, did he continue till the finish line; his reply was, "My country did not send me 5,000 miles just to start the race; they sent me 5,000 miles to finish the race." Akhwari could never win an Olympic gold medal, but he became an example of sheer grit and never-give-up spirit. He was unstoppable.

In life, once we have found our goals and choose to pursue them, we should be unstoppable. Then no obstacle is too big to overcome. Passion, power, perseverance and planning should be the four wheels of the vehicle we ride to move forward unplugged.

Like Akhwari, we are all here to finish the race, to excel, and win in our respective fields and life. We may face obstacles on our way such as ill health, financial setbacks, deceit from those we trust, wrong advice, our own emotional issues – fear, anger, depression, failures, etc. In spite of all that, make it a point to keep on moving at any cost because as soon as you stop, it becomes twice as difficult to start again. Do not let any excuse stop your journey towards your goal.

Let's say that being unstoppable is very much like winning a horse race. The goal is to reach the finish line first and that's all the jockey is thinking about while riding. Have you ever seen the jockey take a break to stretch his arms or allow the horse to wander around? Because he cannot afford to do that if he has to reach his goal, i.e., win the race. Once you know your goal, set a deadline to achieve it, be focused, maintain consistency, ignore distractions and transcend the obstacles in your way.

Unstoppable Aron

Aron Ralston, left his job as a mechanical engineer with Intel in Phoenix, Arizona at the age of 25 in order to pursue a life of climbing mountains. On April 26, 2003, Aron was hiking through a canyon when he went through a terrible accident. While descending a slot canyon a suspended boulder dislodged and came down crushing his right hand and forearm, pinning it against the canyon wall. After five days of harrowing experience, and left with no choice he had to break free by cutting his trapped arm. Aron lived this incident to tell his own story which was later adapted to a movie.

Today, Aron Ralston draws on the determination that brought him back to continue climbing mountains. The arm amputation caused an infection in bone giving him a 50-50 chance for survival. He thought then, that this was not the life he fought so hard to come back from, to get back to. He vowed to come out as a winner, and from that moment he started getting better. The day after he received his first prosthetic arm, he went for rock climbing.

In June 2008, Aron climbed Denali, the highest mountain peak in North America (6194 m) solo and then skied down. He was the first person with disability to ski down Denali. Aron Ralston did not break down after his injury, but he broke the barriers of his thinking. He remained unstoppable. His story inspires many today not because of how he cut his arm, but because of how he started his life again to achieve his life ambitions.

A dancer's tale

In 1981, a 16-year old girl went through a harrowing experience after doctors decided to amputate one of her legs. This was due to a freak accident, when she was travelling with her family. Although she was saved, a mistake by a local doctor resulted in setting in of gangrene in the right foot. The unfortunate teenager was an expert dancer even at that young age. This incident shook her from inside and threatened to end her passion.

However, she did not give up and refused to accept defeat. After getting an artificial leg, she started to practice dance again. It took her two years of sheer dedication and practice to do her first dance show after the accident. She has not looked back since then. Due to her will power, hard work and positive attitude, Sudha Chandran became an acclaimed dancer and an award-winning actor. Her inspirational story was adapted into a highly praised movie. She continues to work in films and soaps and has never let her past incident come in her way of life.

Adversities in our life have their own way to impart lessons. Their role is to make us stronger. People who have undergone severe circumstances in life and have still come out because of their willpower and resolve to succeed are real heroes. These people did not let the unfortunate incidents in their life get better of them. This ability to fight back, to keep on moving despite misfortune and hardships is what makes us unstoppable. Life goes on. So should we. If we stop at any point worrying about what has happened in life or what might happen, we are losing precious life moments.

A simple math

If we take 75 years as an average life span of humans, how many days do we have in our entire life? Exactly 27,375 days. Out of these we lose about 7375 days in growing up. What is left with us is only about 20,000 days. About 5000 days of old age will be a waste as we do not have enough energy left to do what we really want. Balance is only 15,000. Just imagine, only 15,000 days in your entire life. How do you think we should spend these days? Many of us would still have spent half of these days in doing mundane things. How many of us would like to just come to this planet and go back without being noticed? No one, isn't it?

The 'thought' that I am trying to bring in here is simple. Do you think you are born to live an average life? If your answer is 'No', then this book is made for you. If you really think that you are here to excel, to be a winner, to do better than what others expect you to do, live your life successfully, then I am sure you can draw a lot from this book.

'Becoming the best' and 'being unstoppable' are basically mental approaches. We become as we think. If we think of greatness, our life will turn towards greatness. If we think of not looking back and just move ahead in life, beyond our limitations, the universe will help us in doing just that.

Mind matters

To be unstoppable, it is essential to practice discipline and control over the mind. A weak mind is like a dandelion, floating aimlessly, being carried away in whichever direction the wind takes it towards. The dandelion has no control over itself; it is totally at the mercy of the wind. A weak mind will fall prey to many vices.

The storms of our life actually run in our minds. We live in the world of conflicts, wherever we see, inside us, at workplace, at home, everywhere. Conflict creates stress and anxiety. What really matters is not the chaos in our life, but how we react to it. If we have a disturbed mind, even a small thing could agitate us and take us away from our path. The most important lesson is to calm the mind, through which we come out of these conflicts and can look at them as an observer. Only then do we have the power to accept or reject them.

Of course there will be temptations while walking your path. Be aware of the fact that if you want success, you cannot afford to fall prey to such temptations. You already know the time frame to reach your destination. A disciplined and focused approach goes a long way in taking us further on the journey towards our goal. To be disciplined, we have to take control of the emotions that pull us away from our goal or purpose.

Asking for help

We all need help from time to time. There's nothing wrong in asking for help. On the way to our goals, we all may need help at some point or the other. It is the nature's way of growth. If we look around us, we will find everyone around is helping the other to go ahead.

Many times we hesitate to ask for help. We fear being rejected or offending the other person. But why be scared to ask? We don't know from where we may get support or inspiration in our life. Never feel shy or think you don't deserve it. You will be surprised to see how many people are eager and ready to help. But for that we must first ask.

The key is in asking the way it does not offend anyone at the same time we get the required thing or help needed; asking the right way. I have found the best question to ask is "Can you please help me?", and once you get the attention, and then explain your problem. This in my opinion is the most effective, genuine and straight forward way to ask for help. Hardly anyone gets offended if we are sincere in asking.

If you can offer something in return, that's even better. It may not be the same thing or service in return. Most often a sincere "Thank you" will suffice. Asking for help will also help in building up a credible network of people around you. People will want to assist or help you again if they know you genuinely appreciated their help.

Inspirational guidance

Reading books is a very effective way of refuelling your energy. 'Books are the best companions' they say. The best part about inspirational books is that we get unadulterated advice and motivation to go ahead when we feel stuck. Talking to or being with people who have achieved something in life gives a boost to our dreams. The energy and enthusiasm they emit is contagious.

One of the best sources of motivation is biographies of successful people. A great biography can give valuable lessons on life and wisdom. There are so many things we can learn from those who have lived their life successfully. Reading a biography can be very exciting as well, because it is another person's life story. In fact, we find ideas and ways to practice in our own life, through the experiences of others. Find the one which inspires you the most and read it as often as possible. Keep such a one handy, maybe at your bedside so you can read it whenever you are feeling down or depressed.

Another idea is to make a list of people around you who inspire you. Try to meet them as often as possible, weekly or monthly. Just connecting with these achievers and discussing ideas with them will fill you with energy, and keep you motivated.

Collect names unrelated in your field of passion. This will give you an idea on how people in other areas of work think. More importantly talking to them will make your mind filled with fresh new thoughts and ideas; you may come across a new perspective for a problem or a new outlook towards life itself.

Make another list of people (you don't know directly) who you would like to meet before you die. Keep reading their quotes or blogs, listen to their podcasts, and follow them on social media, to keep you charged up.

What inspires others may not be your thing. There may be something else that brings the best out of you. I urge you to find the one that suits you the most. It may be an inspirational movie, or a song or a video or simply dancing on your favourite music. For some, spending time with children is inspiring. For me, spending time and long walks in the midst of nature, or going on long drives works wonders.

Review the progress

It is a good practice to review our progress as we go ahead. Ask yourselves from time to time, "Where will I be ten years from now, if I keep moving the way I am?". If the answer does not take you closer to your chosen goals, think of revising or changing your path.

We can divide our goals into short term and long term. Set a time table for these goals. What do you want to achieve in the next ten years? In the next five years? In the next two years? In the next one year? In next month, or even, week? Once you have a solid plan with a time table, you are more likely to act on it. You should make this plan sacrosanct in our life. Keeping it at a place where you can see it often is a good idea. You can also get it framed and keep it within eye sight. After all, it is your life plan. Isn't it most sacred or important for you to see every day?

The next step is to follow this time table, unless you want your goals to be mere dreams. Have a ready action plan and then take action. Make a to-do list for your monthly, weekly or daily goals. That makes the review easy, and can tell you whether you are progressing towards your goals. Periodic execution, checking and revision of goals will give you the motivation and energy to reach your goals. A great success is the ultimate result of smaller successes.

Be the best in whatever you do

An eagle knows the unlimited freedom of the sky, right from its birth. Similarly, it is our right to experience the boundless joy and freedom of excellence in our life, as humans. We have come on this planet to realize our immense potential and achieve true success. Nothing can hold us back, whether it is a situation, person, thought, feeling or our circumstances. We are born to shine, excel in all respects.

Everything around us is just perfect, the whole universe, our solar system, the planets, stars, our oceans, atmosphere, rivers, mountains, trees and animals. So are we, our life, relationships, challenges, situations, circumstances, rewards, etc., just perfect – a miracle. If it is not, that is for a higher purpose.

We must nurture our goals, our vision for life. Visualize exactly how you feel, see, hear, when you get there, when you experience the fulfilment of your life ambitions and goals, using the best of your imagination. Keep on innovating your ways, constantly learning and updating yourself in the process. Constantly look for better ways of doing things, or achieving our goals. Keep on practicing the talents and improving on the finer skills.

Excellence is a not a single event, but a continuous process of improving greatness. Excellence is a habit to do things in the best possible way. We should always keep in mind that there has to be better way of achieving something, and always search for it. Nothing is impossible if you have confidence in your capabilities. Our dreams can be limitless, as we ourselves are its creators. When you understand this truth and trust your power to achieve them, you can chalk out a plan to accomplish them in real life. Keep on building upon your smaller successes.

Stepping stones

Most of us will fear failure. What we need to understand is that failures can never stop success. In fact, once we learn our lesson from the failures, it leads us to success. Our past failures are actually the groundwork of our future successes. Every time we fail or experience rejection, we get more closer to doing it the right way. We just need to keep on trying despite the disappointments and adversities. We need to put our failures behind and move forward.

Our failures give us the confidence to move forward with a positive intention. Our longing for success needs to be greater than our fear of failure. We must take the right steps towards our goals. The choice is ours. To become great, to achieve the set goals in life and to walk the purpose, one of the most important ingredients is to 'be unstoppable'. At times you might encounter huge roadblocks on the path to success. The solution is to change your perspective of looking at them and march ahead. You just need to break open the trap of beliefs. Once you are able to achieve that, even the sky is not the limit.

At a glance

- *After taking the first step towards your goal, do not stop*

- *To be unstoppable, it is essential to practice discipline and control over the mind.*

- *What really matters is not the chaos in our life, but how we react to it.*

- *Excellence is a not a single event, but a continuous process of improving greatness.*

CHAPTER 6

HAPPINESS

You can be happy here and now

I am happy here and now
I don't care why and how
Sorrow will not touch me now
To be ever joyful, that's my vow.

There was once a merchant who was so busy with his business that he never spent time with his family. One day, his little son asked if he could play with him. The merchant replied, "I need to do a lot of work to be the best merchant in town. When I achieve this, I will be happy and I promise I'll play with you then." For many months, the little boy would run to his father and ask him, "Are you happy today?" in the hope that his father would stay back and play with him, and each time the merchant would say, "Not today!"

Years went by, but the merchant never found a day to play with his little son. When the boy grew up, the merchant asked him to join the family business. The young man simply refused and said, "I'm happy." The merchant did not understand this reply. The son smiled and said to his father, "In all these years, if you have not been happy for even a single day, then why should I join your business and be unhappy every day of my life? I will do something which gives me time to be happy." Like the merchant, many of us have found ways and means to procrastinate happiness. And that day may never come because happiness is in being and not doing.

Secret to Happiness

Someone once asked me, "How is it that you are always so happy?"

"Can you keep a secret?" I asked him.

"Yes I can," he replied. "Well, so can I," I said and we both burst out laughing.

The truth is there is no secret to happiness. It is not some sort of hidden treasure that you will encounter by chance or can hunt for and discover. Happiness is a feeling that stems from your state of mind. And your state of mind is determined by the emotions that are dominant at any point in time. Many people ask me if it is humanly possible to be happy all times. I tell them, of course it is, you just have to tune into the "happy channel" in your mind. Just like we change the channels on TV with the remote, we can change the state of our mind to be happy. Some situations may not be in our control, but how we react to them is surely in our hands or rather in our mind.

Ways to find happiness

Happiness can be found in doing the simplest things we like or have fun doing. Like sipping a cup of hot chocolate with friends on a rainy day, watching a movie, listening to music, going for a nature walk, reading a book, going on a long drive, enjoying a home cooked meal, dancing, singing, writing, painting, spending time with friends or going on a vacation. The list is just endless. Each one of us knows exactly what gives us happiness, yet if you observe closely, sometimes even while doing these things we are unhappy.

The truth is that happiness is in 'just being!' It is a state of mind. Happiness has nothing to do with what we have or what we are 'doing'. A deep sense of calm at 'doing nothing' and 'just being' is also happiness. Be in the moment. Sometimes, happiness is felt in the form of peace.

One day while I was on vacation, I just sat on a couch in the lobby of the hotel and did nothing, said nothing, looked completely at ease, with no stress on my face. After a while the concierge noticed that I was just sitting there. He came over to me and asked if everything was alright. I nodded my head and said I'm fine. After a while, I noticed that everybody passing by the lobby gave me a strange look. I just kept smiling and didn't move from the couch. When my wife came and sat next to me, she asked, "Why are you sitting here and what is that look on your face?" I smiled and said to her, "I'm just being happy".

The problem is we are conditioned to think we need to do something all the time. One of the most common questions we ask someone when we call or meet them is, "What are you doing?" Reading a book, watching TV, at work, cooking, cleaning, studying shopping, anything, but you need to be doing something. The next time someone calls you, try telling them that you are doing absolutely nothing and see their reaction.

If we just sit idle, then it is generally considered that something is wrong with us. Even in doing, we can't do something just for ourselves; it has to be something for our past or planning for our future. If being busy all the time was the key to happiness, then so many of people who run the rat race day in day out and are constantly doing something would be the happiest people on earth. But they are not.

That definitely does not mean one should stop performing one's duties. Happiness has nothing to do with what we are doing, how busy or idle we are, whether we a rich or poor, sick or healthy, alone or in a group.

We have also been conditioned to be happy in certain given events and be sad at certain given events. Happiness is not bound by external factors. Happiness is independent of thoughts, pain and emotions. We can concoct happiness by being in the moment and hoping for the future. Happiness is in our nature, like fragrance of a rose. The rose does not distinguish or discriminate, whether it is offered at altar or at the graveyard, decorated in a vase or crushed to make syrup. Its natural being is to give out fragrance and that's all it does. We are inherently like that, but due to various life factors we forget our true selves.

This is where an attitude adjustment will prove to be magical. Happiness is independent of thoughts, pain and emotions. We can concoct happiness by being in the moment and hoping for the future. In a single moment we can actually make a shift in our mindset, which in turn can change a whole lot of things in your life.

How does it help?

Does happiness pay off? Of course it does! It is the only thing we forever and desperately pursue, yet it is right there within us, in our nature. When we are happy, it shows in our behaviour and attitude, it positively impacts our relationships, health, and work. Every big and small aspect of our life is affected by our happiness quotient.

A friend of mine always said, "If I get promoted, I'll be very happy." When he got the promotion, I asked him, "Are you happy now?" The answer was a 'no', as life had now posed a different set of challenges in front of him. This is what happens with most of us. We always condition our happiness around external things. The probability of something happening or not happening should never be the basis of our happiness.

If I have a car, I will be happy

If I have my own house I will be happy

If I get a better job I will be happy

If I get married I'll be happy

If I send my kid to the best school I'll be happy.

So many ifs! And all these 'ifs' of our life come to merge in a single 'but'. But there is a possibility that all these might not even happen. Then what? Will you continue to be unhappy throughout your life? And as a sad matter of fact, even if we get all these things we assume will make us happy, we are still not! We then start craving for bigger cars, bigger houses, better job and higher position, better pay. Round and round in circles we go. And we don't take a single moment to just stop and ask, "Why am I unhappy?"

Happiness can never be achieved by material gains. To be really happy one has to look inside and not outside. Happiness is inner contentment and inner satisfaction and hence independent of the situation, time or place.

Make happiness a choice

Once there was a young girl full of energy and joy, with a smile for everyone. She worked as a secretary to the director of a company. Her short-tempered boss always found a reason to yell at her. However, the young girl was never affected by his words and the smile never left her face. One day, a colleague asked her how she managed to look so happy every day even though her boss yells at her. The smiley secretary replied, "You see, the HR department has given me a list of duties, and the first and most important one is that I should look presentable and happy at all times. So, I make it a point to focus on doing my job well, and not at the angry words of my boss."

Many may question, how is it possible to ignore someone who is angry or yells at us? It's simple. It is like refusing someone when they gift us a bag of sorrow. We can either accept the gift or refuse it. The choice is ours. The key is to make it a habit to say NO to such gifts that come free all the time. We must not allow external factors to gain control over our state of mind. Only we should be in charge of our mind and no one else. We can either choose to be happy or not.

Ever noticed how children always radiate happiness? That's because they are totally free from the clutches of desires and ego. They are not biased or judgmental. They live in the moment and enjoy it fully, till the time they are subjected to the conditioning that forms their belief systems. As they grow older, they gradually become conditioned to be happy only if their desires and needs are met.

Let's look at a scenario where a child did not fare well in an exam, how would a parent normally react? If we were to do a study of 100 such cases, how many parents would reassure the child and say 'it's alright to fail', 'just cheer up and be happy', 'you can study and do well next time'? Hardly, right?

It is very easy to be happy when you achieve what you want, though this happiness is momentary. But to be happy in a situation, when life plays hard on you is not only very challenging but also a definite doorway to eternal happiness. I am often questioned by many, how anyone can be happy when life has treated them so unfairly.

To my surprise I found the answer to this question in my own household. Our maid hails from a nearby slum. She lives in a rented house with her husband and in-laws. Her husband is an alcoholic and spends most of his earnings on alcohol. She works hard to support her family and her extended family, bears their tantrums, deals with the challenges thrown by the alcoholic husband and juggles three different jobs. When she delivered her first baby, it was stillborn. She went through immense emotional trauma in addition to a huge financial loss in the medical treatment. As if this was not enough, she went through another pregnancy after two years and the baby had to be delivered prematurely and this baby was also stillborn.

Are these reasons not sufficient to go insane? Most of us would. But this girl who has been with for us for five years has never shown any signs of unhappiness. On the contrary we have always seen a big smile on her face, humming happy songs while working. When we tried to sympathize, her reply was, "It was God's wish. Everything will be all right one day." This is a clear example of how our choices make our own happiness. My maid, amidst great misfortune, chose to be happy, in spite of her pain and disappointments. It is very easy to give up, sink and hide behind the miseries life throws at us, but it takes a brave heart to remain happy and smile through these storms.

Life always will test you in every possible way. The situations we face are not in our control but our reaction to them is. Just take a moment to alter the state of your mind and, be happy. Here are a few simple techniques to elevate you to an altered state of mind.

Live in the moment – Most of the time, the cause for unhappiness erupts from the guilt or hurt from the past or from worry about the future. Living in the now and enjoying that very moment will make you happy.

Spend time with children – You will find that children are always in a state of happiness and since happiness is contagious, you will be infected with happiness from them.

Do small things for others – The gesture may be small, but the joy you derive from it will be immense. For example, help an elderly person cross the road, feeding a stray dog, visit a sick, old relative or appreciate your subordinate for his good work.

Be grateful – My mother would always tell me that I should count my blessings. When I actually started implementing it by being grateful for what I have, I realised how fortunate I am and a sense of calm and happiness took over me from within.

Visualising – Many times to trick your mind you just need to fake it. Even if you are not happy, pretend to be happy. It works. Imagine something that you always wanted and believe or visualise that you have received it; you will feel the difference immediately.

Look at the larger picture – If you get dejected by certain setbacks, question how significant it is in the perspective of your whole life. This will make the issue less significant and reduce the feeling of unhappiness.

Recalling a happy memory – This is a quick fix solution for changing your state of mind. If you find yourself in an unhappy situation, recall a happy memory, one in which you felt on top of the world. Your mood will change instantly. It works like magic.

Laugh it out – Many times when you are faced with an unhappy situation that is completely draining your energy, make it appear hilarious as if it's a big joke and laugh with a friend, aloud if possible. Make as much fun of it as you can. Laughter frees you of negative emotions. You will feel much lighter.

Spending time in nature – Nature brings you closer to the source of pure happiness. This is very effective in altering your state of mind because nature is filled with positive energy. So when you feel down, go to a park, beach, or tend to the plants in your garden.

Music and dance – Sing in the shower, lock yourself in a room, and put on some music and dance like you never have before, if your music player isn't around, you can sing aloud or hum your favourite tune. If you don't know how to sing or dance, that's even better.

Watch a comedy movie – Watching a movie that makes you laugh, diverts your attention from the disturbing situation. Also laughing releases enzymes that make you feel in-control and happy. Reading a comic strip also helps.

Research shows that even an artificially induced smile boosts your mood. So act happy, and you will be. Don't waste another second waiting for circumstances to change in order to be happy. Take charge of your life right now, and be happy. The universe presents us with every opportunity to be happy. All we have to do is alter our state of mind and 'Just Be'. When we live each moment of life Being Happy, external factors will stop bothering us.

At a glance

- *Happiness is only a state of mind*
- *There is no secret to happiness*
- *One can be happy in any circumstance. It is unconditional*
- *We must choose to be always happy*

KEYS

"*Thanks, for turning around while I was changing..!*"

CHAPTER 7

POWER OF GRATITUDE

Refuel yourself

I am thankful for, all that I have in life
Friends, experiences, challenge and strife,
Gratitude gives me the strength and power
To make me bloom like a heavenly flower.

My wife is an exceptional 'gifter'. She has this unique ability to gauge what would make the other person happy and goes out of her way to make personalized gifts to make the person feel special. I love to participate in her enthusiasm and help her. I feel immensely grateful that I have a life partner with whom I share common interests.

A few years back, my wife and I created a special gift for a close friend. We invested a lot of our time, energy and money in that gift. But when we gifted them our heartfelt creation, the response was very cold. There came a cursory thank you without any feelings or emotions. My wife was put off by this attitude. I consoled her saying, "Change your perspective of looking at this. We enjoyed the process of creation. Didn't we? So we should be grateful that we got this opportunity, resources and the capability to create something unique."

"I agree, but henceforth I am not going to make anything for her," she snapped.

Our universe operates exactly in the same way. The more grateful we are about the things in our life, the more abundance will flow in our life. If we are truly grateful for the wealth we have (no matter how much), more wealth will flow into our life. The important thing is to be grateful and mean it when we express it.

At any given moment, every individual has a number of things to be grateful of. Even under hardships, it is easy to find things to be thankful for. Every moment we inhale, breathe is a sign of life, it is visible proof that we are alive.

Saying 'thanks'

"Thank you", is such a powerful set of words and yet most do not realize its importance, and hence never say it often enough. Saying *Thank you* and meaning it from the heart is the simplest and most powerful act of gratitude. Being grateful brings joy and happiness to both, the receiver of the benefit and the giver.

Gratitude is a feeling which acknowledges a benefit or a service that one has received or will receive. It is living life as if everything were a miracle, counting life's blessings, appreciating the simple joys of life, and acknowledging everything that we have. One must use gratitude to shift their focus from what they lack in life to what they have and experience a feeling of abundance. Gratitude is a very special and a very humbling feeling. I believe many of the problems the world is facing today would be sorted out, if each one of us could just take a moment, be thankful and mean it.

Gratitude gives us the strength to overcome life problems, by focusing on our positive attributes and using them to find a solution. It has to be a way of life and practiced at every moment, every day. Gratitude is not something to be felt only when someone does something for you. One can be grateful for so many things such as, family, friends, good health, a good job, good relationships, financial security. The list is endless if we decide to appreciate and be thankful. In fact, we can begin with being grateful for this human life we have.

Gratitude has a completely different meaning for some people. They do not look at gratitude as something to express after receiving a benefit and being grateful for it. Rather they feel it is an opportunity to be just helpful without any expectations. Being grateful for the opportunity to serve gives us a sense of purpose in life. It is very easy to be grateful when we receive a benefit, but only very few can be grateful for an opportunity to give. That's an admirable trait to cultivate.

Why be grateful?

Gratitude is a virtue that we all must possess in order to understand and appreciate life. It is one of the routes to happiness. It has been proven through various studies that when we live with gratitude we become more receptive, alert, enthusiastic, determined, optimist, and we experience less depression and we can handle stress. It helps us identify our purpose or goals in life and gives us the strength to move forward in that direction and be happy.

Gratitude is a virtue each one of us must nurture in the garden of our heart and allow it to blossom. Just like a gardener, we have to work on it every single day to yield results. Gratitude is like the fuel, without which a vehicle would come to a stop after travelling a distance. Therefore to keep us going in life and to stay energetic, we must fuel our lives with gratitude. When we are going through a difficult phase in life, turmoil or a tragedy we are vulnerable and easily get attached to negative emotions. But if you shift your perspective and begin to appreciate all the good things you still have, you stand a higher chance to bounce back to normalcy and get over adversity, quickly.

Gratitude is like a life support system which holds us together during times of hardship and difficulty. There is a story of a Zen Master who preached about gratitude in a small village. Every day, in the morning and evening the Zen Master would gather the villagers in their community centre and talk about gratitude and make the villagers feel grateful for all they had been blessed with. The villagers along with the Zen Master thanked God and each other for the abundance in their lives. They started their day with a gratitude prayer and ended the day in giving thanks. They treated each other with respect and took great care of their farms and the farm animals. Each year they were blessed with abundance and they were a happy community.

One year famine struck the village. During this time the villagers faced a lot of hardships. There was scarcity of food, water and the land lay barren. The farmers had to mortgage all their valuables and sell off their animals to distant villages for survival. Even during this time the Zen Master held daily prayer meetings for rain and also to thank God for all that they had as a community.

One day during a prayer meeting, some of the village members got angry and started fighting with the Zen master. They said, "Stop giving us false hope, we have nothing to be grateful for, so why are we pretending to be? There is hardly enough food and water, the land is barren; we have sold off all our animals. We don't know where our next meal is coming from or whether we will make it through tomorrow. What is the point of giving thanks, what are we being grateful for?"

To this the Zen Master replied, "We are being thankful for the strength the Lord has given us to survive through this adversity. I agree that today there is difficulty, chaos and confusion, but we don't know what tomorrow holds for us. As a community we must thank god that we have the support of each other and our united strength to see us through this phase. We have our homes and our families with us, to love us and take care of us. We must not lose faith, and hope for a better tomorrow. Remember that there is a good reason for everything that happens, and there is a lesson to be learnt even from the difficulties we face today."

The next day the village was raided by a group of soldiers in search of food, cattle and strong young men to fight in a war. However, after rampaging through the village they found nothing of use to them. The village had very little food, no cattle and the men were too weak to fight in the war. They didn't find any valuables either as the villagers had mortgaged everything they had. Soon they left the village empty handed.

A few days later, the villagers came to know that many other neighbouring villages had been looted and all young men were taken away forcibly to fight the war. After months had passed, the village was blessed with plenty of rains again. The villagers got to work on their land and slowly got back to a normal life. They paid off their debts and got back their valuables and cattle. When the Zen Master held a prayer meeting to thank God for the abundance, the villagers thanked God for the famine. For had they not been struck by famine, the village would have been completely destroyed by the soldiers and all the men would have been taken away.

All for a reason

As the saying goes, "Everything happens for a reason". We often start complaining about small things in life, not realising that everything happens for a reason and that everything is happening perfectly as per the larger plan of the universe. We focus and complain so much about the thorns that we fail to appreciate the beauty of the roses blooming along with it.

Necessity is the mother of invention, but adversity is the mother of wisdom. It is in times of difficulties that gratitude acts as a pillar of support. It gives us hope and a shift in focus from the present difficult conditions to a better future. Gratitude does not make us complacent; rather, it motivates us to look forward to a better tomorrow. Sometimes adversity is just a blessing in disguise to help us prepare for a better tomorrow. However, what is important is to hold on to our faith and be grateful for whatever we have.

Strengthening relationships through gratitude

Expressing gratitude is one of the many ways to strengthen relationships. It is vital to remember that everyone is dependent on another, in some way or other. We are defined by our relationships with another person in the family, workplace and society. In fact, we share a special relationship with everything we are surrounded by in life, not just the people and the things we have, but also whatever universe provides us.

The nature of the relationships one shares varies with the role played by that person or entity in his life. And each is unique in its own way. When you show gratitude in a relationship towards the entity, you create an opportunity for the receiver to feel valued and appreciated and to feel thankful for their valuable contribution in your life.

Say for example, you have a high pressure job that requires you to work for 10 to 12 hours daily and travel a lot. You have hired a full-time help to cook and clean for you and you have had him for a few years now. Every day when you come home, your house is clean, the laundry has been done, a hot scrumptious home cooked meal is ready and the 'to do' list that you stuck on the fridge in the morning has been taken care of. All you need to do after a tiring day of work is take a hot shower and enjoy the meal.

Now ask yourself, how important is the role of help in your life? How much do you appreciate him and value his work? Paying his salary on time is not being grateful. If you have not taken the time to thank him properly, do so now. Because, his being there for you, makes your life a whole lot easier and adds value to your life. He allows you the free time you have on hand because you come back to a perfect home. When you say thank you to him, say it with real honesty, because the person who has been working effortlessly for you has emotions and it is these emotions that we must value and respect.

The value of gratitude

When a person feels appreciated in a relationship, he or she feels valuable and this motivates them to do better. This in turn strengthens their relationship. Once there was a very hardworking and sincere executive. He was always punctual and performed his duties diligently. He frequently did overtime as and when needed, without showing any reluctance. Due to his pleasant personality everyone in the office liked him, except his boss. His boss thought he was too 'sugary in nature', as he put it, for showing gratitude all the time. When it was appraisal time, the executive realised that everyone except him had been given a raise. When he approached his boss, he was told, "You do not deserve it."

Disheartened, the executive resigned. When his replacement joined the company, it was around the financial year end that saw heavy targets and deadlines. The new executive came and left on time and refused to stay back late. The boss had a tough time and no one to help him out. Eventually, he failed to meet his targets and was refused the promotion he had been working so hard for. When he approached his director, the director said, "You didn't deserve it." This reminded him of the junior executive and how he had treated him. He realised he had made a big mistake by not being grateful for all the hard work of the previous executive.

Sometimes we fail to recognize the importance of a person and the value of their role in our life. In doing so, we lose them and later on have regrets. By the time we realize this, it may be too late. Therefore, it is very important to appreciate every person in our life, no matter what role they play. When we show gratitude in a relationship, it helps us realize how blessed and fortunate we are to have the person or thing in our life.

Living with gratitude also helps us learn to live life as if everything were a miracle, being aware and constantly recognizing how much we have been given. This helps us attribute our achievements and success to the higher self and humbles us. Humility is the offspring of gratitude. When we live every moment in gratitude, we become humble and there is no room for ego.

History shows that ego is one of the biggest enemies of mankind. Many have fallen prey to their ego and have been completely destroyed. Ego is like a poisonous creeper that engulfs our life and humility is the axe we use to chop it off. Being grateful helps us focus on the greater goal of life, which is to fulfil our life purpose. Gratitude not only acts as fuel, but also as a GPS system continuously showing us the way forward. Without gratitude to show us the way, we would certainly lose track, get lost and divert from our life's purpose.

Charity begins at home

It is a great virtue to be grateful for all the people and things that make our life happy and complete. Make a list of people who have contributed to your life directly or indirectly, and show them that you appreciate their role in our life. Openly acknowledge and appreciate the people in your life and let them know how important they are. You can buy a gift for them, or make a kind gesture that brings a smile to them.

When people are aware of our gratefulness, it motivates them to do better and this strengthens our relationship with them. Gratitude extends to "non-living" things too! Consider your vehicle that has been working so well for so long. Show your gratitude by servicing it and cleaning it on a regular basis. Similarly, the house that you live in is also an entity that needs to be appreciated.

Being grateful for animate and inanimate life allows us to appreciate the value the things that we are blessed with. It will enable us to live life as if it were a series of miracles. Be grateful for your present by remembering the hard times that you had experienced in the past. Be grateful that you have been blessed with the strength to overcome those tough times.

Being humble

One of the most important qualities of great people is humility. Humility is a noble asset and he who can master humility attracts success. Each one of us is a special human being. We all are born with unique qualities and a purpose. When we understand this fact from our core, we learn to respect others around us as well. We fully understand their capabilities and purpose of being there in our life.

When you cultivate gratitude, an unexpected outcome is humility. When we live life in humility, we automatically begin to appreciate everything in life and gratitude becomes a part of our nature. Our attitude in life counts a lot when it comes to handling any situation and humility enables us to do it with grace. It works the other way round as well; when we practice gratitude by being thankful for everything in life it humbles us.

Practicing gratitude

If we practice the right gestures, the emotion of gratitude can be activated. Grateful gestures could be smiling, saying thank you, gratitude notes or letters and giving gifts. Ask yourself periodically, "What have I received today?", "what have I given today?", and "how have I been of help to someone in need?" By performing simple gestures of gratitude, you can make a huge impact on your own life, and the life of those who matter to you. Gestures of gratitude make both the giver and the recipient. This will have a ripple effect in turn to make the world a much better place. Imagine a world where everyone practices gratitude and humility! This would indeed be a beautiful world and ego would have no place here.

Have you noticed people who live their life in gratitude wear it proudly on their sleeves and it shows in their behavior? They have a particular style of speaking. They always look at a situation in a positive way and use words that resonate with positivity. They frequently use words such as 'I'm happy', 'Gift from god', 'I'm blessed', 'I'm fortunate'. These are also referred to as 'positive affirmations'.

Practicing positive affirmations allows us to identify the privileges we have and we can easily appreciate them. By practicing positive affirmations, we create a harmonious environment for ourselves where we accept all the good in our life and attract more abundance.

Gratitude prayers

Many cultures around the world practice giving thanks in the form of prayer. In some spiritual traditions, a gratitude prayer is considered to be the most powerful form of prayer, because through these prayers people recognize the role of the universe in their life. A gratitude prayer acknowledges life as a miracle. A gratitude prayer humbles us as we accept that the universe has an important role in making things happen in our life. Inculcate a routine gratitude prayer, for example, in the morning before you get out of bed, during mealtimes, during achievements, during tough times, during bedtimes.

Gratitude is a powerful tool that enables us to see things as a miracle and gives us the power to turn difficulties and challenges. By shifting our perspective and becoming more appreciative, we can trigger amazing changes in our life. Gratitude is a choice we make in life; it does not depend on circumstances. We can be grateful in the most trying times if we choose to. Gratitude helps us forgive easily and become more generous and compassionate. It is the best attitude when we are on the path of fulfilling our purpose in life, it is most important to carry gratitude along with us. Believe in gratitude and practice it daily. The very act allows us to live a more positive life, enables us to make the right choices, be happier and enjoy every moment of our being.

At a glance

- *"Thank you" is an extremely powerful set of words*
- *Having a feeling of gratitude makes us aware of the things we have in life*
- *Gratitude is one of the direct routes to happiness*
- *A gratitude prayer acknowledges life as a miracle.*
- *Those who practice gratitude and humility attract success.*

KEYS

"I am still the best..!"

CHAPTER 8

I AM THE BEST

Boost your self esteem

I am unique, and I am the best
It doesn't matter, what people suggest
I know my place is in the upper crest
In my eyes, I am better than the best.

The other day my wife and I met an old friend Kaira over coffee at Starbucks. Kaira is my wife's closest friend since college days. She was a regular visitor to our house after our marriage. Kaira, hailing from a small town, was a guileless and emotional woman who had come to Mumbai to pursue her career. A chubby, attractive woman, she dressed badly simple because she couldn't be bothered. Her motto was, "One should be beautiful from within... External beauty may not last." Later on she got married and moved out of Mumbai. Now after ten years, Kaira was back in town and we decided to catch up on our old memories.

As we waited in the coffee shop, flipping through the 20 odd varieties of coffee on the menu card and soaking ourselves in the enticing aroma of coffee, Kaira entered. She looked completely different from what we had last seen her. She had lost weight, adorned a smart haircut, and was dressed in a trendy western outfit. We could not believe that this was the same Kaira!

It was an emotional moment to see Kaira and my wife running towards each other like two small kids, as they tightly hugged each other. Both of them were tearful and visibly overwhelmed, totally oblivious of anybody's presence around. As we settled down at the table, my wife said, "Hey Kaira, you look so pretty and you have lost a considerable amount of weight too."

Kaira immediately replied, "Well not really, my mother-in-law does not think so. She thinks I am still overweight. I have to work towards losing more weight."

Now this came as a shocker to me. I started wondering, where is she going to lose extra pounds from? Kaira was in perfect shape and looked pretty enough to attract a few glances at the coffee shop. But she was in complete denial of her beauty.

Having met after ten long years, a heartfelt conversation began between two close friends. My wife asked her, "How do you get along with your mother-in-law, Kaira?"

"Well, not great, to be honest," She replied. "She never accepted me since my marriage with Rajeev. He is her only son and she is extremely possessive about him. Rajeev also loves his mom a lot. She always taunts me, 'My son is so handsome, I really don't understand how he fell in love with you.'"

As Kaira started pouring her heart out and the two friends were lost in conversation, I got absorbed in my own thoughts. It was clear that Kaira was facing low self-esteem. Since I deal with life issues as a life coach, I come across so many people who are suffering from this dreadful disease. Self-esteem comes from your evaluation about your own self.

Depression, suicidal tendencies, anxiety, guilt and anger, lack of energy, not taking any risks, not accepting compliments, unhealthy relationships and giving up easily are typical signs of low self esteem. People suffering from it will often be heard saying, "I am not good enough", "I don't deserve this", "I am a failure in life", "I can't handle challenges", "Nobody loves me", "I feel incompetent and insignificant" and "I always mess up things."

In Kaira's case, she gave a lot of importance to her mother-in-law's opinion. Though she did not get along well with her, Kaira was making all the efforts to go out of her way, to fit into her mom-in-law's mould of an ideal daughter-in-law. Kaira craved for acceptance from this old lady, who did not miss a single chance to criticise her and put her down. For this acceptance, Kaira was ready to change herself completely.

Self-acceptance

People are bound to criticise, but the criticism has to be taken constructively and always with a pinch of salt. It does not matter whether people accept us or not. What is more important is that we accept ourselves unconditionally. We have certain expectations from ourselves due to which we end up critically judging our own selves. And if these expectations are not fulfilled, then we label ourselves as, "not good enough". Or when certain people in our life, such as parents, spouse, in-laws, teachers, a friend or boss have some expectations from us and we are not able to live up to it, we label ourselves as "a failure", many times even "a failure in life". These opinions set a downward trend for the self esteem.

Do we really need to change ourselves just because somebody thinks that we are not good enough? If we are not able to meet somebody's expectations, does it mean we have failed in life? These are the questions we need to ask ourselves from time to time. If the answers to these questions are positive, then we need to truly change our pattern of thinking.

Many times more than the outer critic, it is our inner critic which plays a major role in our misery. We crave for acceptance from other people and in the process loose our individuality. I believe that each one of us has come on this earth with an exceptional set of qualities and abilities and an exclusive purpose to follow. No two human beings on this earth are comparable, because each one of us is different and unique. We are complete in all respects and are perfect. When we fall prey to criticism, we allow someone to change our basic qualities and mould ourselves as per their expectations and in the process loose our originality, our uniqueness. We need to first accept ourselves as we are.

Rounak's story

Rounak joined the driving class along with his younger brother. Their mother would always tell everyone, "My younger one is a smart chap and a fast learner. But Rounak is always slow and laid back. I am not sure whether he will be able to take the car on the roads even after taking driving lessons." Needless to say Rounak never gathered the courage to take the car on the road! He started to firmly believe that 'he was not good enough', especially when it came from his own mother. Rounak's self esteem went so low that he lost the courage to do anything new. Though a brilliant guy and an MBA, he has enveloped himself in a cocoon. He still suffers from inferiority complex, never takes any risks and always tries to please people, especially his mother.

If you are a parent, it is your moral responsibility to develop a healthy self esteem in your children, along with a healthy body and mind. In the formative years of a child, be very vigilant and sensitive of what you feed in their minds. Help your children realise their true potential to excel and never ever compare them with anybody.

Anita's block

Though we don't really inherit self-esteem, it starts building-up or going down at an early stage, even earlier than we can imagine. In my practice as a life coach and a regression therapist, I come across many cases of low self-esteem. Anita, a 30-year-old woman, had very low self esteem which created a block in her progress. Though she was a brilliant girl, she could not take risks in life. She felt totally insignificant and incompetent. This bothered her on a daily basis and hence she wanted to get to root cause of this issue.

When she went through the therapy, Anita found that at the time of her birth, her parents were disappointed, because they expected a baby boy after two other daughters. This disappointment and a feeling of rejection from the people around created such a lasting impression on the new born baby's psyche, that it completely lowered her self esteem. She felt unwanted and rejected from her own parents and the close relatives and therefore was left with a feeling of insecurity. After my therapy where I worked with her through various processes, today she moves in the world with confidence and her head held high.

Self-esteem is a function of two kinds of thoughts. One is "what people think about us" and the other is "what we think about ourselves." Many times, high self esteem is mistaken as ego. I have heard people saying things such as "this person has a high ego" or "is very egotistic". Let me make this very clear, self-esteem is all about boosting our own confidence level. It is about feeling good about ourselves to achieve our goals, be the best, and excel in whatever we do. Self-esteem is a step towards achieving greatness. Even if we are on the path and have not reached there, there's nothing wrong in thinking so.

When we think we are the best, we will become the best. When we think we can achieve excellence in life, only then we can reach there. Self-esteem is not about putting others down, or showing that others are not worth. It does not mean that we are superior to the other person. We should be careful not to judge people around us just because we are moving towards greatness. Each one of us has the quality and capability to become great in life. Only when we think less about others or put others down, or become arrogant, it becomes a bloated ego.

Self esteem is not a static phenomenon. It can increase or decrease due to many factors. It fluctuates with situations, challenges, emotional state and with people around. Though all these factors greatly affect our self esteem, we should work towards building a healthy self esteem that is unaffected by any external or internal factors.

Rejection

When we face rejection from people around us, especially from our close ones, it hurts. This also has a great impact on our self esteem. A lady who recently attended one of my programmes was going through this phase of rejection. Her husband had left her for another woman and she suffered from a very low self esteem. Instead of realising the wrong of her husband, this lady formed a strong belief that "I am not good enough, hence my husband left me". This affected her life adversely.

She suffered from hypertension. She lost her job and she went into severe depression. She held herself responsible for the rejection from her husband and therefore rejected herself. It took me quite some time and lot of efforts to get back the smile and confidence this lady had at one point of time.

Most people operate from their own incompleteness and unresolved issues and therefore behave in a particular way. It is entirely our own choice to accept or reject the rejection! Only when you reject your own self does it became soul-destroying. If you are not too happy with certain aspect of your personality, take steps to improve those rather than rejecting that part of yourself. In the case of things that cannot change, acknowledge the truth they have a definite purpose in your life and simply be!

Bad phases

When we pass through a rough patch we form an opinion that life is bad. We start thinking that 'I have failed in life'. We feel our dreams are completely shattered. Many times the situations in life are not in our control. We can only give it our best shot. The end result is not in our hands at all. In such times, we need to understand that a bad phase is a part and parcel of life. The night is the darkest before its dawn.

Only after the bad phase, will we really value the good phase. Each adversity teaches us some valuable lessons and helps us evolve into a better human being. We need to change our perspective of looking at the so called 'bad phase'. It is imperative, not to let these bad patches in life lower our self esteem. 'This too shall pass' is a powerful mantra to pass through the bad phases in life.

Living by others opinion

We take other peoples opinion about us too seriously. If somebody tells us, in school, that we are not good in studies, we form an opinion about ourselves - "I am not good enough". These opinions formed about ourselves prevent us from living a life using our highest potential. We get so carried away by the opinion of others, that we don't even think that 'well, if I am not good at studies I must be brilliant at something else.' But rather than acknowledging our strengths, we fall prey to others' opinion and let our self esteem down.

We forget that whatever people say or think about us is entirely their opinion, and every person has a right to form their own opinion. Anything good or bad, right or wrong is always a perspective. If someone calls you a monkey, does it mean that you are a monkey? The key is not to get influenced by others' opinion about us. We always have a choice as to how much we should let ourselves be affected.

Not acknowledging our capabilities

I feel deep anguish when I hear youngsters saying, "I am not capable enough". As little children, we all were filled with immense potential. Unfortunately, certain conditioning stopped us from thinking so later on. Even today, irrespective of our age and circumstances, we are full of potential. However, we stop ourselves from taking steps mainly because of self-doubts. It is important that we do not put limitations on ourselves. We have unlimited capabilities to achieve anything that we ever wanted. So believe in your own strengths and powers. Only when you acknowledge them, the world will acknowledge them.

Seeking approval from others

People with low self esteem will always seek approval from others in whatever they do. 'How do I look?' or 'Did you like my work?' or

'Do you love me?' are their common questions. The interesting part is that if the answer to the above questions is negative, these people feel worthless and if the answer is positive, they can't accept it easily.

Seeking approval from others is like living our life on the mercy of others. The other day I was at a close friend's place. His 16-year old son was browsing the computer, looking sullen and irritated. I asked him why he was so glum. After slight hesitation, the boy replied, "I have 527 friends on my friends list. Yesterday, I uploaded a nice profile picture and no one seems to have noticed it. There's not a single like or comment on my picture." Honestly, though I found this reply a little funny but for this young boy, it was a very serious matter. Today in the world of social media, somebody noticing, approving and acknowledging us has become so vital to make us feel important.

Not loving and accepting ourselves as we are

By not accepting ourselves as we are, we strive too hard to become what we are not. Unconditional self-acceptance brings about lot of peace and it helps in better performance. At times we tend to compare ourselves with others. "She is so beautiful, I am not" or "he is so lucky, I am not". Remember that each one of us is on an exceptional journey of life and that we are whole and perfect as we are.

Equating the past with the present

If we have experienced failures in the past, we form a firm belief that life is all about failures. 'I can't succeed" is what we constantly tell our mind. This reduces our confidence and lowers our self esteem, in turn preventing us from taking steps towards a successful life. We should always remember to tell ourselves "What if I have failed in the past? The present does not equal the past. I will definitely succeed this time."

The negative dialogue

Knowingly or unknowingly, we have an ongoing conversation with ourselves. That internal dialogue is continuously on. As a part of this internal dialogue, we also draw conclusions and form opinions about ourselves and others. If you come across somebody in the office doing lousy work, you immediately tell yourself, "I am much better than this person." But suppose you go to a party and after looking at other people there, you feel that you are not suitably dressed, you immediately tell yourselves, "I am pathetic at dressing up suitably for the occasion."

We always need to watch the inner dialogue that goes on within us. As far as the dialogue is positive it is good. But it is very important to scan the negative dialogue and stop it there and then. A negative dialogue acts like a virus that attacks and ruins the self esteem. There is an inner critic in all of us. Its job is basically to criticise anything that is not up to our expectations. For example in the office you are not granted a promotion which you had been long expecting, your inner critic will immediately tell you, "Hey boy, you didn't deserve it anyway!" or "you are always a loser!"

It is extremely important to silence your inner critic. Negative statements like the above will only let your self esteem down.

Patting your back

If you are working towards a goal and you take a successful step towards it, pat yourself in the back. It is of utmost importance to reward ourselves for small achievements. Small encouragements to ourselves go a long way in keeping us motivated to move towards our goals with a high self-esteem. Always be generous in appreciating yourself, so that you don't feel the need to be appreciation by others. Always be proud of your accomplishments, whether big or small. Tell yourself, "I am proud of you!"

Love and pamper yourself

Loving your own self is the most powerful way to boost your self esteem. Always believe that you are the best. The reality that you are a unique person, one of a kind on this planet earth, endorses the fact "you are the best". Say it and believe it.

Many times, we show kindness towards other human beings or animals but when it comes to our own selves we are harsh, critical and judgemental. Always be kind and gentle while dealing with your self. A healthy self-esteem is largely cultivated by self-love.

Anything that may not be 'essential' for us but gives an emotional high is a way to pamper ourselves. Most ignore it as "unnecessary", which is a mistake. Make it a point to pamper yourself from time to time to boost your self-esteem. Different ways of papering yourself could be going to a spa, watching a movie with friends, taking a vacation, getting a massage, go shopping for yourself, etc.

Do things to boost your confidence

An easy and a sure-shot way to boost our self-esteem is to face and do things we are afraid of. If you are scared of public speaking, find an occasion where you can give a speech and go for it. Practise it well, take training if required and present yourself with confidence. See how this boosts up your self-esteem. If you don't know driving yet go and enrol yourself in a driving class. Driving gives a lot of confidence and you feel 'in control'.

Stand up for yourself

It is very important to speak up or stand up for yourself. As mentioned in the earlier chapter, we all have an inner child within us. If the inner child is happy, we feel happy and if it is upset, we feel sad. This state of mind also has a deep connection with our self esteem. Many times, we unknowingly allow ourselves to be dictated or dominated by people, sometimes out of respect, sometimes out of compulsion and some other times due to the lack of courage to oppose. By doing this, we let our inner child down or in other words don't stand up for ourselves. Stand up for yourselves by expressing what you feel, fearlessly and assertively.

Affirmations

Affirmations work miraculously on mind, body and soul. They are like autosuggestions, when repeated get embedded deep in our subconscious mind. Affirmations such as,

"I am the best",

"I love and accept myself, unconditionally",

"I am in full control of my life"

work miraculously towards boosting our self esteem. A personal affirmation can be devised for each person and when practiced daily like a mantra, can create amazing results.

Though our self esteem is constantly affected by so many factors like situations, people, state of mind etc., we need to keep working towards achieving a healthy self esteem. It is as important as having a healthy body and mind. After all, self esteem is our evaluation of us. The world will value us only as much as we do.

At a glance

- *We need to first accept ourselves as we are*
- *When we think we are the best, we will become the best*
- *High self esteem is not ego*
- *Loving your own self is the most powerful way to boost your self esteem*
- *The world will value us only as much as we do*

CHAPTER 9

ARE YOU LIVING IN THE PRESENT?

Present is the only moment with us. That is the life and the only truth. There is nothing more to life than the present. But most of the times in our life we are either living in the past or the future. We are either entangled in the regret, guilt, hatred, anger of the past, or killing ourselves due to anxieties, fears, insecurities, uncertainties of the future; in the process completely missing life which lies only in the present. It is time now to analyse ourselves, whether we are living life in the present or not. Here is a small exercise to help you in this process of assessing this.

Similar to the previous section's exercise, this one requires you to take some time out for yourself and find a quiet place. You can put on some nice relaxing music. Just shut yourself from any kind of disturbances. It a good idea to switch off your mobile phone, and make sure that no one disturbs you.

Keep a pen/pencil handy to do the exercise. You can also use blank sheets of paper if you like. I urge you to be honest with your answers. After all it is the question of your life. Take your time you need to think. Answer the following questions in a *Yes* or *No*. The answer cannot be a *'May be'*. You can freely note down your thoughts that come while answering the questions, or the points you need to work upon for living life at its fullest. Once you finish the exercise you can go back to these points. I have added the next chapter

'Powerful tools to live in the present' to help you in the process.

All the best for the test....!!

		Yes	No
1.	Are you present in the 'now' when you are doing something important?	☐	☐
2.	Are you comfortable being at one place and doing absolutely nothing?	☐	☐
3.	Are you able to keep silent for at least some time during the day?	☐	☐
4.	Are you able to pursue what you love doing?	☐	☐
5.	Are you doing things you are passionate about?	☐	☐
6.	Have you found your purpose of life?	☐	☐
7.	Do you feel that you lose track of time while doing something that you are passionate about?	☐	☐
8.	Are you following your heart while taking decisions?	☐	☐
9.	Do you think you made the right choices in life?	☐	☐
10.	Are you able to say 'no' to things that are unimportant?	☐	☐
11.	Do you believe in your own potential?	☐	☐
12.	Do you have a winning attitude?	☐	☐
13.	Once you decide upon taking a course of action do you take the first step immediately?	☐	☐
14.	Are you comfortable with making mistakes?	☐	☐
15.	Do you feel confident to do what you want without the fear of failure?	☐	☐
16.	Do you feel confident to do what you want without the fear of being judged?	☐	☐

17. Do you feel confident to do what you want without the fear of change? ☐ ☐

18. Are you good in asking for help? ☐ ☐

19. Do you think you are focused and disciplined? ☐ ☐

20. Do you find yourself happy without any reason? ☐ ☐

21. Do you like spending time with children? ☐ ☐

22. Can you laugh without holding back? ☐ ☐

23. Are you grateful for each and every thing in your life? ☐ ☐

24. Do you love and accept yourself as you are? ☐ ☐

25. Do you often stand up for yourself? ☐ ☐

If the answer to 18 or more of the above questions is *Yes*, then congratulations! You are on the right path, and living in the present moment. One just needs to be more aware and mindful to be able to live in the present completely. However, if you have 18 or more *No* answers, then you have a second chance to change your track.

After you finish analysing this test, it is time to revisit the questions where the answer is *No*. Refer to the notes you have made and work upon them with the tools given in the next chapter.

CHAPTER 10

POWERFUL TOOLS TO LIVE YOUR PRESENT

Given below are some tried and tested powerful tools that will help you in living in the present

- **Observe your breath** – Find a quite place, where you will not be disturbed for some time. Sit in a comfortable posture and let your eyes gently close. Now take few slow deep breaths. When you breathe, observe the breath touching the inner walls of your nose and going till the lungs and back. Feel the breath the breath at each point. Observe whether, it is cold or warm? What is the texture? Smell? How does it feel while it goes in and coming out? Anything specific you notice in your breath? After about ten breaths, bring a smile on your lips and open your eyes, feeling the world is your playground to show your best potential. Most of the times we are totally unaware of our breath. By observing your breath your attention comes back to the present moment. This is a very powerful tool that helps us live in the present. This can be practiced anytime, anywhere. This works best in situations when you are stressed out, tense, anxious, angry, fatigued, scared, feeling depressed or agitated.

- **Make an 'Excuse Journal'** – We often take lot of effort about doing things in life. However, we take more efforts in creating excuses if we do not want to do something. We decide to do something, but then just don't take the steps towards it. Our excuses to ourselves or others are always ready. In-fact we are brilliant in making excuses, and they are really creative. So here's the exercise. Every time you make an excuse for not doing something, write it down in a journal. Promise yourself that once you write the excuse in the journal, you are not going to use it again. Slowly, a time will come when you will have no excuses left for not taking steps in your life.

- **List your passion** – Make a list of the things that make you lose the track of time. Things that you are extremely passionate about or you are good at. These could be things you are unique in doing or which set you apart from others. You might feel a great pull towards one or more such thing. You might want to do those thing all throughout your life. This may lead to discovering your purpose of life. Try to do those things as often as possible, and feel the difference in your life.

- **Learn to say 'no'** – Saying 'no' to things that are 'not important', is an extremely powerful tool to uplift your life and your self esteem. You do not have to do things, or listen to something, or go somewhere if you don't feel like it. If you think there is more important thing to do at that time, it is great to say 'no'. One does not have to be rude, but can be courteous and strong. For example, your friends are forcing you to go for a movie, when you feel you need to sleep. Use your discretion, and politely say no. It also helps you feel important, and that your life is the most important thing for you. No one can force you to do something if you don't want to. There is a famous saying that 'by saying Yes to something unimportant, you are saying no to something important in your life.'

- **Face your fears** – Try to do something you are scared to do. Take up at least one thing you are scared about and then try to do it. Initially you may need a bit of training or learning of a skill, do that. It will make you feel confident while you start doing it. It always pays to know the little details or knacks, as it makes the job easier. Always remember that on the other side of your biggest fears lies your greatest success. So face the fears and get over them. You will always emerge much stronger and happier person than you were. For example if you have a fear of public speaking, participate in a public speaking event and prepare well for it. Even if you are not the best you will surely get rid of your fears about speaking in public.

- **Compile a life list** – Make a list of the things you always wanted to do in life, but have not yet started. These are the things which will make you feel good about yourself. Give yourself a target to finish any one particular thing, and take the first step today. This will do wonders to your resolve. For example, if you wanted to learn music since your childhood, but never had a chance to do so, then now is the right time Take the first step. Find out information about the music classes in your locality. Similarly, choose things from your list one by one and take your first step towards it.

- **Laugh out loud** – Never hold yourself back when you get a chance to laugh. Laughing releases stress and makes you feel happy. Laughter is also a therapy which has the power to heal many diseases. Laugh loudly, from your belly, as often as possible. You may even join a laughter club in your neighbourhood. There is none? Then form your own! All it takes is two members to start.

- **Dance!** – Whenever you feel stressed out lock yourself in a room, put some loud dance music and let your hair down. Just free yourself bodily for some time, follow the rhythm with your unique steps. You do not have to worry about how you dance or what will anyone think about you. Just be yourself. Any kind of physical activity, such as dancing, running, aerobics, etc helps in instantly bringing your mind to the present. Other options could be going for a brisk walk or a jog in a nearby garden. You can find your own way to do this.

- **Reading an inspirational book** – Reading something inspirational lifts up your spirits instantly. Specially if you are feeling down or depressed. Another idea could be listening to music or talks which inspires you. My recommendation is reading at least a few pages of inspirational material or a biography first thing in the morning, along with your morning tea or coffee.

Reading inspiring things in the morning will set you up for the whole day and you will keep on feeling good and motivated.

- **Make your own 'Wow! list'** – Make a list of things that make you feel good instantly. Call it your 'Wow! list'. The things could be: coffee with a friend, a long drive, singing a song, taking shower, cooking something interesting, doing something creative, having a quick nap, having an ice cream, going for a quick run, playing a game of snakes and ladders, watching a movie, playing a video game, shopping for yourself (or others), window shopping, playing with a small child. The list could be long. Keep this list handy and do one of the things to make yourself feel good instantly when you feel down in the dumps. This will bring you in the present moment. It is important to come out of a depressed feeling first and quickly. Only then you are able to think positively and creatively to find a solution for a problem or an issue. We cannot think logically or positively when we are feeling low. So feel Wow with the Wow! things from your list and be happy and creative.

- **Fun in planning** – I have found that things which take time in arranging or an enjoyable activity for which you have to plan in advance gives you greater happiness. These could be things you can look forward to. Plan a holiday for the next month, or a picnic with family next weekend or a night out with friends in a fortnight. The longer you plan for, the better. You will have more excitement for that number of days in anticipation of the fun.

- **Inspiring friends** – Make a list of the people who inspire you. The idea is that they should be near you or at least in the same city. Make it a point to visit them or talk with them at least once a week. Talking to anyone who inspires helps in keeping you motivated to live life to the fullest.

- **Say 'thanks'** – Live a life of gratitude and you will always be living in the present moment. If you feel grateful to a friend or family or anybody be good and liberal to express it. Send a thank you note or an email to the person who has done something for you in your life. Say 'Thank you' the first thing in the morning.

This is a great start of a perfect day. 'Always count your blessings' is a common saying. Trust me, it works like a miracle in life. Being thankful for all the things you have or you don't have, brings in a lot of peace in your life. You can also make your own gratitude diary to note down things you are thankful about.

- **Keep a journal** – Before going to bed every night, spend some quite time with yourself. You can write down things you are grateful about during the day in the gratitude diary. You can even list down good things that happened during the day. Then make a plan for your next day; maybe just in brief. A to-do list will also do. This will set you up to take on the challenges or important jobs the next day.

- **Be generous in giving hugs** – Giving hugs to people really helps in making us happy. When you are giving someone a sincere hug, there is an energy exchange between the two persons. The more people you hug in a day, the better you will feel. The point is to give a genuine, heartfelt and honest hug.

- **Lend a hand** – Look for opportunities where you can be of some help to people around you. In fact decide for yourself that during the day you will do at least one thing that make you feel proud about yourself. Helping others in need increases our self-esteem and we feel proud of our own self or our deeds.

- **Positive Affirmations** – Repeating affirmations fills us with positive energy and thoughts about ourselves. Make your own set of positive affirmations, a list that gives you energy and lifts your morale. Here are a few examples of affirmations for living in the present.

  ✓ *Today is the happiest day of my life*

  ✓ *I am the best*

  ✓ *I deserve the best and I accept it now*

  ✓ *I know of my highest potential and am achieving it now*

  ✓ *I am living a fulfilled and purposeful life*

Plan your Future

The future is a matrix, full of possibilities
It's in our hands to design & plan, with our abilities

It is our life, we can plan it on our own
Keep ourselves ready, for challenges unknown

Making a bucket list, is a great virtue
It's a great feeling, when our dreams come true

Visualize, plan, review, we have goals to reach
All we learn ourselves, there's no one to teach

Let's set our targets, and give our best to them
Planning each detail, makes it easier to claim

Always know our heart, shows the right way
Everything around us, is divine energy at play

We must listen our calling, and plan our life legend
Opportunities will be plenty, waiting at every bend

Using our highest potential, challenges we transcend
One who plans the future, is happiest in the end

Our inner guidance can take us out of all the pains
Having faith in ourselves, can surely move mountains

Cultivating great relationships, gives us the strength
And gives true companions, to walk the life's length

Let us not forget, the responsibility to give back
Leaving legacy for the future, before we pack

But being with ourselves, is the only key
To the everlasting bliss, by practicing "just be"

So let us be ready, to write our future story
We are the masters, of our own glory.

"One of these leads to my destination. But which one...?"

CHAPTER 1

FUTURE

Matrix of possibilities

The adventure of my life, lies ahead
My future's tale is yet to be said
Countless options, chances many
I am the maker of my destiny

How can we define the word 'future'? The question was posed to me during one of seminars. Is future an imaginary time where we are destined to go? Or is it just a projection of the present in our mind? It is illusory or real? Is future only in stories when we hear that we have something in distant time? Or is it something we create through our dreams, ambitions, goals, etc? Is future only the latter part of our life? Or is it life of all the generations to come? Is it something created by our fears, anxieties and insecurities? Or does it create our fears, anxieties and insecurities?

I soon came to an understanding that the word 'future' means all of the above, at the same time, none of the above! Some say future is something we create with the help of today's actions. So does that mean future is a thing that is tangible and visible? Some say future is waiting for us and will be revealed as we go ahead in time. Does that mean future is something we cannot create, it's already there, fixed?

I decided to give explaining 'future' a try. I asked the person who asked this question, to imagine driving on a highway. The place we are driving, at any given point in time, is our present, the places we drove through is our past, and the forthcoming part of the highway is our future. In our past, we have had various experiences and remember these in the form of our memories. In the present, i.e. where we are now, we can choose to drive slow or fast, or completely stop because we find something interesting on the way. It's really our choice to decide whether to enjoy the journey by putting on the music, or think about the good or bad experiences of the places we visited before, or just mull over how our journey will be ahead. We can only see a certain distance ahead of us on the highway.

This highway is divided into several lanes, by-lanes and exit points. Signboards indicate the destination and distance of each path, the possible places or destinations you can go to from the present point. It is your choice now to take the lane that goes to your desired destination. There may be some destination which is not directly connected to the path you are on, at present, but you can connect to that lane through a path which can be taken now.

Highway as a timeline

Now imagine that this highway represents the timeline of your life. The past, the present and the future are just the three dimensions of that timeline. In this scenario, the future is the third dimension of time where your ultimate destination or purpose exists. Whether to reach there or not is entirely up to you. It is a part of the many possibilities ahead of you. The future is similar to a game of chess where a single move can either topple us towards victory or defeat. In reality, the future is fluid; it is not fixed because our destination changes depending on the chosen road. Hence, we create our own future based on the choices we at make every moment.

Each one of us has our own time machine. Sometimes we take ourselves back in the past, we call them memories. When we take ourselves forward, we call them dreams. It is actually like a matrix, where the target really depends on what action we take today and each action has a different result. So it is logical to say that the future really is 'a matrix of possibilities'. In the journey of life we are all on our individual paths, striving to attain certain goals or ambitions. Some of us have already found their purpose in life, or set life goals for themselves. Some others are yet to get there or decide on a goal.

Whatever may, we are all travellers on this path. As we move ahead on the journey we come across choices at each point in our life, and we have to make a decision. This decision is critical to the path we pursue, since it eventually leads to the final outcome (some call it destiny). The outcome is always the result of the decisions we have made at each point in our journey and that is how we create our future.

Outcomes and events

In the popular Indian game of snakes and ladders, with every roll of dice the outcome makes us either climb the ladder or get swallowed by a snake. Every time we roll the dice we take a chance and we stand a risk of sliding back to the starting point. Therefore each roll of dice counts when it comes to winning or losing the game.

Similarly, in life, every point of decision making is crucial as each choice will have a different outcome. And the impact of the outcome can be huge or small on our journey to the ultimate goal or destination. The only difference between this game and our life is that in life most of the times we are aware of the result of the choices we make. If we are not aware of the final result and just taking decisions by chance, then we are really living by chance, a dangerous way to live and the outcomes may have enormous consequences. Just like the game of snakes and ladders.

Most of us look at future as something which will anyway happen, whether we work towards it or not. It sounds true, doesn't it? Even if we don't do anything, we will have a future. Even if we don't think about or plan for it, we still move towards a future. Or do we? Is it us or the timeline that is moving, and we just experience the change it brings in?

The changes in life are due to the movement of time. But whatever way it is perceived as, one thing is sure; we do not have to make an effort to move into our future. It is an automatic process. Then why are we even discussing this aspect here? It's because all arguments and hypothesis doesn't change the fact that, wherever we are being taken by this imaginary vehicle of time, the result, the situation, the destination or the outcome at every moment is because of the actions or decisions we have undertaken in the past or present.

Robby's raise

Robby has just received a letter from his HR manager in his company that he has been selected for a promotion in his job and for a handsome raise in his salary. He has been working in this job since last five years now. Today's letter has definitely not come out of the blue. It is only because Robby has worked hard with dedication, and his company has found that he is contributing to the profits it is generating. He has proven his worth to the company in the last few years, and hence received this letter.

Now imagine that Robby had not shown any real dedication in his job. Perhaps Robby had just waited for the future to come to this day without doing anything. Would he have received this letter today? Most probably not! So today's result or outcome is because of what steps or action Robby took in the past. But that past where Robby has worked with dedication was present yesterday or day before or one year back.

One cannot just wait for something good to happen. Rather, one has to work towards it in the present moment. The minimum one can do is be aware of what is happening in the present and see or observe the change. So, here are the three kinds of people going in to future;

- those who let things happen,

- those who work hard to make them happen, and

- those who don't really care what's happening around them;

Where do you fit in? Do you see any similarity between your life and these three types of people? Are you really conscious about what's happening around you, how things take a shape in your life? Do you just let them happen as they take shape and do not do anything about it? Or do you complain about this happening in the way you never expected or blame your situation, society, upbringing, friends, even pets, or global warming for your destiny?

If the above statements feel or seem familiar, it is time to take note. Only when we know the problem, we can allow the change to take place in our life. It is time now to take things in our own hands. To work upon the future, to not just let things happen but make them happen. It is time now, in the present, to think about the time to come, the future. Once we have chosen our destination, life goal or purpose, it is time to plan the journey.

It is important to note that both a plan and planning are important. Moving ahead randomly in any direction has no meaning. The plan is the roadmap, which shows you the way, the path you have selected to reach your goals. Unless you are on this path, you cannot move ahead. At the same time, planning means preparation. You need to sharpen your skills, be aware of your capabilities, work on them or practice them.

The magic of practice

Practice makes a man perfect. We may even need to learn certain new skills to reach there. Take note of the pitfalls on the way and know how to overcome them. It is a must for all of us to have a distinct vision for our future. We should be clearly able to visualize ourselves reaching there, achieving what we have aimed for. And once we are ready to move ahead, we should move with confidence, armed with a positive thinking that we are definitely going to win. Circumstances may change, but our determination should not.

Many times when we are having a tough phase in life, having faith in our own self helps us coming out or sustain. Come what may, the journey must go on. We must keep moving, well prepared, on the right path towards our ultimate goals. Once we do that, be rest assured that nothing can stop us from being a winner, in life. It is we who create our own future. The future is first created in our mind, when we make up our mind to pursue our purpose or to create a better life for us. We first need to be completely convinced in our mind that we are going to reach there. There is no scope for doubt. The mind is really powerful. It is a magic wand which creates miracles if we use it in the right or positive way.

The key is your strong intention to win, to succeed in life, to reach your purpose. Your intent is the force which pushes you forward, gives you the power to soar. The power of intention is the current of wind on which you can sail great distances; it is the fuel which powers your life vehicle. When used in the correct way, your mind power actually gives he hope for a shining future. Once you are convinced and certain about our positive intent, half the job is done. But you have to be careful while we do this.

Our mind can also be the biggest hurdle if we engage it in creating doubts and fears. All our emotions, such as fear, anger, guilt or regret are basically a play of our mind, but it is entirely possible to control them. Doubts and fears weaken intention, slowing down or eventually stopping progress. Know how to manage your emotions and not let them become road blocks.

Action

Once we have a clear intention of our goals, then the next step is to act. This is the other half of the job. Just intention without action is like a car without a driver. It will not move! Without action, the idea of a better future will remain only in the imagination. Action has to follow the intent. Once the power of positive intention and the corresponding action combine, you can climb the highest peaks in life.

Always remember, the past does not equal the future. What has happened in the past by default may repeat itself in the future, only if you allow it to and if you do not make any proactive changes to stop it. Moving towards the future by looking at the past is like driving a vehicle by looking in the rear-view mirror.

A question may be targeted at you: if you were not able to achieve something in the past, how can you hope to achieve that in future? If one has failed attempts in the past, is it possible for him to succeed in future? My answer is a sound, loud YES!

Absolutely! I will politely ask anybody who asks such pessimistic questions to change their attitude. Such people cannot rate the eagerness and intent to win or achieve a goal. In fact, no one should be allowed to judge your abilities and intentions. You are the master of your life, your goals and objectives. It is you who decides what you will achieve in life, the "peaks" that you will scale, and the means or path you will use to get there.

Beware of temptations

Sometimes on our path there may be temptations taking us away from our goals. There was once a young man driving to his office for an important meeting. That day, he had to make a presentation to a key client in the office for a new upcoming project. On the way he stopped at a nearby deli to pick up take away breakfast. While waiting his turn in the queue he noticed a beautiful young girl and started a conversation with her. She asked him if he could give her a lift as she was going for a meeting in the same direction as he was. He couldn't say no to this opportunity, and agreed happily.

After travelling for 10 minutes the girl got a phone call informing her that the venue of her meeting had changed. She politely asked the guy if he could drop her to the new venue which was a bit out of the way. The young man once again happily obliged. They reached the new venue and the girl left after thanking the young man for his kind gesture. The young man then turned his car and started off towards the direction of his office. Unfortunately, on his way back he found that the road was blocked as two trucks had collided. All the vehicles on that road were being guided to take a diversion.

The young man soon realised that this detour is going to cost him a heavy price. It would take him at least another hour to reach his office, making hm late for the presentation. He called his office and informed his boss about his delay. The boss sympathised with him, but asked another executive to do the presentation. The young man finally lost the coveted project to his colleague.

It is most important to stay focused and on course while pursuing your ambitions. Losing focus will cost valuable time and priceless opportunities on the way. Especially when you are close to our target, never take your eyes away from the finishing point. This is the most crucial stage. This stage is like running the last lap of the relay-race, if we slow down in the last lap, we definitely loose the race.

Set intentions to succeed in life, focus on the goals, make a plan, do the planning, then take appropriate corresponding action and never lose the sight of the target till it is reached. Most importantly, be optimistic. Remember, you are the master of your life.

At a glance

- *Our future is only a fluid mesh of possibilities.*
- *We create our own future based on the choices we make at every moment*
- *Once we have chosen our destination, life goal or purpose, it is time to plan the journey*
- *After planning comes action! Act on your plan and reach your goals*

KEYS

"I wonder where I went wrong.....!"

CHAPTER 2

PLAN YOUR TRIP

Be your own navigator

I am ready to reach my goal
My dreams & purpose of my soul
Need to plan the path to the future I create
And reach my destination before it's too late

Most of us go through the journey of life as if we have no control on our life or around us. Even if we have our goals in mind, we are not too worried about how we are going to get there. There is no dedicated, foresight planning or strategy involved. Eventually, we end up nowhere near we would like to be, well, not quite.

During a pleasant weekend, my wife and I decided on an impromptu car trip to a holiday destination with the whole family. We started without much planning, just dumped our stuff in the car and left early morning. The initial drive was smooth; however, by the time we reached mid-way, where we wanted to halt for the night, we all felt extremely tired and famished. We had started without packing enough food for the way and there were no good restaurants on the way. When we reached the hotel of our stay, their restaurant had already closed as it was late in the night. We literally had to request the owner to get us something to eat.

The next day, when we started, I took a wrong turn on the highway, that took us in a different direction. By the time I realized the mistake, we had already travelled 200 kms away from the right road. I had to take a circuitous route to correct the detour but by the time we reached our initial destination, we were all completely drained. We spent an entire day resting and started enjoying the holiday only a day later. I realized then that by not planning ahead for the journey, and not planning the route we were going to take, I had actually put everyone's holiday in jeopardy.

Being spontaneous and following our heart is great as it gives us the freedom to operate. However, when it comes to reaching our purpose or life goals, it's an entirely different ball game. We need to have a specific map, a strategy that can help us reaching our destination much more efficiently. It is important to have a basic road map which will help you move ahead in the right direction. Especially if your life goals are such that you will need more time to achieve. Where do you want to be in 10 or 20 or 30 years from now? Once you know the answer to that, make a plan to reach there.

Realizing our fullest potential in this lifetime, achieving greatness, excelling in whatever we do or becoming the best does not come easy. It is a process where one needs to be consistent. If you want to be the best in your chosen field, you have to work towards it, no shortcut there!

Many people believe hard work is the only way to success. I disagree with this statement to some extent. I have seen people who have been working hard throughout their entire lifetime. However, they could never reach their personal peaks. In fact, they were unsatisfied in the end, as they ended up feeling life has been unfair to them. Even after they have given their best, they could not achieve what they deserved.

Is hard work enough?

Salil's father was a government servant. As a young graduate, he joined work as a lower level officer. He worked twelve hours a day as he wanted to reach the top of the ladder in this office. However, by the time he retired after 40 years of service, he was still somewhere in the upper middle level post. He was worn down physically, suffering from high blood pressure, diabetes and heart trouble. He was discontented with his life; he had constantly sacrificed his home life for his work, and thus his relationship with his wife and children was just okay to say the best.

Let me share with you a startling fact. Salil's father is not in minority. Most people who have worked hard all their life will feel this way. They live the last part of their life dissatisfied, unhappy, frustrated, and dejected. They blame their own self, situations in their life, circumstances, near and dear ones, friends, ex-colleagues, their office management, their own upbringing, their parents, in fact anything and everything, for their state in life. They fully realize that it is too late for them to start again in this life to seek their goals.

Where did people like Salil's father go wrong? You will say they all worked very hard to achieve what they wanted. And hard work is the only way to success. Sure enough! I agree, but only partly. It is impossible for just hard work to take us far, if it is not backed by a road plan. Working hard without a plan is similar to running on a treadmill. We end up at the same place. That's why, planning our trip is important if we want to reach our goals, and in time. In my profession, I have observed that most people are so busy in fulfilling their mundane duties and living by someone else's version of life, that they hardly ever think what they want to achieve in life, what is their real purpose in life is. All of us are blessed with capabilities and talents that are beyond our imagination. However, the sad part is that only very few of us are able to recognize or discover the talents and a much lower number of people are able to use them for reaching their life goals.

Passive lives

Most often, when it comes to our life, we don't think about ourselves in stages - the adult stage, the midlife stage, the retirement stage. We feel that life will just happen. Even if we do not make efforts, we do not take enough risks; we live a secured or settled life, hoping that things will take their own shape.

We are here to excel, to be who we are. Our first responsibility is towards us, to utilize our fullest potential and rise to phenomenal heights in whatever we are; to take risks and succeed; to live our purpose. Our mission is to try new things, make enough mistakes, fail in our endeavors and then when we rise, to shine like the brightest star. That's what we are here for.

If you think the same way, then this book can help you reach there. To lead a spectacular life, one needs commitment, planning, perseverance, hard work and risk taking ability. You must first decide where you would like to be, i.e., your destination, and then make a detailed road plan. Only when you decide your highest goals and then plan to reach there, can you strive to achieve them through hard work and dedication.

The journey will not be easy, as greatness or excellence is only a factor of resilience and hard work. But once we have a road plan, the hard work will not go waste. Any work we put in helps us move towards our target destination. Planning is nothing but a path from the start to finish, or the stretch from intention to the manifestation. Working or going ahead with a plan helps us in staying focused on our life goals. We are able to move efficiently towards the destination, without wasting valuable time and energy. Here are few tips to plan the future to achieve the life goals.

Make a Bucket List

In my workshops, I ask people to prepare a Bucket List – a list of the things one wishes to do or accomplish before 'kicking the bucket' (a slang that means 'before dying'). It is quite an exercise where we are required to think only our own life and what we want to achieve. Most found it difficult to verbalise or write down their wishes. We are ready to think about everything and everyone around us, but when it is our own life, we have neither time nor inclination. Even if we know what we want to do, we are not sure if we are able to reach there. By preparing this Bucket List, our focus shifts to our own life. This helps in clearing our mind from the mist of uncertainties and confusion and gives us an idea of our exact goals. Well-defined goals are more likely to be achieved than vague ones. The clearer we are about our goal in our mind's eye, more focus and energy we will be able to give to it.

While defining your goals, make sure that they are *tangible* and *achievable*. Each goal should be attainable; otherwise it becomes the single factor to dissuade you from achieving it. It is good to have big dreams, but ensure that we have a practical way of achieving it too. Setting tangible goals does not in any way undermine the capability of the individual trying to achieve a goal or the belief that anything is possible. Remember, nothing is impossible, but a sensible approach is the one where we bring in practicality while setting goals.

Again whether a goal is tangible or not depends on the individual and the circumstances. The goals should be such that they can be measured by some means, so that we can check the items on the list once they are done. For example, instead of writing, "I want to be adventurous in life" we could say, "My goal is to climb Mount Everest by Dec 2020." It is also important to give it a time limit.

Want it and believe it

Once the goal is defined, it is good to be extremely passionate about it. That goal should have the top priority in your life. Passion is the feeling of loving something with highest intensity, and the feeling of a burning desire to achieve the objective. Be restless till you reach your goal, and before that, believe that we can reach our goal. Self-confidence plays a big role in helping us believe our potential. Do not let self doubts creep in.

Visualize

The prerequisite for planning is creative visualization. It is extremely important to visualize the person we want to become, our social, financial status, relationships we would like to have, while being aligned to our values. We must allow ourselves to dream how do we want to accomplish what we have set out for, how we achieve our purpose and goals.

The visualisation should be as vivid and creative as possible. Give it your own colours, details of place, detailed timing and people you think or want to be associated at that time of the goal completion. Feelings are an important ingredient of these dreams or creative visualisation. Imagine for a moment, someone is telling you that you cannot fail; that all your dreams would come true. How would you feel? Ecstatic? Imagine the joy, confidence, peace, excitement, security you would feel as a result of imagining that you have achieved your goals. We need to actually feel that we have reached there, as if it is happening now.

These feelings form a bridge between our intentions and their manifestation. They give us the essence and energy to transform our dream into reality. The more intensely we feel and the more vivid our imagination is, the more the likelihood that we will reach our destination.

Write down the mission

Once you have chosen our goals, and have visualised them, then it's time to write them down. This can be in any creative statement through which we are able to capture the spirit of the goals in words. Just like writing a mission statement, writing down your goals make them more concrete. The more vividly we can describe it, maybe in an emotionally charged language, the better. You may also like to put your signature on it, as it is your own contract with yourself. You are now committed to achieve that aim of life.

If you are more creative, draw a diagram of the mission along with a map to reach there. It is a great idea to cut out pictures of your goal or destination from magazines or news papers and make a collage out of it. You can call it your dream chart. Keep it or hang it at a place where you can see it often. You may even make it the desktop design of your computer.

Since writing involves our mind, hand and eyes, it takes the message deep in our subconscious mind. As a result, it stimulates our whole body to act accordingly. By writing down our goals, we send a message to the universe about the things we want to achieve in life. And once we ask, nature does create situations for us to get help and support on our path. Writing down the goal several times helps in reinforcing it. Say you have a certain goal to achieve. Write it on a paper or notebook 20 times every day, similar to when we write an affirmation, in present tense. It definitely helps to programme our sub-conscious to become ready to achieve it.

Split it up

The next step is to split the goals in distinct, smaller components. Every component may have a different requirement which we may need to prepare ourselves for. For example, if your mission is "producing and directing a film", just the enormity of the goal may stop you from taking the first step and thus achieving the goal. The simplest thing is to break it up in to smaller components. Ask yourself, what are the smaller tasks you must achieve to get to the final goal? What are the things you need to reach there? What are the skills you need to learn? You would probably first need to join a school for film direction. You may need to prepare a business plan to get an idea of how much capital will be required. Then need to think about arranging the financing for the film (if you don't have it already).

Schedule it

Once you have set a goal, made a plan or road map on how to achieve it, the next important step in the process is fixing the time frame. Without scheduling the goals, you cannot reach far ahead. Prepare a detailed time table for the next one year (short term plan) with specific targets, and a ten or twenty year time table which is more flexible (medium or long term plan). This will help to prepare for the journey towards your goal.

Although there is no fixed time line that decides these short, medium and long term goals, it varies from person to person and individual goals. Two people who want to lose 10 kg and 30 kg weight have a common goal, which is weight loss. However, the time this weight loss would take will be different depending on various factors.

It is important to know this fact when you classify your goals into long term and short term ones, so that you can prioritise accordingly.

Say your short term goal could be to buy a house and your long term goal could be to travel around the world. Precisely know the way we you are going to reach our goals and the estimated time it will take you to achieve. Set personal deadlines to maintain motivation and interest. If this road map is rigid and does not make allowance for life's twists and turns, it leads to frustration and disillusion. Keeping flexibility in our plan is important as well; then there is a chance to change the course if something does not go as planned. Even if plans go wrong at any point, keep our eyes on the long term goals, the mission. Always keep the bigger picture in mind. As a film director, you will need the creative freedom, but at the same time you also need to set a time frame for a particular project completion. Otherwise there are chances that the project will never see the light of the day!

Review it

Without periodical review, there are chances that we may be going off-course. Keep track of your progress, keep re-evaluating your plans from time to time, and cross the smaller targets already achieved. We can know whether we are going faster or slower than required. If we think we need to re-evaluate our original goals or mission depending on our self development, growing awareness and understanding, we should do that as well.

Consistency, discipline and perseverance

Once a decision is made, it is important to remain consistent in our actions throughout the journey until you reach our goal or achieve our purpose. You must be as solid as a rock when faced with adversities. There will be many such factors, people around us, society, circumstances, and temptations, to name a few. Keep moving on your journey and do not let these factors become a distraction.

Consistency and perseverance are the key ingredients of a successful person. A disciplined effort will help us reach there without getting diverted from our path. People who are disciplined and determined are also self-motivated to achieve their goals. Sometimes, challenges may come in the form of physical constraints testing our determination. For example, you wish to run the marathon, but you are highly over weight and are suffering from high blood pressure. This is a limitation that can be overcome with time and discipline. You can start exercising, go for long walks and plan a diet to lose the excess weight and take care of your hypertension through medication. Then once you are fit, you can practice for the long distance running. Some constraints can be overcome and others not, however we can always find a way around a constraint to suit the need.

Be a visionary

Most people think only about what they will do today, tomorrow, next week or maximum next month. But those who look forth, beyond several years, are the ones who can truly envision the future. They can visualise the situations in future and take steps in the present to move towards it. It is like going into the future through the mind's time-machine. In order to achieve greatness, we must reach that level when we plan for our future, well ahead. In fact, we must cultivate the habit of having visionary thoughts *all the time*. Think about how we can do day to day activities differently in the future. Today's problems will have a solution in the tomorrow. Realising this solution today makes us a visionary. This ability will help us rise above the average and excel in our life.

In an age where flying was just a figment of human imagination, Orville and Wilbur Wright (the Wright brothers) made it a reality by inventing the first airplane in 1903. They were true visionaries of their time. History has given the world many such great visionaries. The point is to take inspiration from these visionaries to become one. Here's a small exercise to find out if you are moving in the right direction in life.

Sit in a comfortable position. Be sure that you are not disturbed for the next few minutes. Take a few deep breaths. Focus on your breath and be conscious about each breath. Slowly as you feel more and more relaxed, gently, let your eyes close. Go deeper and deeper into your own self. You are now about to embark on your life's journey in future. Now visualize a white screen in front of your eyes. Your life's movie is being projected on this screen and you have a remote in your hand.

Slowly take your thumb to the fast forward button of your remote and press it. Your life movie goes in a fast forward mode and comes to halt on the last day of your life. Look at yourself on the screen. How do you look? What do you feel? Do you have any regrets? Are you completely satisfied with the way your life has gone? Do you feel that you have lived life to your highest potential? Have you made a difference in people's lives? Or do you feel, "Had I got just one more chance to live, I would have lived differently,"?

All the answers to these questions will write the script of your life. Even if you have the slightest doubts that you could have lived differently, it is still not too late. This is the point in life where you can choose to live differently and make a difference. You can rewrite your own script. The future is anyways a matrix of possibilities. Decide how you would like to leave this world. That will set your goals for your life. That will define the purpose of your life. The planning will navigate you through your life to achieve that goal and help you live your purpose.

At a glance

- *Planning our life's journey gives us a direction to move ahead*
- *Working hard without a plan is like running on a treadmill. We end up at the same place.*
- *Consistency, discipline and perseverance are all needed on our journey to our destiny*
- *Make a bucket list*
- *Think ahead of time. Be a visionary*

KEYS

"My wife likes practicing her archery skills....
on me....!"

CHAPTER 3

HONE YOUR SKILLS

Opportunities come unannounced

Practice keeps me ready to go
To take on my life, spring or snow
Be it smooth sail, or a stone wall
I'm always prepared to take the call

"I will prepare and some day my chance will come," said Abraham Lincoln. And it did. This attitude gave America one of its best presidents ever.

Opportunities and challenges always come unannounced. But once they arrive, they don't wait for long. If you are not prepared when an opportunity comes your way, you'll lose it, sometimes forever. Likewise, if a challenge comes and we are unprepared, it will sweep us away. But what exactly is 'being prepared'? Let the following Chinese fable illustrate the meaning:

In the small hamlet of the Shanxi Province in China, there lived a man named Zhan-Shi. He belonged to a warrior tribe that was very vulnerable to attacks from the neighbouring tribe of Mongolian bandits. The men of the village had fought many battles and won and Zhan-Shi was one of them. After winning a series of battles, there was peace in the hamlet as it had not been attacked for years. The men were relaxed and spent a lot of time in merry-making, eating, sleeping and drinking.

Zhan-Shi was the exception. He spent all his days sharpening his Jian (a Chinese double-edged straight sword) and practicing his battle skills. The villagers ridiculed him and thought he was crazy. Zhan-Shi's mother tried many times to persuade him to take up a work in a farm and enjoy life like the other warriors of the village; however, nothing could distract Zhan-Shi from honing his battle skills.

One day, the Mongolian bandits launched a surprise attack on the hamlet. When the villagers saw the bandits charging towards them, they started running helter-skelter in fear. The men ran into their homes looking for weapons. However, as none of them had expected something like this to happen, they were not ready for battle. But one man was, and he stood strong in front of the Mongolian bandits with his Jian that shone bright in the sun.

Seeing his bravery, the villagers stood behind him with whatever weapons they got hold of. When the bandits saw that the whole village of warriors gathered together and in front stood a man with a shining sword, they retracted, as they were afraid of their fate at the hands of the warrior tribe. But in reality, it was only Zhan-Shi who was prepared with his weapon for the battle. Zhan-Shi had devoted time to sharpening his sword and practicing his battle skills. Because of this, he could be in the forefront to fight with confidence.

Zhan-Shi was prepared when the unexpected happened. We do not know what the future holds for us; therefore it is important to be prepared for all eventualities. When we are prepared, we can face them fearlessly and overcome them with zeal and vigour.

The farmer's returns

Once there was a farmer who worked his fields every day preparing the soil for planting. The other farmers thought he was crazy as the village had been affected by drought for two consecutive years. The land was dry and the air smelled thick with dust, the lakes and rivers had dried up too. The others farmers sat around their huts all day long either complaining or whiling away time in mundane activities.

But this one farmer, along with his family faithfully went to the farm every day and worked the land. After a hard day's work he and his family would gather in the farm and say a prayer to thank the universe for keeping his family healthy to work the land. The farmer and his family would then happily come home looking forward to return the next day.

This went on for several weeks and one day, suddenly it started raining non-stop. The other farmers were caught unawares, not expecting this sudden change in weather. Hence, their land was not ready for sowing. The next day, the farmer and his family as usual went to the farm and started sowing. That evening the farmer prayed again thanking the universe for the rains and the opportunity to sow. That year, the farmer had a bountiful harvest, received good returns for his crop and there was enough for his family to be happy.

The best time to prepare for an eventuality is when there is no eventuality. We must keep ourselves prepared as we never know when opportunity knocks on our door and when the opportunity comes we must be fully prepared to en-cash the benefits. There is a saying, "When opportunity knocked at my door, I wasn't properly dressed to welcome it." Well, the truth is that opportunity does not visit by prior appointment; it can come anytime, anywhere and to anyone. The question is, are we prepared? If we are not, then you will end up like the other farmers in the story above! That's the wonderful thing about the future; no one really knows what it holds. We can anticipate, be hopeful, even predict but we can never be sure. Therefore, it is important to 'be always prepared'.

Blessings in disguise

Sometimes opportunity comes disguised as misfortune or a disaster too. Such times present a true test for our faith and our ability to focus on honing our skills. Each one of us is born blessed with a special talent; all we need to do discover this talent and polish it. Silver may lose its lustre over time, but it does not cease to be silver. All it needs is a bit of polishing and then it shines as new.

The same applies to us, when we neglect our talent or skill it loses utility. Some skills are acquired by learning (for eg. going for computer training); others are natural. In both cases, we need to hone them if we are to make maximum use of them. Otherwise, when the opportunity presents itself, we shall not be ready. If you do not practise swimming after learning it, you will forget some of the techniques and lose your confidence.

Rishon's regret

In life, we acquire many skills, but it is also important to be equipped with the basic skills which could prove be to be very useful in times of need. My friend Rishon is a computer software engineer and works for a medium sized IT company with a decent salary. For quite some time, Rishon wanted to enrol in a short course to learn the newest technology in his field. However, every time he was ready to enrol, something would come up and he would postpone going to the institute.

Recently, Rishon got a call from his dream company. They were offering him a good designation and salary. However, one of their most important requirements was having proficiency in the newest computer application, the same one that Rishon never found time to learn. Till today, Rishon regrets procrastinating about enrolling for that class. Had he taken the effort, he would have lived his dream as a manager in this big firm.

In today's information age, when technology and knowledge is ever progressing and changing, it is even more important to hone our skills and keep ourselves prepared for new challenges. Even if we are the best at what we do, tomorrow the method will change or it may become totally irrelevant and obsolete. Keep abreast with the latest skills and technology. For eg, at one time, music composers recorded music with a live orchestra in the studio. Today, music can be created on the computer. So a music composer too needs to keep updating his knowledge.

Similarly, the technology of photography changed in an instant. Several photographers, who had perfected the art of converting negatives to positives, had suddenly no purpose for this skill. My friend

Meirah's father Abner, who was a great photographer, also went through the stage of change to digital photography. While many grappled with shock and were filled with resentment because of the new technology, Abner was quick to buy the latest camera. He did extensive research about the new technology, read many books and learnt Photoshop from friends. Within a few months he was able to master the new technology. He continued to be one of the best photographers in the city because he kept himself at pace with the changing scenario.

Change with the times

No one could think about social media being essential for marketing, 10 years back, but today it is an integral part of it. Rather, by itself, social media has become a lucrative career option for many. It's important to know that there's always something more and new to learn, whatever our field of interest be.

It is important to be constantly prepared for both eventualities and opportunities as both may come unannounced. The best examples for people who constantly hone their skills are athletes, who keep on practicing whether there is a game or not. Their entire lives are dedicated to perfecting their skills, as without that they would fail to perform when the time comes. This applies to all of us in life, if we become complacent and lazy we will lose touch of our skills and then one day suddenly when an opportunity arrives we will be thrown out of gear. To be prepared, we must nurture and exercise our skills and talents, keep going, keep practicing and stay ever focused.

At a glance

- *It's a good idea to be prepared for all eventualities*
- *The best time to prepare for an eventuality is when there is no eventuality*
- *Opportunities or challenges mostly come unannounced*
- *We must keep adapting to the changing times*

"I have a feeling we may have a surprise guest tonight.....!"

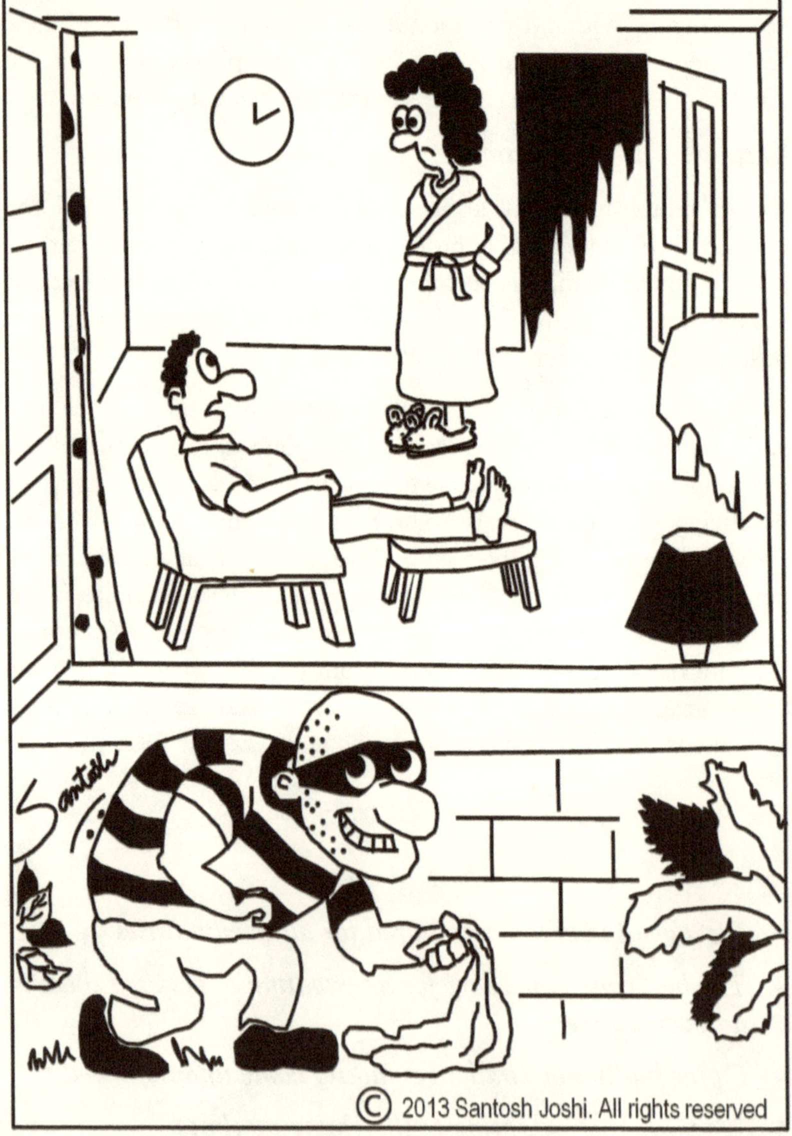

CHAPTER 4

DECODING THE MESSAGES

Tune in to your inner voice

Universe keeps on guiding me
Unlocks the doors with divine key
I just need to keep my heart in tune
Nothing can come in my way to moon

Have you ever heard the trees talking to you in the quiet moments of dawn? Have you ever looked into the eyes of animals and had a heart-stirring experience? Have you ever felt the tears of Mother Earth dry out in oblivion? Sounds bizarre, doesn't it?

How about these? Remembering someone, then accidently meeting that person or receiving a phone call from him or her. A solution is suddenly presented in front of you for a certain issue that seemed impossible while you were mulling on it. You somehow know who is calling you even before you answer the phone. You just know that a certain incident is going to take place. I am sure you must have certainly experienced such moments at some point in your life. What would you label these experiences as? Coincidences? Well, I would call them 'a heightened sense of awareness'. I will try to substantiate this view as follows.

We are normally aware of the things happening around us through our sense organs. Our perception on the physical level, which many times is also referred to as *gross level*, mainly comes from our five senses – sight, smell, sound, touch and taste. We form our opinions, beliefs, views and knowledge-base throughout our entire lifetime based on what we see, hear, smell, touch or taste. In fact, the whole basis of science, as we see it now, is this.

In today's science (I call it today's or modern science because it is only few hundred years old, whereas human existence is said to be present since a few thousand years), everything around us is proven or discovered only after we perceive it or its effects from our sense organs. Today's science does not believe or prescribe to anything which cannot be perceived by our senses. Our awareness on the gross level is limited to the abilities of our sensory perception.

However, if that is the case, then there is definitely an issue with our general sense of awareness. We already know the basic facts about our senses, or to be more precise, their limitations. For example, our eyes can see only the visual spectrum of violet to red colours, our nose can sense only about 100-200 smells out of 110,000 smells in nature, ears can hear within the frequency band of 20 to 20000 Hertz, skin can sense touch of roughness only above 75 nano meters and tongue can taste only above 0.05 parts per million of a substance.

There is so much more

It is quite clear that our perception, if solely dependent on our sense organs, is extremely inadequate to say the least. Many of us, however, will still be dependent only on these meagre resources throughout our life for their knowledge base and still not know the difference. In today's times, as we are moving from the information age to the age of higher consciousness, we need to know and experience more. That's where our higher capabilities come into picture.

We all know that there are many things happening around us that we cannot even perceive. Small examples could be mobile phone waves which connect us to any part of the world, or wireless signals of Wi-fi / Bluetooth, etc, or heat energy waves. Our entire planet is now connected together and any information can be sent from one place to another. To do that, we just need a transmitting device and a receiving device; a transmitting device to send information to that *info-sphere* and a receiving device to tap or receive the information. This sphere of information, *info-sphere* is always present and we just need to stay connected through our devices e.g. mobile phones/laptops/tablets, etc.

A similar property of sending and receiving information in the form of signals is inherently present within us as well. Human beings are made up of the physical body (the gross level element) and the consciousness (the subtle level element). Our consciousness is present in each cell of our body and that what is giving life-force (or *prana*) to us for our day to day functioning.

Consciousness is the quality or state of being aware of an external object or something within oneself. Although, the term itself is impossible to define, consciousness can still be explained as awareness, sentience, wakefulness, the ability to experience or to feel, or having perceptions, thoughts, and feelings. Consciousness cannot be perceived by the sense organs but can only be felt. Most times in life, we live from the gross level of existence i.e., from the physical state or physical body. However, many times we also operate from the deeper or subtle level. That is when we are living in the heightened state of awareness or from higher consciousness. I call this a heightened state of awareness, because our awareness state is actually high when we are here.

In this state we are able to perceive things which are on the subtle level of existence. We can receive or send signals through this subtle network of energy which is pervading all over the universe. We feel that we can experience things that are outside the purview of our limited sensory perception. These experiences have no rationale or logical explanation whatsoever. To put it in other words, these experiences are beyond logic and the mind.

In South Africa

In the year 2004, when I was on a business trip to South Africa, my dad who was 78 then, developed some serious health issues. I was in a meeting when I received a call from my wife, sounding a little anxious. When I called her back after the meeting, she said,

"You know it may sound a little weird. But while I was meditating in the morning, I suddenly saw your Dad's face and the words 'stomach cancer' kept flashing in my mind. I am not sure what it means. I really wish it is not true." She was very nervous by then.

"Are the investigations done?" I asked, feeling equally nervous myself but did not want to sound like it.

"Not yet, I will be taking him in the evening for the tests," my wife replied.

A little relieved, I said, "Don't worry, everything will be fine." I was really hoping that what I said becomes true.

I must admit that I was scared, because somewhere deep within, I knew that my wife had got an intuition regarding my father's health, a message from the divine, which I blatantly refused to accept. Well, the next day, the medical reports said it all. My dad was suffering from colon cancer.

Many times we keep receiving such messages from the universe in various forms. They sometimes warn us of the situations that are lying ahead of us. These messages come to us in the form of feelings, visions, sounds or simply knowing. Sometimes these messages also come to us in the form of dreams. One of my friends narrated that she dreamt of an aeroplane hitting a tall building just a couple of days before the 9/11 World Trade Centre's twin tower tragedy.

The universe is always guiding us on our path. And it has its own way of talking to us directly or indirectly. Sometimes, when we are stuck or confused in our life, we suddenly get a call from the person who has not been in touch for a long time or come across a book that was lying in our library but we simply had not read it, as if these were just the answers we needed at that particular time.

Guideposts

Life is always full of ups and downs. When I started on this path to follow my purpose, I had these experiences at every step. This is not an easy path at all. I went through my own low phases when I felt like a huge bolder blocked my path. I was just unable to see what lay ahead. Whenever this happened, invariably I would come across a message, "Don't worry, I am there with you."

This message would come in various forms. It would just flash on a hoarding, or in the newspaper or in a book or suddenly while I am driving, a car would come in front of me with this message inscribed on its rear. This message always reassured me and gave me renewed energy to cross the road-block in front of me. This also reinstated my faith in the power of the Universe.

Many times when we get such messages, we do not give them enough credit. We may think it is just our mind playing games. For example, you may have heard stories from people that they miss the train and later that same train meets with an accident. At that particular point, we fail to understand the larger plan and curse our destiny and God for the disappointment and for everything going wrong.

In one of my seminars, a lady came to me and shared her experience. She said, she got 'messages' as a child and saw visions of things which actually happened later. Her parents were scared and took her to the family doctor, not knowing how to handle this. She narrated one such incident when she had been to an immersion ceremony which marked the end of a religious festival in India.

In the middle of the celebrations, she suddenly told her friend that she can see death approaching. Her friend ignored her then. They were shocked, when the very next day, it was reported in a local daily that four boys drowned the same day at that place.

Children and ESP

I would like to mention here that when children say things like "I can see something" or "this is going to happen", we as adults or as parents are unable to handle that. In fact, all of us at a very young age, or as children, naturally have a heightened sense of awareness. You will observe that when somebody with a negative intention or thoughts comes near a child or when a child is taken to a place where there are negative energies, he/she will start crying. The child is able to sense and feel those energies, but cannot talk, hence will express his/her feelings by crying.

One of my very close friends went on a vacation with her husband and her six month old baby to Goa. They decided to hire a bike and ride around the area for sight-seeing the next day. That night, the baby suddenly started crying hysterically in the middle of night. They had never seen their baby cry like this before, but they just failed to understand the real reason. They somehow managed to calm the baby down.

The next day, when they went for sight-seeing on the bike, they met with a severe accident. The accident has left a permanent scar on their lives. We may also see this as a coincidence. But my friend, who is a logical person, also started seeing the previous night's incident as a signal when she put the events together.

Each one of us is a pure form of consciousness when we start our life as a child. As we grow, we slowly get covered by layers of conditioning and our pure self gets buried deep within us. Our inner voice, however, is always talking to us. But we cannot hear that voice in the outer chaos of life. Our focus is so much on the outside, on the gross level of existence that we simply fail to hear or acknowledge that voice.

All through our lives, in fact at each step, we are being guided by that inner voice. If we listen to our inner voice it will always guide us on the path towards our purpose. However, most often we are unaware of this and therefore have an indifferent attitude. In case of a problem or if we feel stuck at a point we should always ask for guidance and we will immediately receive it. This inner voice or the heightened sense of awareness is also commonly known as intuition.

Intuition is related to the right quadrant of the brain which is the creative side. An artist coming up with a masterpiece is totally using the right part of the brain without logic and is guided by that inner voice. I had the good fortune of being taught by one of the greatest musicians in India. He used to say, "Music cannot be learnt, it has to be felt from the heart. The music notes are already there, in the air... we just need to catch them." This is exactly what I am talking about.

Intuitive abilities

In our daily life, we notice that some people can foretell future or have the ability to understand what is going on in other people's mind. But the fact is that each one of us has been blessed with this unique ability.

Intuition is like a doorway that connects us to all the wisdom in the universe. Our intuition speaks to us directly or sometimes in subtle ways. The medium could be through pictures, words, feelings, visions, urges, voices, flashes of insights, etc. Certain things might be revealed to us through our dreams. These things could be external or internal.

Once, while I was still working in the corporate sector, I had misplaced an important document. I searched every nook and corner of my home and office in vain. After wasting one full day doing this exercise, I finally surrendered and asked for divine guidance and help, before I went to bed. The next morning when I woke up, I had a gut feeling to look into one drawer. I quickly got out of bed and opened that drawer and bingo… the document was there. I was stunned! I had looked in the same drawer the previous day as well and logically I would have never looked into it again, had I decided to overlook my hunch.

In retrospect, I realised that this was a very subtle way of getting the message from the universe… it was just a feeling and could have been easily overlooked. But since I was so desperate to find that paper, I paid heed to each and every thought and feeling. This desperation also led to the heightened sense of awareness. I had received the higher wisdom, that we just need to ask for guidance and it definitely comes our way.

Intuition is an inherent gift given to us by the universe. We just need to tune in and decode it. Once we are able to do that, it can lead to beautiful transformations, solutions and miracles. Having worked with few of the top Indian and international business houses for 17 long years of my life, I had the opportunity to closely interact with quite a few corporate bigwigs. I have found that most of these CEOs or directors believe in their gut feeling or 'knowing' when it comes to taking crucial decisions or to hire people for important positions.

Once, I travelled to Sydney for a job interview, my first one in an international business house. I was interviewed by the chief of marketing who was of South African origin. He is probably one of the finest gentlemen I have seen in the business. I later came to know that he had made the decision to hire me within the first couple of minutes, although our meeting lasted for almost an hour. I also learnt that his decision was based on his hunch. He told me years later that when I made an eye contact with him during the interview, he immediately felt that I was the right candidate for that job. I felt satisfied and happy when he told me that in the following years I proved his hunch to be right. These feelings come from the heart and I believe that the heart can never be wrong.

Living in the present

One of the most common and easy ways to live in the heightened state of awareness is living in the now or in the moment. When we live completely in the present time or moment, our energies are concentrated. Our focus lifts our consciousness to a higher level. We are experiencing that particular moment without wasting our energy in regretting the past or worrying about the future. This gives us an opportunity to receive and understand the signals from the universe without any distraction. Living in the present moment is in itself a very powerful form of meditation.

Meditation

Through meditation, one can connect to the vast reservoir of knowledge and wisdom with us, the sub-conscious, or inner self. This inner self is directly connected to the subtle energy network pervading all over the universe. This subtle universally available energy network or layer has all the wisdom, knowledge base, information of the whole universe, which can be accessed while we are connected to the sub-conscious mind.

Think of this subtle network as the subtle World Wide Web, www in common parlance or the subtle level internet. As we all know, internet is becoming widely available everywhere and through this is a vast amount of information and knowledge is accessible. A simple modem or a dongle is enough to tap this huge reservoir of knowledge. Once we are plugged in, we have access to any information we can think of.

On the similar lines, there is a subtle level reservoir of universal information and knowledge. Unlike the web which can still fail at a certain situation because the servers are ultimately being managed by humans, the universal reservoir or network is infallible. This super-consciousness or super-server can be accessed at any time from any place in the universe, and this system never fails or "the uptime is 100%".

The simplest and best way to access this network is by connecting to our sub-conscious through meditation. We can not only know about past, present and future through this (our own or others'), but also communicate with other beings through the language of nature. This language is through our feelings and normally termed as telepathy. Sometimes the messages may be abstract or sometimes direct but mostly may contain a solution to one or more of our current issues. They are very personal and individualistic in nature pertaining to a particular situation. The key lies in decoding of these messages.

There is no standard way or method or a dictionary to decode these messages. When we get such messages, the best thing to do is be alert and conscious of what is happening. We normally connect to our sub-conscious even while we are sleeping. That's when we receive messages about our past or future through dreams. Our sub-conscious is talking to us regularly through our dreams. That is the reason, why sleep is often also called unconscious meditation while meditation is called conscious sleep.

Telepathy

Telepathy, from the Greek, *tele* meaning "distant" and *patheia* meaning "to be affected by", describes the purported transfer of information on thoughts or feelings between individuals by means other than the five classical senses. (Ref. Webster's Dictionary)

Whenever we were in a conversation with a group of people, my wife used to speak the exact words that I was thinking at that particular moment, and vice-versa. In the beginning, I used to wonder how she knows what I am thinking; she too, was amazed and asked me, "How do you pick up the exact words that I am thinking and say it before I do?" When this started happening very often, we were both surprised at the frequency and spontaneity of these incidents.

As we started moving further on this path of self discovery, many answers started revealing themselves slowly. Many people may call such experiences as metaphysical. We understood that it is nothing but telepathy and happens very naturally to all of us. We all naturally transfer a lot of information to each other without any physical interaction. I am sure you must have had these kinds of experiences in your life at some point or the other. Telepathic abilities can be increased with practice.

Creative connections

Being a keen admirer of art I don't miss any opportunity to witness a creative act or indulge in some kind of creative activity. I have a friend who is a sculptor. Once I visited my friend's workshop, where she was working with clay. She was in the process of creating a beautiful piece. When I went there she was completely oblivious of my presence. She was so engrossed in what she was doing that probably she had not realised that her clothes and face were completely covered with clay. She seemed to be in a state of meditation, operating from the inner self or the sub-conscious mind, trying to make the piece more and more beautiful.

Whenever we do anything creative, we directly connect to the sub-conscious mind or the inner self, as creativity comes from deep within us. It is then that we experience the heightened state of awareness. One does not need to be an artist to be creative. Even our routine work can be done creatively. We can cook in the most creative way, or dress up in a creative way, or solve a particular problem creatively, or even arrange our wardrobe in a creative manner, or we can delegate work to our subordinates in a creative way. Whatever we do in our day to day life, can be done in a creative manner.

Another friend who had never held a painting brush in her hand throughout her life, suddenly started painting at the age of fifty. She is now thinking of putting up an exhibition of her paintings. She said, "When I did my first painting, I experienced bliss like never before. During the process something deep within prompted me that this is my purpose in life, and I simply decided to follow it." Only when we are completely at peace and in a state of bliss can we connect to our deeper self and can draw messages. Hence, it is good to indulge in any creative activity or do anything creatively, which takes us to the heightened state of awareness.

Synchronised events

Swiss psychologist Carl Gustav Jung first began using the term "synchronicity" in the 1920s to describe the experience of two or more causally unrelated events being observed as happening together in a manner that is meaningful. Just as events can be grouped by their cause, they can also be grouped by their meaning.

In his research, Jung noticed that some occurrences were connected in such a meaningful way that they seemed to defy the laws of probability. At some time or another it has happened to all of us. There is that certain number that pops up wherever you go. Vehicle number plates, street addresses, phone numbers, Hotel rooms - its haunting presence cannot be escaped. Or when we are in our car, absently humming a song, we turn on the radio and find that same song is now pouring from the speaker.

There are many different explanations for the theory of synchronicity, but most occurrences go by one of the three following explanations:

- Synchronicity is connected to our psychic abilities. We can get a message from our inner self while being connected or get an intuition when a certain event is going to occur. This is why we start thinking about that event even before its occurrence.

- Mysterious connections. At a higher or subtle level of existence we are all connected. Synchronicity simply makes these connections visible.

- We can manifest what we think. As per the principle of subtle energy flow or flow of life force energy, wherever our attention goes that's where the energy flows. By giving energy to a certain thing or event, we can actually manifest that in our life. This is also known as law of attraction.

Here is an example to understand how these explanations work out. A young man came to me for guidance on his profession. His hobby was dabbling in design and art, and I noticed that he was very good at it too. However, his dilemma was that he was a commerce graduate and was only looking at career options in commerce and finance fields.

During this meeting, he agreed that he will also try to find a suitable job opportunity where he can use his artistic skills. When he reached home that day, he was surprised to find an email in his inbox from a recruitment agency that had last been in touch with him some five years earlier. This agency had invited him to apply for a two year contract with a packaging firm as Creative Manager for their new products.

That is synchronicity. According to the three explanations given above,

- The young man had a premonition that this agency is going to contact him, and hence he started to look for a job.
- The crossing of his wish to take a new job in the area of his liking with the email from the agency was a significant indication that this is the correct action plan.
- He probably manifested a job or the email for himself because of his strong thinking in this direction.

Whichever explanation applies in this case, few things are clear.

- Synchronicity is a call for action
- A synchronic event is a personal message from the higher self or universe.

If we simply disregard the message, possibility is that we may be losing a valuable opportunity. If we act upon the secret message that is revealed by synchronicity, we can invite many good things in our life.

Synchronicities occur in our lives every time but they usually go unnoticed or they reveal the meaning post-facto. My grand-mother passed away in the late 1970s. She was quite old and emotionally much attached to my mom. We lived almost 1000kms away from where she was. One morning, my mom narrated a dream where she saw my grandmother. My grandmother hugged her and cried a lot. My mom was a little anxious that day. Since communication was possible only through letters or a telegram in those days, she decided to write a letter to her mom. Even before the letter reached my grandmother's place, we received a telegram saying that my grandmother passed away on the same day almost at the same time when my mom saw the dream. If you remain observant, you can notice that similar synchronicities take place at every moment in your life.

Decode the messages

Our lives are filled with messages and signs that seem to be designed just for us. They appear on our path to teach us lessons, to help us make decisions, or simply to give us a preview of things to come. Since they're hardly ever noticeable, they can be quite easily overlooked or ignored. Most often these messages are very personal, and one can relate to them only if he is connected to a particular issue or question or situation. Here are some examples when signs and messages are particularly easy to spot and decode:

While driving or walking – Many times what we see along the road while driving or walking is an indication of what's happening in our life pattern on a larger scale. For example, witnessing an accident while driving is usually a message to slow down the pace of our life. We may see messages either at the back of the vehicle in front of us or on a billboard on the side, which are directly applicable to our state of mind at that point.

Through music – The meaning of a song being played might apply directly to our life in some way, perhaps to give us strength, or offer clarity about a decision.

Overheard conversations – If you overhear some talk about a vacation or a holiday, maybe it is time for you to take a holiday, or to give yourselves some time to relax.

Number patterns – Different numbers have different meanings, so if we happen to see the same numbers frequently, take a note.

Home front – If we face a problem at home, it may mean that we need to do some extra work on our inner self as well. Water is a metaphor for our emotions, so a leaky tap or a plumbing problem may mean that we are feeling emotionally overwhelmed. A clogged drain may indicate that we have a suppressed issue or blocked emotion within, and we need to let it go.

Other situations – When I wanted to buy a new car, I had a particular brand and model in mind. I found that most of the cars I noticed on the road were of the same model and brand, sometimes even the same colour which I was thinking of buying. This actually made my resolve stronger to buy that car. We can see sometimes an incident or combination of incidents makes us stand up and take notice.

Silence – The best times to receive the messages or communicate with our higher self is while we are silent. In silence, we can hear the inner voice very clearly and can also understand the message. It is a good practice to be silent for five to ten minutes every day, focusing inward. This gives us a chance to be in touch with our inner world, and also think creatively within the chaos all around us.

Connect emotionally

Telepathic abilities can be increased when one is able to strike the emotional chord with the other person. This happens when you open the love centre or the heart centre. When you feel exactly what the other person is feeling, you will also be able to know what that person is thinking. This is because magnetic field of the human heart is about 5000 times stronger than the field of human mind. By being more sensitive and opening ourselves, we will be able to emotionally connect.

The messages are on the subtle level. If a message comes, we must trust it and believe it. Our higher self knows all and sees all, but we must not doubt or question its powers. Guidance comes as a feeling, an inner awareness, an overpowering hunch whereby we know that "we know". It is an inner sense of touch. We must follow it with the simplicity of faith.

Practice brings heightened awareness

The state of heightened awareness can definitely be brought in by practice. There are a few small exercises for increasing these abilities.

- Next time when you get a phone call try to guess the caller.
- When you are talking to a friend over phone, try to guess the colour of the dress the friend is wearing. Try describing the surroundings and validate the description.
- Next time when the door bell rings predict who must be at the door.
- For this exercise, you require a partner and paper and pencil. Tell your partner to think of 5 fruits, 5 colours and 5 flowers and write it all down. You then have to guess what your friend has written.

All these exercises are very useful but please don't get discouraged if things go wrong at the first few instances. With practise you can definitely master this.

By studying the synchronicities from the past, many a times we can find a beautiful pattern emerging in our life. Everything goes around in cyclic patterns. We can find the repetitive cycles in our life. This can also give us guidelines for the future course of events that are going to occur in our life.

At a glance

- *The universe is always sending us messages*
- *We must be willing to listen to them*
- *Intuition is like a doorway that connects us to all the wisdom in the universe*
- *Decode the messages and take a call - you will be pleasantly surprised*

"*Have faith... you'll feel better...!*"

CHAPTER 5

FAITH

Your support system

On my life journey, when I feel alone
Gripped with worries and fears unknown
My faith gives me company, & inner strength
And supports me through my journey's length

Once all the villagers decided to pray for rain. On the day of prayer everyone gathered, but only one boy came with an umbrella!

I always feel there is a lot to learn from the children around us. Children have such pure consciousness that they exhibit the finest of the virtues very naturally and effortlessly. They are an amazing testimony to faith.

Recently, I had an opportunity to baby-sit my neighbour's 18-month-old child. This baby had just learnt to walk and was so excited about his new discovery that he would simply run and try to climb everything. As we were playing together, my phone rang and I went to the other room to answer the call.

When I came back I was astonished to see this baby standing on the top of our dining table which was about two and a half feet high and proudly waving his hand as if he had accomplished a big feat. With a huge grin on his face and a confident look, without even a second's delay, he just jumped!

I almost skipped a heartbeat, as I leaped to the table to hold him in my arms. It was such a sudden and unexpected situation for me that I just sat there gasping. I thanked God as I could make it, just in the nick of time. While I was still petrified at what the consequences could have been, this baby seemed to be extremely proud and in a state of bliss, clapping and smiling wildly. He seemed ready for the next feat.

Children arrive on earth with an inbuilt virtue called faith. As children, we don't even know what doubt or fear is. When we start our journey on the planet, we have the knowing that we will be taken care of, that we will be protected at each and every step. We have complete faith. But then as we grow up where does this faith disappear?

Well, it is still present but it gets covered by layers of doubts. Because of our conditioning at the growing stages of our life, we form our own unique sets of doubts and beliefs. For instance, if someone asks us to jump from the first floor of a building, will we do so? Definitely not. Over the years we get conditioned by certain dos and don'ts. We believe that we will fall, more than we believe that we will be protected. We believe that we will be hurt than be safe. We believe that we will fail rather than succeed. Slowly, these belief-systems start forming up and the faith get buried deep within.

The role of faith

Faith has the power of holding us and everything around us in life. Faith plays a role when the odds are against us in life. When each and everything seems to be crumbling down, the whole world seems to be going against us, and our life seems to have come to a standstill. All our wisdom, which we have been preaching to the world, goes out of the window when we need it the most.

Our idea of faith is something which keeps changing, although we may not seem to agree to this. So what exactly is faith? Faith basically is of two kinds: (i) faith is our own self and (ii) faith in the universe. For a successful life, we need to have a balance of both.

Faith in our own self is the best gift we can give to ourselves. Lack of faith in one's self is the sole reason for all of today's problems, illnesses, diseases, stresses, relationship issues and fears.

Having faith in ourselves is not the same as ego. It does not mean we can be arrogant or possess a superiority complex. It means that we have complete trust on our abilities and potential and can make use of these in growing ourselves at the same time in helping others when they are in trouble. Faith in our self is that light which can show us the way in difficult times when we are immersed in hopelessness and self-doubt.

While having faith in ourselves gives us a solid foundation, having faith in the universe keeps us stable. It gives the feeling of completeness and continuity. The belief that everything around us is happening as per a larger plan and for our own good, gives us the maturity to understand life in its totality.

Faith becomes our main driving force in times of crises. Faith gives us the hope and energy to go forward towards our goals. It has the power to take away our worst fears and insecurities, the main cause of today's despair and sadness. In our life, we can either have fear or faith. Both cannot exist at the same time.

Fear comes when faith is not there, and faith destroys all fears. Fear is opposite of faith. It is actually lack of faith. Similar to how darkness is the absence of light, and cold is the absence of heat. When we have faith in our own self, our abilities, and in the universe, fear cannot touch us. When we do not accept ourselves as we are or when we reject our own self, we are filled with fear. We may go into depression and even think of ending our life.

Faith is unconditional

There is an interesting story. Once a newly-wed couple were crossing a river in a boat. Suddenly, the weather turned for worse and it started pouring. The situation was such that they could drown any moment. The wife was frightened and started shouting and screaming. But her husband who was a warrior was calm and unaffected. She could not stop her anxiety and asked him, "Aren't you scared? Both of us may die!"

At this, the husband suddenly took out a sword and held the sharp edge an inch away from his wife's throat. The wife was confused and thought that her husband had gone insane. He asked her, "Aren't you afraid? I might just slit your throat and kill you. And there is no one around here to save you."

The wife replied, "I am not afraid. You love me so much and I cannot believe you will hurt me."

Putting his sword away, he said, with a gentle smile on his face, "This is exactly how I feel. I have complete faith in the universe. How can it let me die? I know that I will be taken care of and whatever is good for me will happen. Why worry?"

Faith is unconditional. It is not with the expectation of any result. Faith is not biased. Faith has the power to calm us down even in the most difficult situations. When we live in faith we detach ourselves from the results and responsibility of our actions, which leaves a calm deep within us. This helps in bringing out our best potential and in leading a healthy, fulfilling and successful life.

Like in everybody's life, I have also had my share of my rough patches… days when everything seemed to go wrong. In 2004, my wife was hospitalised, my dad went through a major surgery for colon cancer, there was a financial crunch, and my mother was full of anxiety. I was unable to concentrate on my job as I had to look after my wife, my father and my old mother. As a result, my job was also at stake.

During this period my faith was my only saviour. I decided to just hold on to it. "Whatever happens is for larger good," was my mantra. This really helped me maintain my calm and composure. One of my friends could not stop himself from asking me, "I am a witness to all the challenges you are going through at this point in time. How do you manage to be so calm and always carry that gentle smile on your face?"

I said, "I have a choice to get disturbed by whatever is happening or just hold on to faith that whatever happens is for good. And I choose to live by faith."

"But how can all the bad things happen for good?" he asked.

I told him, "Well I have faith and faith has no logic."

Faith results in miracles

I have experienced a lot of miracles in my life. Its only when we acknowledge faith can we experience miracles. The very fact that you are alive and reading this book is a miracle, isn't it?

I once went on a business tour to Geneva. While alighting from the cab at the hotel in Geneva, I forgot my expensive phone in the cab. I realised this only after checking in the hotel and settling down in my room. As soon as I realised this an unknown fear gripped me. Losing the mobile phone meant losing all the contact details, and moreover I was in a country where I hardly knew anybody. It was already past half an hour since the cab had left, I thought.

I was little disturbed to start with but somewhere deep within, I always believe that I am divinely protected and nothing can go wrong with me. I knew that this was a test of faith. I went down to the reception with this knowledge, to inform them about the incident and see if there was some way of getting my phone back. To my surprise, I saw the cab driver standing right there with my phone enquiring about the passenger who left it. It really was a miracle!

In the same trip, on the way back I missed my Geneva-Zurich flight because of tight meeting schedules; because of that, it looked like I would also miss the next Zurich-Mumbai connecting flight resulting in a huge financial loss. And it was only a miracle that I could be accommodated in the next flight without an extra penny, though it initially appeared fully booked.

Faith is like the sun. It gives us lot of energy to sail through the worst circumstances. We say that the sun sets, but the sun never really sets, it's only that the earth moves and therefore, we cannot see the sun. But the sun always exists. Similarly, faith exists. Faith is when we believe in something, when our logical mind says not to. Faith always comes from the heart. Whatever we perceive, is from our limited senses, oblivious of the bigger picture in life.

Faith is much beyond the perception of our limited sense organs and our logical understanding. Faith is the power that comes from a brave heart. When a brave heart trusts, miracles happen.

Faith is like a life support system. It gives us hope to march ahead in the future with renewed zest. It helps us in pursuing our plans for the future.

Faith Heals

In today's world, people are gripped by inner rather than external demons. Demons such as fear, worry, anxiety, insecurity, etc. happily reside in the body due to absence of faith. They create havoc inside the body, resulting in multiple diseases at a physical level. The only way to counter these demons is faith which is abundantly available. We just need to hold on to it.

Miraculous healing can take place even at a physical level by faith. Many methods of faith healing have become popular in the recent years. In fact, all alternate therapies are based on faith healing. There are so many examples of people suffering from terminal illnesses, who have been completely cured by faith healing.

Affirmations play an important role in faith healing. Any statement in the positive, present tense said with complete faith gets embedded deep within our subconscious mind, and starts working there to create a positive result. For example, "I am completely healed," this is very effective in case of healing. Faith is believing that 'God will' and not 'God can.'

My mother who is now 78 years old insists on visiting our family doctor for every small ache and pain. At times, the doctor is at loss as to what medicine to give her, as most of the times there is nothing wrong with her medically. But now since the doctor knows my mother for almost 12 years, he has a special medicine for my mother… sugar pills! The most interesting part is that she gets completely cured even by those sugar pills! Faith heals.

Faith means complete surrender

When we ask for support and guidance we generally have an ounce of doubt. We are not sure how it will happen or whether it will happen at all. Instead of worrying about the future, have faith that things will work out; maybe not as they are planned but as they are meant to be. Sometimes our doubts overpower our faith. During the counselling sessions when I tell people that they need to hold on to faith, when planning for the future, they say they cannot have 100% faith.

Well, the fact of the matter is that either you have faith or you don't. It cannot be quantified. Absence of faith gives rise to doubts and fears. Whereas, faith gives rise to hope and hope can be used as an oar to wade through the strongest currents of the ocean of future. Faith is there. It already exists; you just need to acknowledge it. It is a phenomenon that cannot be experienced by any of our sense organs. We cannot touch, hear, feel, see or smell faith. We just need to tune in to faith. Once this is done we start experiencing miracles.

We say that our faith is shaken when life plays hard on us. But faith is something that is indestructible. It is the knowing that whatever happens, positive or negative, victory or defeat is for our highest good. Faith is that concrete bridge on which we cross the river of time, fearlessly, though we have no idea where it is leading us.

Faith and love

When we live in faith we connect to our inner core – our true self. Like love, faith is also the basic nature of our true self. We cannot create or cultivate faith. We don't need to do that. We just need to live in faith. By living in faith, you are expanding your inner consciousness. When we live in doubt and fear, we are living superficially. Hence, we also feel disconnected. But when we go deep inside, crossing all the superficial layers, that's when we get answers, we are shown the light.

Faith is 100% surrender. And 100% surrender means, no ego. They say, "Let go and let God." I am sure you must have experienced this many times. When we say I am doing this and I am doing that, and things don't seem to work out. We lose confidence and belief in ourselves, and when we completely surrender, everything just starts falling in place. Complete surrender closes the gates of ego and opens the gates to faith. Complete surrender to the higher self instils faith and frees us from the grip of worry, fear or anxiety.

At a glance

- *Faith has the power of holding us and everything around us in life*
- *When we have faith in our own self, our abilities, and in the universe, fear cannot touch us*
- *Faith can result in miracles*
- *Affirmations play an important role in faith healing*

KEYS

"You have still not accepted my friendship request...!"

CHAPTER 6

CULTIVATE RELATIONSHIPS

They stay forever

My friends are my biggest treasure
Always with me, pain or pleasure
Ready to help, when I need the most
Best security for life, I can boast

Recently, one of my childhood friends was in town on a business trip. There is an unsaid pact between us friends to meet up whenever any of us are in any other's hometown. Childhood friends are the ones with whom we have spent some enchanting years while growing up. I am sure you will agree with me that childhood is the time we all cherish. We share our dreams, our fears, and our aspirations without the fear of being judged or ridiculed. We cry, laugh and play together. We also play mischief and immediately point a finger at the other when caught.

So here I was waiting for my friend at the coffee shop recalling all the priceless moments we spent together. Thanks to the technological revolution and social media, we got in touch with each other after 15 years. When my friend arrived, the first thing we did was turned our mobile phones to silent mode. As we got busy talking, a group of teenagers occupied a table next to ours. This reminded us of how we friends met practically every evening at Indian Coffee House, which was a famous joint then.

I still remember one such evening when one of our friends cracked a joke and all of us broke in to a roaring laughter, totally oblivious of the place and people around. The manager had to come and request us to be quiet as it was causing nuisance to others. My friend and I exchanged smiles as we knew exactly what the other was thinking. We expected something similar to happen on the next table.

But to our surprise, these guys ordered their stuff, took out their smart phones and started chatting with their other friends or playing games. Occasionally, they exchanged glances or smiles, or shared a text joke. They finished their coffee and left after a while. There was hardly any conversation between them. My friend and I were baffled. How can you not talk and laugh and shout when you are with friends? I realised that technology has really revolutionised every aspect of our life from physical to emotional relationships.

Riny, a young engineer works with a multinational company. The job is so demanding that she hardly finds any time for herself; leave aside her family and friends. So she makes it up by connecting with them via social media. The other day, when we were talking about relationships, she said, "I have a lot of my friends on FB. I make it a point to chat with them once in a while to keep in touch. It may sound strange, but the fact is I don't know what to talk about when we actually meet. I am more comfortable chatting."

Today, the world has become smaller, distances shorter, and connectivity greater than ever. We are able to communicate with a person in any corner of the world. Due to the advent of social media, we can locate and connect with even our childhood friends. Some are connected to each other just because they were in school together, or worked as colleagues in a company maybe decades back, or met at a camp and so on.

No doubt it is possible to be connected with them electronically but is it possible to be connected to them emotionally as well?

My dad once told me, "In our times, there was no communication network. The only way one could connect with a relative or a friend living far away was through a letter or telegram. But our bond was very strong. For us, a relationship always came first. Their need was our priority. Our relationship was based on sacrifice. In our times, relationships were like an insurance against all odds." Then somewhat frustrated, he added, "Nowadays, people don't even know what true relationships are."

My dad, a witness of the changing times from 1950s till the current age of e-living, made some valid points. Our priorities have changed and probably so has the definition of relationships. We have become so busy with our work, earning money and meeting deadlines that in the end, we realise that we are left only with money and things money can buy. We are generally very meticulous when it comes to investments and financial planning, etc.

But the real question is, are we equally particular about cultivating relationships? How much time and energy do we invest towards building relationships? How much quality time do we spend with our family, our friends and most importantly with ourselves? On days when we have some free time what do we do? Go to malls or watch a movie or watch TV or play video games? Do we really catch up with some friends or relatives, visit them and spend quality time with those who we have not connected for a long time?

I have a friend who works almost round the clock and has reached a high position in his career. He travels most of the time and when he is in the city, he is busy with his emails, phone calls and laptop. He has earned well for himself and has been able to provide the best facilities to his wife and children. However, he had to pay a huge price for all this. While focusing on his career, he missed out on the growing years of his children. So much so that now he cannot even relate with them. He has not been able to develop his relationship with his wife. He has lost the big group of friends he once had.

The other day, I happened to ask him, "Do you still meet up with your group of friends? I remember, you told me about the fun times you shared with that group." He said, "Hardly! I am so busy that I don't even have time for myself. I have lost touch with all of them." It is sad that he doesn't have time to maintain the relationships he had so lovingly cultivated. The result is that he has lost the zest for life he once had; and is now a loner.

I'm just trying to stress on how important it is to cultivate relationships. Especially, ones those are truly deep, long-standing, motivating, inspiring and soul-nourishing. We must ask ourselves, who would be the person I would call in the worst of situations when I need help? Who is the person I would call without hesitation in the middle of the night when I am feeling low? Even if we are able to think of just two names, it's a hint that we've done a great job cultivating relationships. But if we have none, it's a hint to change something in our life really fast.

Recently, one of my acquaintances met with a serious accident, while returning from a holiday. He was with his wife and child when his car was hit by a truck loaded with iron rods. The impact was so severe that one of his ears and a thumb was chopped off and he sustained multiple fractures on his skull. His wife and son were also badly injured. They were about 600 km away from home when this accident took place. The first person he called, as soon he came back to his senses, was his friend.

As soon as his friend learnt about this incident, he informed a few others and they immediately rushed to the spot. They made arrangements to take him to the hospital and took great care of him and his family for almost three weeks until they were discharged from the hospital. When I went to see him in the hospital he looked very positive and cheerful. He said, "You know, the biggest lesson I learnt from this incident is that I have the most valuable treasure in the world – my friends. I would have never realised their worth if this accident had not happened. I have now learnt to value my relationships even more."

This is an incredible example of how cultivating relationships over the years, plays a crucial role in life. In today's world, where we don't have time for our own self, this guy had a hoard of friends who were selflessly at his service round the clock. This is the biggest asset people can build up in their lifetime.

Cultivating relationships

The most important ingredient in a relationship is the emotional connect. This bond is independent of age, gender, religion, place, social status, educational background, etc. Great relationships can exist between siblings, spouses, parent and child, friends, colleagues and even boss and subordinate.

Such relationships always speak the heart's language and that is love. You may or may not be connected on a daily basis, but that doesn't matter. You will never judge the other person and will never let ego play its role. It is a beautiful space two individuals share irrespective of the external factors. You know that 'you are there for each other'. It is simply based on trust and love. It is a space where you can speak your heart and not your mind. You can just be what you are. No pretence required. You don't need to seek approval or acceptance neither do you need to justify your actions. Such relationships are beyond the physical limits. They are simply divine.

But these relationships need to be *cultivated*. They don't happen overnight. They need to be nurtured. Just like a seed when sown needs love, care and attention till the time it grows to become a tree. This nurturance makes the roots stronger and the tree is able to withstand any storm and give shelter and fruits. Similarly, a relationship well developed and cared-for gives us the support when we most require.

You have to invest time and energy into cultivating relationships, as these will never fail you, even in the roughest of weathers. There are chances that your financial planning may go haywire because of fluctuating external factors but a well-nurtured and true relationship will not. Only a true relationship will give us power and courage to sail through the roughest patches of life. It's also essential to teach our children to cultivate valuable and enduring relationships. This is one of the best legacies we can leave for our children.

Students and relationships

When I was a student, I chose friends who thought like me. The students who joined me when I wanted to bunk classes, became my best friends. As I was not too good in academics, I felt less comfortable with the ones who topped the class. This may be because of my own complex, but I always ended-up spending more time with the mischievous ones.

Of course, I also had a few friends who were good in studies and helped me in my submissions or during exams. Like me, at that age most students will probably choose friends who share the same interests. The studious ones usually stick together, and then there are the sports fans, the movie buffs, the music freaks, etc. The friendships we cultivate at that time stay for a lifetime. Even if we meet these friends after 10 or 20 years, there's no hesitation. We can hit it off any time, in an instant.

In that stage, although we cannot be too conscious about choosing whom we are spending time with, we can at least say no to the unwanted ones. It's better to say no to things you do not feel right about, than regret it later. This is the age when we can get swayed by false attractions.

Kunal and Adi were best friends in college. They spent most of their time together during and after college hours. One day in one of their college parties, Kunal asked Adi to try inhaling a strange substance. Adi did not know what it was, but saw others who had tried it, in a state of trance. Kunal and the other boys seemed exited to try it and started coaxing Adi to join them. However, Adi felt something amiss and made some excuse to leave the party.

Later, Kunal became friends with the boys he met there and attended similar parties together. They frequently invited Adi and tried convincing him to join them, but he could no longer identify with them. Slowly, Kunal started drifting away from him. Adi could have gone against his better judgement and joined Kunal in his new "hobby", but chose not to. For a couple of days, Adi felt lonely but he stuck to his decision. Within a few days, he found new friends who had similar interests as him.

There's a very important lesson to learn here. Today, most teenagers will do anything to become or stay popular. But just because we don't want to be alone, we don't need to keep cultivating a relationship that is harming us.

Relationships and business

Whatever we give comes back to us. This is a universal law and it never fails. Even in relationships, we need to really put in sincere effort, quality time, and should be always ready to give. Trust, support and a genuine disposition play a very important part when it comes to relationships in business. Business is not only about commerce, it is also about cultivating relationships. Customer-supplier relationships, trading partner relationships, professional-client relationships, boss-subordinate relationships, relationship between working colleagues, and relationship between companies. We would like to do business only with the person or company we are comfortable working with.

While I was working for an international business house, my job was to set up their marketing office in India. I had to do all the ground work, and really work hard to establish the credibility of the company and their product. For this, my approach was to concentrate on building rapport with the customers, as I firmly believed in building bridges. My basic premise was to work on trust, honesty and transparency. This worked so well that I not only established their market in India but also got in some sustainable business. The business relations I developed then were so strong that even after I switched on to a completely different profession and after so much time gap, our equations have not changed. This, I feel, is my biggest reward.

Relationship with self

One evening, I was quietly standing in the balcony, looking at the breathtakingly beautiful view of the sun set. The birds were chirping, hurriedly moving towards their destination. The sky was filled with the hues of yellow and orange. I was deeply absorbed in my thoughts, completely unaware of the surroundings. I came back to senses only when I felt a gentle tap on my shoulder. I turned around to see my mother standing beside me with a worried look on her face. I looked at her dazed, as if out of deep trance, which increased her worry even more.

Before I could understand what was happening, restlessly, she said, "You have been standing alone here like this since half an hour now. Do you have any problem? Talk to us son. Your dad and I are there for you, we will sort it out." I was a bit confused at this statement but soon realised where the concern came from. I told her, "Relax Mom, there is no problem. It is just that I got absorbed in my own thoughts, looking at the beautiful sunset."

My mom was not convinced with my answer. It is very difficult to convince her, once she forms an opinion. So to escape this conversation, I had to change the topic. I escaped the situation by cracking a joke and left her smiling.

Being alone does not mean being lonely. If we are sitting quietly and not 'doing' anything, it is often misunderstood as we are either worried or depressed. We are so conditioned to think that we need to 'do' something all the time that we completely miss out on the benefits of just being with ourselves. Only when we do not 'do' anything can we be with ourselves. Swami Vivekananda beautifully said, "Talk to yourself at least once a day. Otherwise you may miss a meeting with an excellent person in this world."

It is very important to communicate with ourselves and cultivate our relationship with the self. It is great fun to be in our own company. It really helps us focus on our inner well being, know ourselves, and realise our highest potential. I make it a point to just shut off all my senses connected to the external world and take a deep dive within, whenever I get a chance. This state of mind allows me to introspect, contemplate, dream, and plan for my future. During this time I come up with the most brilliant and creative ideas.

Many times, instead of focusing inside we turn our entire attention outside. In the process, we lose the opportunity of knowing ourselves and land up in despair as in the case of Simi. When Simi got married in a typically Indian arranged marriage, her top-most priority was to win over her in-laws. She tried to please everybody around her and did win the best daughter-in-law award but at the cost of her own identity. Simi started dressing, talking and living life as others wanted her to live. As a result, after a few years of marriage she was a depressed soul, at war with herself, edgy, and frustrated. Slowly, it started affecting her relationship with other members of the family.

After a few counselling sessions with me, Simi realised that she was trying too hard to be what she was not. She was almost living a life of pretence. This was the root cause of her pain. She needed to accept herself the way she was. This will happen when she spends more time with herself and develops the relationship with her own self.

Only when we love and accept ourselves can we love and accept others. Once we are at peace with ourselves, we can go ahead and cultivate wonderful, enriching and long lasting relationships with everyone around us. Since smart phones are helping us stay connected to the word through various apps, I am just waiting for the day when a smart phone company develops an app that helps us talk to ourselves. That one would really have many downloads!

Dealing with relationships teaches us so many things about life and helps us develop virtues such as trust, unconditional love, patience, forgiveness, gratitude, etc. Good relationships can really help us develop into a better and evolved human being. Good relationships can inspire and motivate us to walk ahead on our path, even in the worst of times, and can really give us soul stirring and life changing experiences.

It is still not too late if you do not have a few great relationships. You can start on cultivating them now. Make your relationships your strong point. Give time to cultivate them, nurture them so that you can proudly say, "I have great friends."

At a glance

- *Relationships are like plants; they need regular care and nurture, without which they die*

- *Only relationships give us power and courage to sail through the roughest patches of life*

- *We must invest time and energy towards building true relationships*

"My grandpa left this for me. I wonder what's it for...!"

CHAPTER 7

LEAVE A LEGACY

Make your life count

I feel for the world, the people around me
For those not as lucky, as I found me
My heart goes out for those in pain
Really don't want my life to go in vain

Oxford Dictionary defines "Legacy" as an amount of money or property left to someone in a will. Most people will think of legacy as mainly leaving or gifting of personal objects, family house or villa, money etc as a part of the will or otherwise for their children or heir. But legacy is not always about material possessions.

Legacy is not so much about the material objects we leave as is normally thought. I believe, legacy is something much more than just material gifts or inheritance. Legacy is leaving something for the family, society, world, and the next generation. Most often it is how we touch other people's hearts and life, for them to create a better life. It is about becoming a pillar of truth, care, kindness or whatever we stand for.

We are actually creating the legacy every moment, each day whether we know about it or not. Once, an old man was planting a mango sapling. He was doing it with lot of enthusiasm. On seeing this, his other old friend said to him, "You are so excited about planting the mango sapling, but sadly you will be long gone before the tree bears fruit. You won't even enjoy the fruits of your hard work." The old man smiled pointing at a child playing nearby and said, "But he will".

Leaving a legacy essentially means being grateful for what we have received in life. We have been looked after so well - first by parents, then teachers, community, our friends, even people who are not directly connected to us. We express our gratitude towards them by giving back or contributing in our own way to balance the energy. We can give back in various ways, for example, giving back to our parents by being good human beings. This will give them immense satisfaction that they did a good job in making us what we are.

We can give back to the society by contributing to its betterment in our own ways. We can express our gratitude to our planet or nature by helping prevent the destruction of environment and forests for the future generations to have better quality of life.

It is important to make sure that when you make these contributions, you do it unconditionally. Don't do them to get acknowledgment or for other people to applaud you. It does not matter how big or small or the nature of the contribution, what matters is the willingness to give back. Regardless of your financial status, you can at least do a small thing. A good way of doing this is by treating it as a part of our responsibility here on earth. We may not realize, but if every single person planted a single sapling, the world will be saved from the devastation of deforestation. If each one of us plans to give back in our own small way, that would make the world so much better place to live in. What is required is only a conscious effort from our end.

Nothing is permanent in its physical form. Law of conservation of energy states that energy continuously keeps on changing its form; but overall, energy always remains constant. Matter is also a form of energy, as quantum physics has already proven. Any matter which is in physical form in the present will be in a different state or form of energy in future. Our physical body is no different, and shall go through the same universal law.

We are born in this physical form in this lifetime, grow up to our optimum size, level, health etc, and then our body slowly becomes a part of the cycle of degradation, as per the second law of thermodynamics. We in our physical form go through the universal process of increasing entropy and eventually result in equilibrium with the nature – or die and mix with the five elements. However, it's all about balance of energy throughout the universe. What we create here during our lifetime, we leave here. We have to give back what we receive during our lifetime. Nothing, which has a physical form, can be taken back with us when we leave. It is up to us as to how would we like to balance that energy or pay back.

Although this is an automatic process, being conscious about the process helps in our own development; and gives us peace and satisfaction. Most of the time, we would go through this process unconsciously. If we are aware of the process, we can contribute to it in our own way. It is a great way of living if we consciously make an effort to give back in a way we feel suitable. The world is a much happier and better place to live in when each one of us makes a sincere attempt towards it. We must take some time to find a cause and make our best endeavour to stand up for it.

If we look at life as a transit lounge, then in reality each one of us is just waiting to board our respective flight which will take us to our final destination, our home. So why should we be hoarders and not givers? Imagine if you had to revisit this transit lounge, the earth, how would you like to find it, in an utter mess or in order? If your answer is the latter, then this is the time to do your bit and contribute towards making earth a safer and liveable place for the future generations to come.

Finding the meaning

The greatest question you can possibly ask yourself could be, "What gives meaning to my life?" If you find it hard to get to an answer, then it is time now to really work upon this question. In an event of face-to-face with "life and death", people report that their life flashes in front of their eyes like a film. This situation comes when we suddenly find ourselves facing our end; it might be a case of terminal illness or a terrible accident.

In such a state we are be forced to think about this question, and many times end up with regrets about not doing enough. Most realise that they have wasted the precious time in their lives doing mundane things, or spent a lot of valuable time simply in front of the television or computer screen. Life could have been much more than that, much more passion, possibilities and action. But then it is probably too late.

The point is, why do we need to wait till such a situation arrives in our life? We can do this 'simple but powerful' thinking even now, by reaching deep within ourselves and discovering how our life could be. Our life's mission could then have a much deeper meaning and purpose, doing away with what is meaningless and false. Imagine our life if we consciously live every day as if it is our last day. What would you like to do on your last day if you knew you were going to die tomorrow or the day after or the next week? How would you live life differently than you are at present?

The merchant of death

Dr. Alfred Nobel is now a household name, as almost everyone must have heard about the Nobel Prize. But how did it all happen, makes for an interesting story.

In 1867, Alfred was involved in the study of making safe explosives, when during an experiment he came across a mixture of nitroglycerine and an absorbent. This mixture worked well, which he then patented by the name Dynamite. Nobel became a wealthy entrepreneur and made a fortune through his invention of the dynamite and other explosives that were used by military as weapons of mass destruction.

In 1888, when his brother died, a French newspaper wrongly reported that Alfred Nobel has died with the head line "The merchant of death is dead". The newspaper carried the obituary saying, "Dr Alfred Nobel, who made his fortune by finding a way to kill the most people as ever before in the shortest time possible, died yesterday." He was shocked to see his own obituary and horrified on how his reputation is going to be after his death. He went on to change his will giving away most of his wealth to an institution for a series of prizes, including the Nobel Peace Prize.

Alfred Nobel was fortunate to be able to change his life story. Unlike him, we may not get the same opportunity to evaluate our life when we are still living. Our chance is now, today. We can create our own legacy by planning and doing something for a larger cause today itself. We can always ask these questions to ourselves. Is there a better way I could have lived? Could I have given more love to the people around? Was it possible for me to have served the society or community in a better way? What I could have done that would have made the life of people around me better? What better life could I have given to my family? Did I live a life which could make earth a better place to live? Was I able to pass on the knowledge and wisdom I acquired, to the next generation? Was I a burden or a blessing to my family and people around?

By thinking about the answers to these questions, we will get clarity about the purpose, or meaning we would like to give to our life. It is not necessary that everyone should follow the same path. We must try and listen to our own truth and then try to mould our life accordingly. It is really not what possessions or wealth we leave for others that is important; it is how we have made a difference in their life that matters most. It is about leaving behind our spirit, what we stand for. That is the true legacy we can leave for the world. That is what humanity needs from us. So we must serve others, love to our fullest, live a life that becomes a shining example in itself. It is we who can create our own legacy today.

Giving back to nature

In 1979, a teenager felt miserable with the plight of animals due to heat on a barren sandbar. He wept looking at the bodies of dead snakes and other animals that died due to excess heat. Informing the forest department was of no help as they said nothing could grow at that place. He was asked to try growing bamboo. He started slowly by burying seeds along the sandbar to grow a shelter for wild animals. He dedicated his life to this purpose and started living there to work full time. In 30 years, Jadav Payeng has created about 1300 acres of forest in the Indian state of Assam on his own, now called Mulai Reserve.

We must begin by respecting the needs of Mother Nature; a lot of harm has already been done and we cannot undo it. However, we can do our bit to stop further damage being done and save the earth. Can you imagine an Earth without rivers, lakes, waterfalls, greenery and animals? Charity begins at home and therefore we should not waste a single moment but start right away in our own way to save and give back to mother earth.

The problem is that we wait for something to go wrong until our antennas are up or worse, till we wait for someone else to take the initiative. We must inspire ourselves, to be our own leader. We can do something within our means, our reach and capacity. There are many organizations doing great work to help preserve the planet, we can become part of them or start something where others can join in. The key is in starting now. The time of contemplation and procrastination is over; it is time to put everything into action.

Giving back to the society

Another way to contribute is by doing something for the community or society we live in. This can be done by participating actively in making our society a better place. For example, if your community is taking up a good cause of rain water harvesting, then become part of this project, learn and contribute so that everyone can benefit.

I know of people who have done great work for their communities and as a result everyone has benefitted. Life is about give and take and that is how we strike a balance. You can take up a cause and do something in your own small way and request your community to join in. Like building a school for the underprivileged, providing safe and clean drinking water for a village, providing seeds for poor farmers. Once again the list is endless.

When you give, give with love, give and walk away. Sometimes doing a good deed in itself is a reward to the self. A landless farmer from Bihar, India, dedicated his whole life to create a road for his village, with just basic tools available such as chisel and hammer. Dasrath Manjhi started carving a 1 km long road through a hill, all alone, when his wife died because of an injury she got while crossing the hill. It took him 22 years (from 1960 to 1982) to complete this about 9 meter wide path.

Earlier his village people had to travel 70 km to reach the nearest medical facility. Due to this road, the distance was reduced to 7 km. His motivation was that he wanted to make it easier for his villagers to reach hospitals, schools, markets etc. Dasrath did this job selflessly without any expectation of recognition or awards. He passed away in 2007, leaving his legacy for the villagers. There are many such people who have given back to the society selflessly, without any expectation of name or fame. Many have already dedicated their lives; many more are still doing it. Legacy is not only what we leave behind when we are no more. It is also when we touch people's hearts by making a difference in their life. It is what we live, create or contribute while we are living.

My wife's grandfather was a qualified lawyer. But he chose teaching as a full time profession in a small Indian town in the state of Maharashtra. A noble soul that he was, he dedicated his entire life teaching poor students for free. Although he went through major financial crisis himself, it did not deter him away from his chosen path. He believed in the principle that 'every child has the right to education and knowledge, and it should be available free of cost.'

Throughout his life he lived on a meager salary of a school teacher, while supporting a huge family. He could have earned a comfortable life for himself and his family by practicing as a lawyer, but he chose to live his legacy. When he breathed his last in the year 2000, many of his students poured in, even from faraway places, to attend his funeral. They all had tears in their eyes. I came to know later, that he was revered by his students not only for teaching them free of cost but also for touching their hearts. They all still remember him even now, although many of them have achieved great heights in their respective lives.

Randy Pausch was a professor of computer science at Carnegie Mellon University, Pittsburgh, Pennsylvania, USA. He was doing great in his work in the university, authored books and many articles, and was also involved in a research with Walt Disney Imagineering. In 2006, at the age of 46, Pausch came to know that he had pancreatic cancer.

Almost one year later he was told that his cancer is terminal, and he had only three to six months to live. It was then that he delivered his inspirational "Last Lecture" with the title "Really Achieving Your Childhood Dreams" at the university. This lecture became a phenomenon which also became a bestselling book "The Last Lecture".

Pausch died in 2008 leaving a legacy of his thoughts and messages through his lecture and book. "Too many people go through life complaining about their problems. I've always believed that if you took one tenth the energy you put into complaining and applied it to solving the problem, you'd be surprised by how well things can work out," said Randy Pausch in his book "The Last Lecture".

It should be our endeavour to live a life in such a way that it becomes an example in itself which others can follow. Our life should become the light that shows the way of selfless service to everyone around us, even to the people who are not directly connected to us. Recently there was news that a group of more than 200 Japanese pensioners, all above the age of 60, were volunteering to help dealing with the nuclear calamity at the Fukushima power station. They said, it is the old who should be facing the hazard of radiation, not the young. There are countless other stories such as, an athlete stopping to help an injured competitor across the finish line during a track meet or a man giving his shoes to a homeless girl in Rio de Janeiro. It is up to us to live fully, inspire, spread love and awareness, and help the ones in need. Let us take up the cause and become a guiding star to the world.

At a glance

- *Legacy is giving back for whatever we have received in life*
- *We can leave a legacy for the next generation, mother earth or the community*
- *It does not matter how small your contribution is*
- *Be the change you want to see*

CHAPTER 8

HAVE YOU PLANNED YOUR FUTURE?

Future is just a matrix of possibilities. At times it is our own projection of our life, as we perceive it. Future is first created in our thoughts before it manifests in reality. We just need to focus on what we want from life and plan towards achieving it. Knowing whether we are prepared for our future is therefore a great exercise to do, as we are the masters of our own creation. Hence it is important to asses where do we stand, to know if we have really planned for our future. This is an exercise to help you analyse.

Again, like earlier exercises, I suggest you take out some peaceful time and place for yourself. It is necessary to focus on the questions, and not on the outer noise. Make sure that you are not going to be disturbed for some time.

Take a pen/pencil and start on the exercise. Feel free to use blank sheets wherever needed. Be honest to yourself, answer whatever best you feel. No one is going to judge you from your answers. This is only for you. So take your time, think and answer in a *Yes* or *No*. Other than the *Yes* or *No*, if you feel like noting something down, do that. It's all about your life. This is for you to work upon your planning for the future. After you finish the exercise, you can go back to your notes to check on your observations. You can then refer to the next chapter 'Powerful tools to plan for your future' for help in guiding you to plan your life.

		Yes	*No*
1.	Do you think future can be planned?	☐	☐
2.	Have you made your bucket list?	☐	☐
3.	Have you planned the path to reach your life goal?	☐	☐
4.	Do you give importance to health and finance planning for your future?	☐	☐
5.	Do you think you are prepared for any opportunity that knocks your door?	☐	☐
6.	Are you well prepared for the adversities in life?	☐	☐
7.	Do you listen to your inner voice often?	☐	☐
8.	Do you believe in telepathy and intuition?	☐	☐
9.	Are you creative in whatever you do?	☐	☐
10.	Have you experienced synchronicity in your life?	☐	☐
11.	Does building relationships come to you naturally?	☐	☐
12.	Do you feel you can closely relate to yourself?	☐	☐
13.	Do you give importance to cultivating relationships above other things in life?	☐	☐
14.	Do you have faith in the universe?	☐	☐
15.	Do you have faith in yourself?	☐	☐
16.	Do you believe in miracles?	☐	☐
17.	Are you working towards leaving a legacy for society/planet/future generation?	☐	☐
18.	Do you think you give love to people around you?	☐	☐
19.	Do you think you have always been of help to people in need?	☐	☐
20.	Do you meditate?	☐	☐

If you have answered 15 or more of the above questions in *Yes*, then 'well done'. Know that you are very much there, on the right way. You just need to be more aware and be consistent in your planning and execution. However, if 15 or more of your answers are *No*, then it is still not too late. Don't worry; you have a chance now to plan for your future.

After you finish doing this test, you can go back to the questions, where the answer is *No*. Refer to your notes and start working again. I am suggesting few tools in the next chapter to help you in doing this.

CHAPTER 9

POWERFUL TOOLS TO PLAN YOUR FUTURE

Given below are some tried, tested and powerful tools that can help you plan your future

- **Make a bucket list** – Making a list of the things you want to achieve before you die is high on my list of recommendations. Don't wait till you are old and left with no energy to pursue what you wanted to do. We are often so stuck in situations of life that we realise about the things we wanted to do in life only near the end. But that's too late. That time we will only end up with regrets. So make a list for yourself now and set targets. Review it every week if possible, or at least once a month. Believe that the things on the list will be accomplished.

- **Visualize** – Develop the habit of visualization. Visualizing what you want to achieve to the minute detail brings in clarity and helps it manifest faster. Visualization stimulates your wishes and operates your mind's mechanism towards it. Whatever you think and give attention to, that's where the energy flows. The more you think about something in a positive way, the more are the chances of that manifesting in your life. Here's an exercise you can try on visualisation:

Close your eyes and take a few slow, deep breaths. Now focus on your breath and count up to twenty breaths, observing each going in and coming out of your lungs. Now imagine yourself in a beautiful garden. Appreciate the beauty of nature all around you. Feel the breeze of air touching your body as you are looking around in this beautiful patch of nature. Now imagine yourself walking on a path which goes through the garden towards a gate. You can clearly see the wooden gateway at the other end of the garden as you move towards it very slowly. This is the gate for your dreams, for your life goals.

As soon as you open the gate and cross it, you find yourself in a different time-zone. You can clearly see yourself in the time when you have achieved your dream or goal. Experience, how it feels having achieved what you always wanted to. Feel each and every emotion at that moment. You can clearly see how you achieved it, in detail. See all the steps you took to reach there, which path you undertook, what were the challenges you successfully faced till that point.

Experience fully the joy, the feeling of victory, that feeling of ecstasy and satisfaction. You have fulfilled your dream. Thank the universe for helping you reach there and in achieving your life goal. Feeling elated and satisfied, now slowly start walking back towards the gate. When you cross the gate, you will find yourself again in the garden. You can spend some time in the garden, taking in the positive energy of nature, before gently opening your eyes with a bright smile on the face.

Spend 10 to 15 minutes doing this visualization. This will also help you in detailed planning of the road to your goals. Regular practice of this visualization exercise has the potential of bringing in positive changes in your life ultimately taking you towards your dreams.

- **Dream chart** – This is like a road map to your dreams. You can be creative and graphical in making this chart, which will also add to its clarity and functionality. Feel free to use colours, drawings, symbols and pictures to make it more interesting. Your dream or goal in a chart form or graphical shape engages your brain in a much effective way. This becomes more effective when you start adding more routes to reach your goals or add any insights about a step you want to take. You can also take cues from mind mapping. Indicate your goals as clearly as you can, and then show the path you have chosen. You can indicate the milestones you might reach on the way. Giving a timeframe to activities will help you in pacing your journey. You can create a nice collage or wall hanging out of this and put it right in front of your bed so that you see it first thing in the morning to give your day a kick-start.

- **Learn a new skill** – If you follow the same pattern of life for a long time, you will end up feeling not very happy about yourself. Learning a new skill every now and then keeps your brain active and keeps you versatile. The more skills you learn, the better you are prepared for new projects or opportunities coming your way. It makes you feel good about yourselves. Life is all about new changes, even new ways of doing the same old things. You could learn anything new such as driving, a new form of dance, classical singing, sketching or painting, writing, any foreign language, graphic design, any other art form, a new cuisine or recipe; try anything you can think of. You can even learn a new basic skill such as, changing a tire or making a Spanish omelette. Don't wait for too long. Pick a skill that attracts you and start learning. There is no age bar to learn new things.

- **Develop Intuition** – You can learn to develop intuition and to receive messages and insights. These messages are mostly about your own life and provide guidance in your decisions. Everyone has intuition power. The more you know about it and practice it, the more accurate it gets. One can practice intuition in many ways. For example, do a blind reading of cards, or guess who is calling you or who is on the door. Regular meditation helps in developing your intuition power as well.

- **Help someone** – Make it a point to do at least two acts of kindness in a day (you can do more than two; more is better). It could be anything, helping a child in homework, helping an elderly cross the road, giving food to a hungry person, feeding an animal (other than your pet), guiding a person who has lost way, letting someone go ahead of you in the queue, giving up your seat for someone, giving water or fruit to the delivery guy, giving a compliment about your waiter to his manager, helping someone replace a flat tyre, buying an inspirational book for someone, writing a thank you note, helping maid's children with their studies. You can think of new ways to help, or take any opportunity which comes your way to show your kind heart. If each one of us makes a sincere effort to do a few acts of kindness in a day, the world will become such a better place. The important thing here is not to expect anything back when you do your act. Also try 'not' to make it known to everyone around you or 'declare' your acts; keep it with yourself and see what difference it makes in your life.

- **Spend more time with your friends** – Studies has shown that people who spend time or interact with close ones, friends, neighbours, relatives more often, lead a happier life. Spending more time with your friends has many hidden benefits which ultimately helps you in becoming a better human being.

- **Meditate** – Meditation helps us heal our past, live in the present and plan for our future. How much time you should meditate daily? The thumb rule is, minimum 30 minutes and after that, on an average the number of minutes equal to your age. For example, if you are 35, then you should meditate for at least 35 minutes every day. Always keep in mind, Meditation should be like brushing your teeth, one cannot miss it. You are the real expert on yourself. So try to find the wonderful things or method that works best for you

- **Positive Affirmations** – It is said that there are 6 billion paths to paradise, and your path is your own. Choose it wisely and make it a happy one. Here are the affirmations to recharge you and to take away your fears of future. You can repeat these affirmations as many times as you want during the day.

✓ *I am safe and secure at all times*

✓ *I have complete faith in my abilities*

✓ *I am blessed beyond my fondest dreams*

✓ *I am open and receptive to all the abundance that universe offers*

✓ *All my relationships are loving, harmonious and healthy*

Santosh Joshi

THE NEXT STEP

Congratulations! on completing the book. Now, you are aware of the three powerful Keys. Reaching this chapter is an indication that you have a strong intention and have started living the HLP way.

Slowly, you will have a completely light and healed past, awareness of your true potential, and the wisdom to handle any eventuality and opportunity. Just remember to listen to you inner voice and make the right choices. Be sure, you will soon achieve everything you've always wanted – a stress-free and regret-free life, better vision for the future, great relationships and overall success. During your journey remember to contribute to the community, society, mother earth and the universe.

Look back to Keys in times of need

Remember, HLP is an ongoing process. Don't hesitate to go back to the book or a chapter when you are stuck at any point in your life. The HLP process is not a onetime thing, for hurdles will keep coming your way.

We continuously create a past which in turn will affect our present and future. Life is full of unforeseen obstacles and circumstances, but keep Keys handy and you will never fail. It will help you keep focus on your ultimate goal.

Take help, give help

Stay connected with people who follow the HLP principle. If you're having trouble in some aspect, seek support from these friends. Also, help others follow Keys. One of our responsibilities is to help others find their journey and purpose. So be the Key in someone else's life and push them ahead. Gift this book to those who really need it and be a reason for change in their life.

Give the best to your Organization

If you are the team leader, boss, regional director or CEO of your company, you can take even more advantage of Keys. If an employee follows the HLP principle, he will have a completely healed past, will be living in the present and planning for the future effectively; making him a better performer and a greater asset to your company. Keys will enhance team work as HLP also deals with forming effective relationships. With Keys, your employees can give their best to your organization. This in turn will help your organization achieve greater heights. To aid this I have specially designed a Corporate Workshop under the name of SKY Pro. This transformational workshop is based on the HLP philosophy and I also teach the 12 min SKY Healing technique which I have developed. This technique works miraculously in reducing the stress levels instantly.

Form a Key-chain

Before the launch of the book, I organised a reading at my home. Even though the event was meant to generate criticism for the book in order to improve it; after every chapter the group started discussing the ideas presented and shared their personal stories relating to it. This lead to the idea of starting Keys discussion groups. Reading and understanding the ideas of HLP is important but discussing it with a group takes it to another level. It's like a support group enabling you to learn from other people's experiences and mistakes as well. You can motivate and inspire each other. And grow together.

Of course, I am also available for any assistance. I can be contacted through my website www.santoshjoshi.com or Facebook and Twitter. I conduct regular workshops which you are welcome to attend.

Go ahead, live your life to the fullest and enjoy each moment.